THE GODDESS
OF PROMISED LAND

GENESIS
BOOK ONE

Rachael Roberts Bliss

Jan-Carol
Publishing, Inc
"every story needs a book"

The Goddess of Promised Land: Genesis
Book One
Rachael Roberts Bliss
Published February 2022
Broken Crow Ridge
Imprint of Jan-Carol Publishing, Inc.
All rights reserved
Copyright © 2022 Rachael Roberts Bliss

ISBN: 978-1-954978-38-6
Library of Congress Control Number: 2022933085

You may contact the publisher:
Jan-Carol Publishing, Inc.
PO Box 701
Johnson City, TN 37605
publisher@jancarolpublishing.com
www.jancarolpublishing.com

To all the women in my life,

youth and elder,

who have made me believe

in the Goddess.

Author's Note

As a spiritual person, I invite readers to imagine with me a feminine version of the Holy Spirit, incarnated as a fictional woman and sent to Planet Earth to model the power of the Divine Feminine. Her goal is to teach humans how to solve problems threatening the future of our world. Thus in *Genesis*, we meet Sophia-Emma as a baby whose mother is Loving (Amanda) Foster, a goddess herself in little Sophia-Emma's baby eyes.

Jesus Christ, the second person of the Christian-based Trinity, almost saved the world, but patriarchal followers misrepresented his teachings through the centuries. Into this violent world enters the *Spirit-Goddess* herself, who intends to finish the job of bringing peace to the world. She ushers in with her the skills and tactics of the *Divine Feminine* as an alternative to patriarchy that had its chance and failed to bring harmony to the world. Can the girls succeed where the men failed?

Will young Sophia-Emma and the important women in her life bring a new consciousness to the world, one based on compassion, wisdom, forgiveness, collaboration, intuition, and nurturing?

The Goddess of Promised Land: Genesis takes you to the beginning of a new life born in a world needing transformation. Can a *Spirit-Goddess*, incarnated as a powerless baby of color, even survive in a world of the Old South where Jim Crow still rules and white supremacy doesn't want to give an inch?

Foreword

By H. Byron Ballard, writer, priestess, witch

S hh. Listen. Everywhere you can hear it—the sound of a long-held breath being released. With a sigh, a grunt, a fierce scream. The Divine Spirit who is Goddess and Goddesses, singular and plural, has crept back into our world and our lives. This force has been deliberately repressed for so long that She seems new now in Her returning, new and also impossibly old. Elder, mother, sister, and child to those who have held Her in their hearts and bones for so long. Too long. She has returned when the Earth and our species needs Her most—and we welcome Her.

Chapter 1

"So God created human beings in his own image. In the image of God he
created them; male and female he created them." (Gn 1:27 NLT)

The ghosts of Promised Land were wailing as Amanda Foster parked her ancient VW van, called Very Wicked, at the end of a rutted private road that led to the Alabama River. The young anarchist wasn't far from Promised Land's big house, where another argument with her mama was on the midday agenda. But for now, there was only the river and the land—and those souls who loved neither.

The ghosts had screamed at her since she was a child, the Foster's youngest heiress. Indigenous hunters stricken down by colonialists. African slaves beaten and raped before being condemned to shallow graves. Their anger soaked the black dirt, blood mingling with the reddish tint of the meandering river—once bountiful with fish, once the path carrying slaves to never-ending bondage. This was where she'd been raised up, where she'd listened to the ghosts many times. But for now, there was only the river and the land—and those souls who loved neither.

After a few steps, she came to a few meager stones honoring Sally, Ellie, and Cecilia. Nearly hidden by stubborn weeds, next to Cecilia's grave, was a much smaller rock that bore the scratched name of Sofie on it.

"Probably Cecilia's child, who died of yellow fever," her family's maid, Tillie, had told her back in the 1990s, when she herself was a little girl.

Buried near the "wenches" were the "bucks," as the masters had called them. Splintered wood crosses, some looking like scattered pieces of driftwood, marked these graves. Amanda knew not their names, but she reckoned Ellie, Cecilia, and Sally knew them as sons, fathers, brothers, and lovers. These folk were just the tip of the iceberg and represented probably hundreds of other battered souls who had sweated, labored, and died for masters whose blood now flowed through her.

Amanda had repeatedly told the ghosts that she wasn't responsible for their lives and deaths. But she knew her people were. For years, she'd run away from these voices, but now she was back.

Then she heard a new cry. The cry of a baby.

"Can't be," the tanned heiress of Promised Land told herself. Could this three-year span of living in her van be driving her crazy?

She knew she was the only descendant left who might one day own the thousand-acre estate. Her mama's expectations, which were steeped in the Jim Crow tea from the fifties, left no room for compromise. Today, she'd level with her mama. She would not birth any grandkids for the Fosters. No blue blood son-in-law, either. And if her mama didn't like it, she'd lose her only heir. Amanda's two brothers had already died fighting in the Middle East.

The calm, wide river beckoned to her sweating body. Already barefoot, she waded into the lazy waters up to her waist. Her tie-dyed skirt formed a circle around her, like a rainbow floating on the water's surface. On this hot, sticky September day, the waters refreshed her aching body.

She hadn't slept in a real bed for months. The last time had been when she'd stayed at her friend Chaos's apartment one April night when she'd paired up with Redhot. Too bad the relationship had bombed, as she had sure enjoyed wrapping herself around her lover and mentor, Peter Zinn, in Chaos's sturdy four-poster bed, which she'd found alongside US 43 back in 2004. These days, her bed consisted of a piece of egg-crate foam in the back of her cluttered van.

Amanda leaned backward into the water, floating downstream to mingle with the scenic Cahaba. Like every other day, the Cahaba would rendezvous with the Tombigbee River and the Tensaw downstream before finally becoming the great Mobile River herself.

Raggedy brown dreadlocks floated around Amanda's oval face, forming a battered halo around three-quarters of her head. Her loose, blue, sleeveless, see-through blouse accentuated her fully formed breasts, making them look like melons ready for the picking.

She remembered when she'd first noticed her breasts, back when she was in third grade, more than fifteen years ago. Back then, she'd worn her hair short and had worn school uniforms and Adidas sneakers. That little girl would cringe in fear if she saw Amanda today. All they had in common were the aqua blue eyes and the unquenchable love of warm watermelons right out of the field.

In those more innocent years, Amanda had been proud to call herself a Foster. Her family had lived in a big, old house in Dallas County, where all of her friends who wanted to ride horses with her would get lost trying to find her home, which was located nearly a dozen turns off Dallas County Road. It was before cell phones and texting, so those girls' moms and nannies would drive around, over and under, on old plantation roads, and across wobbly bridges, and if they were lucky, they'd get to her house by four o'clock

Amanda would greet them on the big, stark-white, wrap-around front porch. Tillie would serve up ice-cold lemonade, and they'd run out to the barn to ride Willie and Sillie through what seemed like endless trails. As Amanda grew older, she pointed out to her friends where the huge cotton crops had once grown, where enslaved humans had lived, and where her dad had hidden his moonshine (tucked way back where no one would ever find it).

Deep in her nostalgic thoughts, Amanda waded back to the river-bank to sit in some heat-exhausted, prickly grass. She wrung out her dripping clothes and dreadlocks. Her feet were not the only naked parts of her body anymore.

She let her eyes follow the darkening white clouds above her, seeing in them images of a wolf, a horse (of course), mice, and roosters. This had been a way she'd entertained herself when she was a little girl.

"A little Scarlet O'Hara," Peter would tease as they gazed at the stars above them at their campsite.

Snapping back to reality, she stood up and slowly twirled 360 degrees. If she had been taking a panoramic picture, she would have captured her rambunctious Alabama River and its flat floodplains, nearby pastures burned by a hot summer sun, and white stables with wooden fences of the same color. There was also the tobacco barn; the machine shed; the corn crib; the old spring house; the work house and milking barn; rows and rows of corn; alfalfa fields; a garden now full of pumpkins, melons, and potatoes; the apple orchard; the pecan grove; and the struggling vineyard. Much was now neglected. Tillie was in no shape to maintain it, and no one wanted to work for the old woman Amanda called Mama.

In Antebellum days, the place had fed more than sixty people every day. The family who'd lived in the Big House got the best fruits. The house slaves and their overseers preserved most of the rest before giving the near-rotten, bruised harvest to the field slaves. Amanda got nause-ated when imagining those days and thinking of the sharecroppers who did much of the same work, but for little pay, while living in nearby shacks, their rent due every month.

She tried to envision what this land had looked like in the days before her family had settled it. What did this land say as it felt the weight of European boots on its soil, when it had been free to grow whatever seeds fell on it? Did it miss the days before it had been culti-vated and stripped of its nutrients by greedy landowners who saw it as income rather than as a living, breathing organism? Today, Amanda saw Promised Land with tearful eyes and an aching heart.

As she returned to Very Wicked, she heard the baby cry again.

Chapter 2

Louise Foster, matriarch of Promised Land, suspected that Amanda would probably be late because that old junkyard van of hers had broken down somewhere up the road. She attempted to calm herself by listening to classical guitar and flute on her Magnavox stereo. She wondered why she'd never taken music more seriously when she was younger, but this wasn't the time, however, to lament the past. It was time to look to the future beyond 2005. Her vagabond daughter would be showing up any minute with a new sob story that both of them would drink to. Maybe a little too much.

But the two remaining womenfolk of Promised Land had excuses to drink and cry into their liquid refreshments. They were the only survivors of the Foster clan, who were now buried up on the hill that held the majestic red oak. The oak seemed to savor its role in providing shade for those weary and respected souls. Louise and Amanda were the last homebodies who could pass their family story on to the next generation.

Louise realized the task before her. Before she'd let herself die, she was determined to convince her daughter that the Foster story had to be preserved. If Amanda wanted the rolling hills and bottomland, plus the money and the prestige that went with them, she'd have to cooperate and do more research on the Foster family, who'd made this land a homeland for generals, landed gentlemen and fine ladies, and even thoroughbred horses.

So far, Louise and Tillie had woven together an impressive document that featured eight pages of distinguished gentlemen. Now was the time to study the refined women at their sides. When these women had found the right sires, it had made the Foster name renowned throughout the county.

The man she would choose for Amanda would also have pure blue blood, as vibrant as the morning sky. Amanda would have the children she was destined to bear. After they were born, money would be set aside to ensure they received only a superior and proper education. They would learn how to make the Foster line prominent in both the state and the south.

Louise opened her cedar chest and took out the big wooden box of files, which she had put together over the past twenty years. She noticed that some pages were yellowing. Perhaps it wasn't too late to get them laminated. They were certainly important enough.

Why did her maker have to put her into a family that mattered? Louise would rather have been born into a family like the Lunds, who lived down the road. So many evenings, she'd hear them partying into the dawn. Occasionally, a couple would sneak over to her back pasture to copulate. First, he would initiate, and then she would follow. Louise wondered how this good Earth could put up with their kind. Nevertheless, she envied the abandonment they exhibited, like puppies and kittens delighting in all that could be touched, eaten, or drunk.

Louise knew the saying, "For of those to whom much is given much is required." This had been the model for her life. To be truthful, this was the advice her mama had given her right after she'd beat the devil out of Louise for coloring on the wall—the one with the pretty pink tulips and dazzling white daisies on it. Louise had wanted to tell her mama that she had been coloring on the wallpaper because there hadn't been enough purple in the flowers. Wild violets were too mild in color. Passion flowers were needed here and there. She learned on that day, however, that her opinion would count later on, and on far more important issues than the color of wallpaper.

Her mama did a remarkable job at teaching her children how to carry their heads high. She told them to only look down when an adult of good breeding addressed them or gave them a compliment, which was very seldom.

"The worst thing one can do to a child is spoil them," Louise's mama would tell her when she was a new mother. Louise had had three children with her husband, Lawrence. That in itself was a miracle considering that most nights Lawrence had been too drunk to do more than conk out on top of the bedspread. Poor man. One had to pity him in his later years, when he considered it his duty to warn the world that black people would take over in national politics, putting old white families in dire straits. Poor Lawrence died of worry. Now it was up to Louise to keep the family from being contaminated by trash like the Lunds, the Yoders, and, worse, the foreign and dark scoundrels.

Louise wheeled her chair over to the mirror. Her jet-black hair had taken the dye better this time. Her deep-blue eyes were bloodshot as usual. How she'd love to stand up and study her figure, which Lawrence had once commented was the sexiest in the entire county. And he knew what he was talking about. He got around. He had to; people needed to be aware of the impending days of doom.

She practiced "the smile"—the one powerful women of well-bred families knew from the time they could walk. *Don't show too much of your teeth, but let others know that you have them and that they fit nicely in your mouth. Use enough blush so that it looks like you're embarrassed about a mild joke. Keep your nails long, but don't have claws like the ones those wild women down the hill wave around. Keep your shoulders back and your legs crossed at the ankles, if they must be crossed.*

Having finished assessing herself, and passing with exceptional marks, Louise looked around her parlor. There were dark, subdued colors, such as burgundy, gray, and cinnamon brown. Her Indian tapestry on the wall was showing its age, but that was a plus in her world. Along with a moss-green plush sofa, the room held a fainting sofa, a mahogany card table with padded chairs around it, and three over-stuffed easy chairs. Her floors were dark hardwood, made from the chestnut trees that used to thrive in the local forests. Rounding out her parlor were portraits of Lawrence's mama and papa, grandmas, grand-pas, and great-grandparents, plus a few cousins, aunts, and uncles. She imagined that when she passed on, her portrait would hang over by the piano, as she'd always appreciated music.

She looked over at the grandfather clock on the south wall and noticed that she still had enough time to smoke a cigarette out in the courtyard before Amanda arrived. She reached deep into her loose slacks and took out a Marlboro and her lighter, then wheeled into the courtyard for a breath of fresh air, which would nullify any bad air that would get trapped in her lungs while she smoked. She had it all figured out.

In the courtyard, she noticed an eagle flying in circles over the old pasture, which was near the old slave graves. She hoped his eye was on a rabbit and not on a baby pig. (Another eagle had found one quite delectable a couple of weeks back.) She also realized that the rest of the wildlife had become silent, most likely hiding, fearing they might be the next meal.

A breeze from the west was picking up, and Louise saw that thick clouds were moving in. Everything needed a rain. Because of big losses on Wall Street, she had laid the landscaper off, and now the property only received monthly trimmings. Her shrubbery and flowers were on their own most of the time now and were thirsty.

Louise heard the front door slam abruptly, and she had to throw her cigarette butt into the nearby bushes. She went back into the parlor, and in strolled a wet Amanda, her long dreads bouncing and dripping up and down as she glided over the floor. Louise could see the nipples on her daughter's ample breasts through her see-through blouse. Amanda was also wearing a long, loose skirt, something she had probably picked up at Goodwill years ago. As usual, she was barefoot, the pads of her feet tough and black.

"See you're smoking again," Amanda jokingly accused her mama. "If you insist on smoking, I can bring you some weed, and then at least you can die mellow."

"Don't you dare bring that stuff into this house, Amanda. You know what I think of illegal drugs. I wish you'd learn a few of my good habits," Louise said angrily. "You know, someday I'll be gone, joining your father, and it'll be completely up to you to save our land."

"Mama, get off your high horse. I've been frank with you for years now. This isn't hallowed ground to me in the same way it is to you. We stole this land from the Indians. Then our ancestors beat their slaves so they would whip this land into the manicured piece of crap it is today. I know you think it's God's gift to the Foster family, but my universe tells me that it's time to give it back to its rightful owners, although I may give some acres to the families of the former slaves as repar—"

"Amanda," Louise vigorously interrupted, "we've been through this a thousand times. I will not let you do such an idiotic thing. My will absolutely forbids this. This land is the burial ground for your grand-parents and ancestors from many generations back. They sacrificed all they had to settle this prime farmland, and everything they did was legal at the time. Didn't you ever do your history homework? We spent way too much to send you to that prestigious boarding school and then Brown University up there in Rhode Island. What a waste!"

Amanda went to check what was in the refrigerator to drink. She found a full bottle of Chardonnay and was about to pull out the cork when she overheard her mama call Mr. Perkins, her lawyer. Probably checking on the wording of her will, which would saddle Amanda to this haunted land for the rest of her life. She grabbed a couple of tall wine glasses from the dishwasher, inspected them, and decided they were clean enough. With glasses in one hand and the bottle in the other, she slithered back into the parlor. She filled her mama's glass half full and her own up to the brim.

"Now, let's talk about your plans for me, Mama, as your only living child."

Chapter 3

Louise took a long drink of the wine and commenced with the little talk she had rehearsed for Amanda earlier. "My dear daughter, you're all I have in this world," she pleaded. "You're the only one left to carry on the Foster name, perhaps even revive it in politics, statesmanship, and law. There's nothing I won't do to see that you're properly prepared for the task and—"

"Mama, I want to leave a mark on this planet," Amanda interrupted. "My task is to correct all the mistakes y'all made in this part of Dallas County. You're lucky I'm even being frank with you about this." She stared into the wine glass, which had an Old English F embossed above the stem. "I know my attire, or lack of it, makes you think I'm a loser. But I'm far from it. Like you, I love my ancestors. What I plan to do will release their souls from the guilt and regret they're dealing with beyond these walls and, to be perfectly frank, within these walls right now."

Louise was completely baffled by what her daughter was saying. The Episcopal Church didn't speak about delivering ancestors from their sins once they were dead. Besides, the Fosters were very reputable people. They tithed. They gave to the Salvation Army and United Way at their extravaganzas every year. They saw that their children were properly educated and disciplined. Most tried to live chaste and holy lives because, after all, the neighbors were watching and they had to lead immaculate lives like the Fosters before them.

"You're talking sheer nonsense, Amanda. Who's influencing you? Those anarchists? The monsters who wear black masks and look so evil? If anyone were to hear that you so much as spoke to any of those ruffians, I'd be scandalized."

Amanda smiled and winked at Louise. "Well, get used to being scandalized, dear Mama. The man I love is a leader. And there's no way I'm going to separate from him. And yes, we've had sex out in the open, beneath the trees at Bud's Place, where we live together in my van."

Louise's eyes widened to the size of lemon drops. "You're doing no such thing, Amanda. You're only trying to make me angry so I'll disinherit you. But my mind's made up. You'll bring vitality to this land once more. Your children will run through our woods, pick flowers from our rose bushes, and celebrate birthdays and weddings here. They—and you, their mama—are my only hope."

"Seems we're on different wavelengths, Mama." Amanda poured herself another drink, then offered Louise a partial fill-up, as well. "Do you really want to come to some sort of compromise here? I personally don't know where to start. I know you don't like the man in my life, who, if you were lucky, could become your grandchildren's father someday. You don't want to split up our hundreds of acres or pay back the families of our ancestors' slaves, who never earned a damn dime here. You want me to become the matron of this haunted land, where souls on both sides want mercy, forgiveness, and justice. What in the devil can we agree on? Nothing!"

Louise agreed that she still wanted Amanda to take over Promised Land someday, but what that would entail was completely the opposite of what her once-sweet Amanda wanted to do. If only she could put Amanda into a deep sleep, perhaps hypnotize her, long enough to get a few children out of her. Then Louise would just have to live long enough to successfully groom a male child and add some masculine energy to this place.

The two women stared out the window, gazing at the old pasture behind the house, while they sipped the wine. *There has to be agreement somewhere*, Louise told herself.

"Would you like to use this land to start your own organic garden, maybe raise hops so you can brew beer? To save my homeplace, I would even be willing to let you sneak in a few marijuana plants." She looked around to be sure no one else heard her. "Maybe you could invite your unconventional friends to help out. Then, with your profits, you could dedicate the north side to the Cherokees, open it up for hunting. Isn't that mostly what they used their land for anyway? Buy some mules for your black families, but don't give forty acres to them. Impossible."

Amanda started laughing. Surprisingly, Louise laughed along. Funny how a bottle of wine could help them laugh at their disagreements. Better to laugh than to attempt to fix the unfixable.

Both noticed the eagle drawing closer to its victim on the ground beneath it.

"Mama, I'm going to see what's out there that Mr. Eagle is about to snatch. I'll be right back."

Louise, seeing a chance to squeeze in another cigarette, grimaced and told her to go ahead.

Chapter 4

Amanda couldn't help but feel nostalgic as she galloped out to the back pasture, hoping to catch the little critter that might soon be dinner if the eagle swooped down before she shooed it away. Soon, she noticed that the object wasn't a small animal; it was a tiny baby wrapped in an old flour sack. She did a double-take. The baby, perhaps a newborn, was letting out a hungry cry.

From the corner of her eye, Amanda saw a small creature run into the adjacent woods, which separated the Lunds from the Fosters. She let out a big yell. After she surveyed the grove, she realized it was one of the Lunds's mutts running home, most likely to search for dinner elsewhere.

Admittedly not the mommy type, Amanda hesitated before picking up the baby. But in this circumstance, pity for the baby overcame her hesitation. She picked up the tiny being and cradled it in her awkward arms. Standing there in the field, now eye to eye with the newborn, she wondered where this dark-eyed, sandy-toned baby had come from. Who could have deposited it in the middle of a field, leaving it to be meat for vultures and the patient eagle still hovering above?

Amanda—often a rabble-rouser, anti-establishment free bird who flew from one nest to the next—was actually holding a baby. Later today, she would drop it off at social services, and that would be that. She smiled as she grew more comfortable holding this little piece of humanity.

One thing was for sure: this child wasn't a Foster. Fosters had straight light hair, sky-blue eyes, and fair skin. Most tended to look anemic. This child, in comparison, had feathery black hair and almond-shaped dark eyes that were highlighted by a golden complexion, as if it were a combination of all the world's babies. And it was boisterous, seeming to want more than cuddling. *Maybe it needs nourishment or a dry bottom,* Amanda thought.

She did her best not to read too much into the finding of this baby. She was a hero, for sure. Would the newspaper want to do a story on this? Or the TV station in Montgomery? No matter. She would continue to live her life as she normally did.

For now, she would get a kick out of studying her mama's reaction to the baby. Maybe she would play with her a little. Pretend that she wanted to adopt the baby, to bring it up as a Foster. *That could give her a heart attack,* Amanda thought sarcastically.

Louise, who was now in the courtyard, saw it all. The closer Amanda got to the Big House, the easier it was to make out what this creature in her arms was. It had some dirt on it, and its little limbs were kicking. It looked somewhat like a baby. My God, it was a baby. A little heathen child, not like one of her own. She put out her cigarette, tossed it into the bushes, and went back into the parlor.

Amanda came in, the babe in her arms. "Mama, I have your new grandchild right here, delivered to us from the wings of an eagle. Isn't it beautiful?"

"I see you've got a baby in your arms, but he or she isn't destined to make their life in our home." Louise forced a laugh as she finished the little wine that she had left in her glass. "I know that, and so do you."

"No, I believe in finders keepers, losers weepers." Amanda put the crying baby up to her shoulder. "Got any old diapers around here? This baby's full of shit, just like my mama. We can also find out if it's a boy or girl."

"Tillie, come in here with some rags and a couple of safety pins," Louise ordered. "The rag drawer has some old diapers in it. I need some right now."

Tillie had been with the Fosters since Amanda was a baby herself. The shuffling servant put her garden magazine aside and went from the dining room to the kitchen. Both Louise and Amanda could hear her slamming cabinet doors and drawers in the ample kitchen. The kitchen was a kingdom that belonged to Tillie alone, as neither of the other females saw any use in cooking when Tillie was around to do it so well.

"That wasn't a nice thing to say to your mama, Amanda," Louise said, referring to the "full of shit" comment. "You never learned language like that from me. Never. It's those anarchists who're putting these filthy words in your mouth. That's no way for a real Foster woman to talk, or even think, for that matter."

Tillie came out of the kitchen with an armful of rags that used to be Amanda's diapers. They were no beauties, but at least they were absorbent. *That's all that matters*, Amanda thought as she stretched the infant out on the nearby velvet couch.

"Not on the sofa, Amanda," Louise yelled. "Take that little urchin into the bathroom and change it there. And wash it up good. No telling who hatched it. It does have a strange, unfamiliar odor about it."

"Mama, I know what I'm doing, and I'm doing it here." Amanda put a diaper under the baby and proceeded to strip the soiled rag off the child. As she looked at the fat little body, she saw that the girl's umbilical cord was still fresh. *Interesting*, she thought momentarily, then screamed out, "Tillie, I need a warm, wet cloth to wipe this little one's butt! And by the way, Mama, you got yourself another girl child."

"This child isn't ours, Amanda. You will bring me children—children of our blood, yours and mine—who will appreciate what this land means to our family."

"Mama, if you want a descendant, you're looking at it, because I intend to bear you zero children. I don't have time for such diversions."

"You're talking nonsense, child. Just wait. Even anarchist women have female hormones that want to reproduce. I can be patient a little longer. Now, as soon as you get that little half-breed in clean diapers, I'll let you make your departure, and we'll talk again when you want to talk sense for a change."

Once she was in a clean diaper, the baby stopped crying. Amanda knew that what her mama had said was partially true. Even anarchist women had female hormones. They drove Amanda to hold the baby as if it were her own, as if she'd given birth to it herself.

It was time to head to social services to turn in a lost newborn.

Chapter 5

Amanda laid the swaddled babe on the floorboard in front of Very Wicked's passenger's seat. Social services wasn't just around the corner in Promised Land. It was twenty miles from Selma, then another fifty to Montgomery. She told herself she would only drive the speed limit, and if she still happened to be pulled over because she looked like a messy-haired troublemaker, she would give the baby to the cop. This time, she was doing nothing wrong. Nevertheless, she had no love for the Highway Patrol in Alabama. Never had and never would.

Before going to Montgomery, Amanda decided to stop off at Bud's Place, where she and Peter, her lover, were camping. She couldn't let this opportunity go by. She had to show the baby to him before continuing her trip. *Plenty of time*, she told herself as she shaded her eyes from the sun, which was still high in the sky.

She realized that soon her favorite season would be here—autumn. When the extreme Alabama heat would turn moderate before the onset of chilly weather in mid-December. She had spent six winters up north, in Connecticut and Rhode Island, at boarding school and Brown. There, her autumns were always whipped away much too soon by early winter winds and snows. She usually never had time to wash her fall school jacket even once. In Alabama, however, fall went on and on, melodic bird songs waking her in the mornings and deep lullabies from croaking frogs putting her to sleep in the evenings. Even now, she could feel fall just around the corner. Summer breezes were calming and welcoming, and there were less heated blasts from the sun.

Amanda parked Very Wicked in her regular campsite, under the trees at Bud's Place, and treasured the view from her van window. She saw her partner, Peter Zinn, pulling paper out of his Royal typewriter. He was sitting in his favorite lawn chair; it was handmade and was made of olive-green wooden planks that he had recovered from a ditch near Mobile three years ago. She assumed he was pulling out the letter he intended to send to other radical groups. It discussed plans to cause a stir in downtown Montgomery in support of gay rights in Alabama.

Amanda loved to watch her boyfriend as he edited his letters. (They were nothing fancy. After all, he wasn't editing a computer document. Grassroots changemakers like Peter seemed to enjoy their work in the rough. That way, they wouldn't be confused with public relations corporations, who themselves were agents of the corporate culture.) If only she had access to her camera—the afternoon sun was casting a glow all around Peter, almost as if the universe was blessing his work—but it was still in the top drawer of her bureau in her bedroom at the estate.

Her morning laundry was still hanging on the twine rope that she had tied between the maple tree and the young oak. The clothes were begging to be freed from their clothespins and folded. The park's grill seemed to be begging for some hot coals, as they usually warmed its insides around this time of day. She felt a sense of peace as she watched nature, her man, and the tiny baby next to her. She felt warm goosebumps all over her body. All she wanted to do now was make love with the world.

"Hey, Peter, come see what the eagle brought me today at Promised Land. She's as cute as your little butt."

Peter gave her a perturbed look. After all, he was in the middle of looking for a bunch of addresses that he had put in a special place he would never forget. *So much for good intentions*, he thought to himself.

He walked over to the passenger side of the van, looked in, and stepped back in shock. "What are you doing with a kid, Manda? Didn't we say no kids?" He took another prolonged look. "But she is kinda cute. Got a name for the little lioness?"

"Do you think we should name her, Peter? I really want to, but I thought that if I gave her a name, I wouldn't want to leave her with the State." Amanda was feeling the mama pull again. "Let's name her now. I'll go with Sophia, the Gnostic goddess of wisdom."

"You know I'm not into religion, woman. So how about Emma? After our heroine, Emma Goldman, mother of anarchy in ye olde US of A."

"Both are good. Too bad we only have one baby here. Since I found her, I get to name her. But I do love you, my man. Therefore, on this day in 2005, I name this sweet little baby girl Sophia-Emma Foster. I wish we had some water so our christening would be complete."

Peter frowned, and Amanda knew why. "Too religious," they said in unison, then laughed.

They both shifted their gaze to the now-sleeping bundle in Amanda's arms. Religious or not, Amanda couldn't help but compare this child to the fairy-like angel she had fanaticized about as a child, when she was up in her spacious, spooky room while her mama and papa partied with the elites down in the parlor and courtyard. The only way she had been able to ignore the laughter, the clanging of crystal glasses, and the abundance of tobacco smoke creeping under the door was by gazing at the picture of the little angel that hung above her bed.

"Aw, I'm too emotional to take this little charm to the State today. I'm going to keep her overnight. Here, take her for a bit while I run over to Moses's to get a baby bottle, some diapers, a blanket or two, and, of course, some formula. You can boil some water for me to mix with the formula when I get back."

"Now, Amanda, I think you're letting this baby thing get into your head a little—"

Amanda interrupted, saying, "Don't worry, Peter. I know what I'm doing. This baby's not going to take me away from you. I've got everything under control. See ya!"

She thanked God for the little money her dad had put into a trust for her before he died. Otherwise, she'd be over at the intersection with a cardboard sign that said, *Will create havoc for food*, or something stupid like that.

The store was about to close, but she ran for the door and made it inside. She debated over which formula had the least amount of preservatives and food coloring. She didn't want fireproof blankets because of the chemicals in them, but she realized she would have to go with disposable diapers because that was all that was available. She was amazed by the size of her bill at check-out. All the more reason not to make a habit of this mothering practice.

Pete was walking with little Sophia-Emma when Amanda got back and put her van into park. She grabbed her merchandise and ran to relieve her partner, who was grateful. Dinner that night was simple: hamburgers, with canned pork and beans over the campfire. Most of Amanda's attention was on the baby, who, she told herself, would be given over to social services the next morning. But the more she thought about it, the more she dreaded it.

"You know, Peter, I agree that we shouldn't bring any more children into this unjust world, but what about the ones who are already here? Some folks have to care for them, right?"

"Guess so, Manda, but don't think those folks should be us. We're always on the move, you know, and marching, chaining ourselves to trains and road equipment, and landing in jail. And we would scare kids with our black masks," Peter explained as he licked his plate clean. "I think our job's to make the world better for kids who're already here, not to do the actual raising up. Don't you?"

"Now, don't get too bossy, Mr. Bossman. I'll do what I want to do. I'm a big girl."

In the night's wee hours, Amanda was beginning to understand a little of what Peter had meant. Little Sophia-Emma was waking every other hour. For the first time in months, she saw what Lady Dawn looked like.

Peter was normally a late sleeper, as well, and this morning was no different. Amanda was kind of relieved that Sophia-Emma's antics the previous night hadn't seemed to affect his sleep at all, as he would be busy organizing groups for the march that weekend. (The anarchists who made up their group weren't the type to call on the police for protection, as the police were often part of the problem.) Amanda let him sleep while she mixed some instant Quaker oatmeal with cinnamon and brown sugar.

As she ate, Amanda looked over at little Sophia-Emma, who was now resting comfortably in a padded lawn chair. She was glad no bears had been spotted nearby, as the baby would've been just a good couple of bites for such a critter.

Amanda started arguing with herself about how much the baby weighed. Seven and a half or maybe nine pounds? She had no idea. Then she wondered where Sophia-Emma had come from. Was she Indian? Part Black? Asian? Part white? A female Moses? It was too soon to tell. Then she got depressed, knowing that after that morning she might never see the baby again. She would never know. She wanted to take a cotton swab and wipe the inside of Sophia-Emma's cheek, then send it off for DNA testing so she could know her genetics, but she decided that it would be a stupid idea.

She sipped on her fire-hot cup of coffee, burning the tip of her tongue. Sophia-Emma was stirring. It was time to make some fresh formula in a clean bottle. She kind of liked being needed by this helpless being. Peter and Amanda loved each other, but they didn't depend on each other like this child depended on her. Their relationship was one of egalitarianism. Neither ranked below or above the other or the cause.

Amanda began to think more about Peter and herself. Would they last in the long term, or were they just biding their time until circumstances changed?

When she had first met him back in 2002 at Brown University, Peter had swept her off her feet during a tour she was giving him of the campus. He hadn't been interested in the buildings, and she knew it.

But they'd had to do this mating dance—the first touch, a kiss, the fon-dling of a breast—before they could lose themselves in the pure energy of sex. Afterward, she had made up her mind that there was no way she would not follow him and fight corporate power, bigots, and inequality with him. She'd quit college and went off to fight the pigs. Yes, they were both passionate about taking corporations off of Uncle Sam's tit, but they also drank in the chemistry of love, which intoxicated them before and after the battles.

The fight for gays and lesbians, and the fight against white national-ism, was spreading throughout the country, but eventually folks needed to make some dough, sleep in a real bed. That was when she'd used a chunk of her trust fund to buy Very Wicked. She and Pete had driven to places of civil unrest, like Seattle, Cincinnati, Quebec, Edmonton, Benton Harbor, and Montreal. Now there was work to be done in the South, especially in Alabama.

Just recently, anarchists had started to see that equality meant more than just equal rights for all races; it also meant equal rights for people of different sexual orientations. Some even thought gays and lesbi-ans should have the right to marry. Meanwhile, the KKK was almost broke because of recent civil lawsuits, but the more sophisticated white nationalists and Europa groups were organizing to go mainstream and pick up political clout.

Right now, though, all Amanda could think of was her man, who boiled with passion for their causes and her body. She never tired of gazing into Peter's tantalizing emerald-green eyes and staring at his little copper goatee, which was divided into three braids about three inches long. His hair matched his goatee in color, but it was curly like a Brillo pad, begging for a woman to civilize it. To this day, Amanda hadn't been able to accomplish that simple goal. How in the world did she think she could make him into a daddy?

Sophia-Emma didn't care about Amanda's rambling romantic thoughts. She was hungry. And thanks to the woman who had found her yesterday, soon she had a bottle in her mouth and was wearing a dry, comfy diaper. Best of all, there were muscular, soft arms holding her, making her feel safe and connected to some kind of wonderful world that she would one day explore, maybe even thoroughly change herself.

Amanda met the little baby girl's black and curious eyes. Their eyes seemed to focus on each other like laser beams. Amanda began to sob quietly. She didn't want Peter to see her like this, but there was some kind of love going on between her and the baby. Amanda noticed how Sophia-Emma fit into the crook of her arm, much like how she fit beside Peter's entire body. Love between a man and a woman and love between woman and child—so much alike and yet so different.

My, what a lack of sleep will do to a person, Amanda thought. If that were the case, then she'd been sleeping too much before last night. This morning, she was thoroughly in love. She remembered a new mother once telling her that holding a baby and making eye contact stimulated the love hormone, oxytocin. That must've been why she felt so euphoric at that moment.

Peter peeked out the back of their van, which they had recently renovated so they wouldn't have to camp on the hard ground in their simple tent. He saw his lover caressing the baby she had found. At first, he'd reacted to the baby much like he'd reacted when Amanda had found a puppy in the bushes a couple of weeks ago. But now he could see that this was something different. He didn't feel slighted, but he knew that what had happened yesterday could change their lives forever. He hated moments like this. He had just become comfortable with the way his life was going. Women!

Peter knew that Amanda had strong nurturing instincts. He had seen that when she'd adopted the puppy, especially after little Scamper had been struck by a car. For days, she'd spoon-fed him, soothed him with warm wraps, kissed him, and held him tightly, even as the puppy took its last breaths. She'd mourned Scamper's death for days afterward, which was one reason they had never looked for another pet. The vulnerability of bonding with another living creature was too much for Amanda...until this baby. He suspected that she had changed her mind when she'd met Sophia-Emma.

Amanda looked up from the baby and gave a "Can't we keep her?" smile to the man in her life. He was caught. They couldn't possibly take in a child, especially considering the kind of life they were living, but if he protested too much, he would probably lose Amanda. From experience, he knew that she always did what she considered to be right, no matter what. He smiled back and told himself he was reading more into this moment than he needed to. She had said she would take the baby to social services today, so what was he worrying about?

"Come eat your oatmeal and say hi to Sophia-Emma," Amanda hollered from her chair. "As you can tell, we're getting along just fine. Hope she didn't keep you awake all night."

"She was fine. Are you about ready to drive to Montgomery and hand her over?" Peter asked as he looked for a clean spoon. "We don't need any cops chasing us because we have someone else's baby. Admit it, Manda. Someone out there is missing a baby."

"Oh, I know, Peter." Amanda dug a clean spoon out of her pocket and handed it to him. "But what if someone put her out there because they didn't want her anymore, making little Sophia-Emma bird food for vultures?"

"This baby could end up in the news, and those very same parents may come and reclaim her." The guy who usually downplayed risks was now exaggerating the risks to Amanda.

Amanda could see what he was doing. But she understood. There were risks if she kept the baby. That was why she planned to be on the road within the hour.

"Don't you think she's the cutest baby you've ever seen, Peter? I wish circumstances were different, but the real parents deserve to get their child back. I gotcha."

"Good. Like we agreed earlier, we fight for all kids but don't make one our own." Peter washed his dish and spoon and poured himself the rest of the coffee. "Can I ride with you into Montgomery? Need to figure out the logistics for Saturday's direct action. You're going to help, aren't you?"

"Wouldn't miss it, love," Amanda reassured her partner. "Let's go out for a pizza tonight, okay? And then let's make love like it's our first time."

"I'll buy that, hon." Peter smiled. "Now, why don't you do what you have to do? Then we'll get on the road. Busy day!"

"Sad day, too," Amanda mumbled under her breath as she packed up the rest of the diapers, formula, and bottles.

Within half an hour, they were buckled up in the van, heading to Montgomery. Sophia-Emma, on the foam rubber mattress in the back of the van, fell asleep as the motor serenaded her. Amanda looked over and saw that Peter had followed suit.

She dropped Peter off by Dexter Avenue Baptist Church, the historic church that Reverend Martin Luther King Jr. had pastored during the Montgomery Bus Boycott more than fifty years ago. On Saturday, participants would be attempting to fight for equal rights for those who loved who they wanted to love. Talk about risk! And the conservative Christians were planning to turn out, too, with their flags and crosses.

After saying goodbye to Peter, Amanda found her destination just a few blocks away. She scooped Sophia-Emma up from the back of the van and held her in her arms. *But gee,* she thought, *the day is so nice.* She saw mothers strolling with their babies on the sidewalks, and she ached to do the same. After all, she did have all day to release little Sophia-Emma. What was the rush? She could even go to Goodwill and, if lucky, pick up an old stroller. Maybe some baby clothes, too.

Quickly, she settled Sophia-Emma back into her little nest on the passenger side of the van. She drove under the speed limit and took the two of them to Goodwill. As she proudly carried Sophia-Emma into the store, she crossed her fingers, hoping they would have the darling stroller of her dreams. A stroller like the ones she saw in old black-and-white movies—a little bed on four wheels, black with white trimming. She rummaged around for about half an hour and saw nothing, so she accepted defeat in the stroller area. She did, however, find some great bargains on tiny baby clothes, which Sophia-Emma really needed. As she piled them on the counter, the saleslady asked if she'd found all she was looking for.

"I really wanted a stroller, but I see that they're all gone," Amanda said.

"Now wait a minute. I saw someone drop one off a few minutes ago. It's probably being priced this minute. Do you have time to wait while I see what I can do to speed this up a bit?"

"You'd better believe it," Amanda responded. "I'll go ahead and pay for this, then wait to see what you find."

"Well, this total is $32.22." The salesclerk started stuffing the clothes into a huge plastic bag. "Cash or credit?"

"Cash," Amanda answered as she pulled a wad of bills out of her pocket. "While I'm waiting, I'm going to slip into your restroom. But as soon as I'm back, I'll check with you."

"Sounds good, young lady," the clerk said. "And oh, by the way, I love your dreads."

Normally, when anyone complimented her hair, she told them why she wore dreads and explained how they could go that route, as well. But right now, she had some baby-changing to do. Thank heavens the restroom had a changing table. She wiped it down and laid Sophia-Emma on it. She couldn't believe she was really playing mama, and even more unbelievable was that she was having a ball with it. As she looked down at her little sweetie, she could see and feel their bond strengthening.

She chose the little green outfit that was gender neutral. What was particularly appealing at the moment was the fact that the bottom included a built-in pre-folded diaper. She took off Sophia-Emma's current diaper and saw that it was soiled. Amanda was shocked. Her poop was nearly black, just like yesterday's. Was her baby sick? She didn't have a fever, but something was going on, and it had Amanda stumped.

Since she couldn't take Sophia-Emma to a doctor, as she wasn't hers, Amanda decided it would soon be time to turn the baby over to the authorities. But in the meantime, she would get the stroller and talk to some mamas near the social services office. She stuffed the old diaper into the garbage and returned to the clerk. Beside the saleswoman was the stroller. *Perfect*, Amanda thought.

"How much?" Amanda asked.

"For you, we'll charge $10."

"It's a deal!" Amanda pulled another bill out of her purse, laid a receiving blanket on the bottom of the carriage, and laid Sophia-Emma on top of it.

Amanda stood over the baby as if she were in a trance. A woman behind her tapped her on the shoulder, bringing her back into the real world. "Oh, excuse me, ma'am. Guess I got carried away looking at this new carriage with my baby in it."

The woman huffed and whispered to another woman next to her, "Probably high on weed. Think so?"

That was enough for Amanda. "Ladies, if I may interject, the only thing I'm high on is love for this child. Why don't both of you concern yourselves with other kids who need love instead of picking on those of us who are freely giving love to babies like mine?"

With that, she stomped outside. The day remained bright, like the blue Caribbean Sea, with floating, fluffy, boat-shaped clouds changing shape in the breeze.

As she strolled around the outer edges of the parking lot, she realized that she hadn't had any weed for almost a week. Yet she could see why those old hags had accused her of being high, because she was.

This wonderful little human depended on her. The world was applauding her by giving her a beautiful day full of purity and beauty. How could any day be better?

However, today was also the day she had promised Peter she would give Sophia-Emma to the State. The more she postponed the task, the harder it would be. Kind of like putting off going to the dentist even though your tooth aches ever so slightly, knowing that if you wait too long, you might lose the whole tooth.

She wheeled the stroller to her van, gave Sophia-Emma a little hug, and laid her in the spot she had carved out for her. She momentarily thought that she should have looked for a car seat while in Goodwill, but soon that need would be gone. She would just drive carefully.

Sophia-Emma was getting hungry and fidgety, so Amanda dug through her pile of necessities and found a four-ounce, warm, sealed bottle of formula that had been sold with the nipple already on it. She dreamingly fed the baby nestled in the crook of her arm. Life couldn't get any better.

Chapter 6

Amanda's idyllic moment was interrupted when she noticed that Louise had called her cell phone while she was in Goodwill. She gingerly put Sophia-Emma on her van's floorboard and grabbed the phone that had fallen into the car earlier. She hurriedly returned her mama's call.

"Yeah, what do you want?" she said as Sophia-Emma fussed, searching for a good burp.

"Amanda, what do I hear? Do you still have that baby with you?"

Amanda groaned and admitted the truth. "Yes, Mama, you hear right. I'm feeding her now and will be dropping her off with the authorities in a few minutes. But the longer I talk to you, the later it'll be."

"I'm calling because I wanted you to know that I've decided to fix my will. Now, the only way you'll ever receive any of our estate is if you promise to live here with your lawfully wedded husband, and you'll have to pass it down to your biological children. I'm doing this so I can sleep at night, knowing Promised Land is safe."

"Mama, you're not going to get my cooperation with threats. Maybe I don't want your old estate that's falling apart. Did you ever consider that? And since you sent both of my brothers off to die in Afghanistan, hoping they would become proper gentlemen who would inherit your place, totally leaving me out of the plan, you now have yourself in a pickle. If I were you, I would be real nice to your only living descendant, but right now that's not happening. So, goodbye, Mama. I've better things to do than put up with your dementia-based plans."

"Well, I never—" Amanda heard her mother curse, but she promptly hung up and turned off her phone.

Picking up Sophia-Emma again, she put her to her shoulder and patted her back until she heard a couple of good burps. She felt a warming on her baby's bottom and knew she was having another bowel movement. After a few minutes, she laid Sophia-Emma in the back of the van and found a clean diaper to exchange with the dirty, wet one. Once again, the dirty diaper was full of black, tarry poop. She remembered that she needed to discuss this with another mother before relinquishing the infant to the authorities.

"Okay, little wisdom, time to go talk to some other mommies and their babies," she told Sophia-Emma, tucking her into her little spot one more time.

Amanda started driving to the Department of Human Services. Traffic on the way back downtown was heavier than usual. She also noticed more cops out than normal. She concentrated on going with the slow flow and not doing anything that would make her look more suspicious. She turned on the local radio station, which seemed to be broadcasting a late breaking-news alert.

"Authorities are not releasing any names at this time, but it appears that a young man in his early thirties was shot and killed about an hour ago by a drive-by shooter. The shooter was in an old, black Ford pickup truck with an Alabama license plate. The suspect has not been apprehended. Call Montgomery Police Department at 241-2651 if you see anyone driving a vehicle like the one just described. Stay tuned for further developments in this story."

Weird, Amanda thought as she coasted along with the traffic. She hated to hear stories about innocent, or even guilty, people being shot. But a drive-by, in particular, was a senseless, cowardly act.

She reached for her phone, remembering that she'd turned it off after the rant from her mother. Maybe Peter was trying to call her.

When she looked at her phone, she noticed that she had indeed missed a call from Peter. She clicked on his message.

"Amanda, where are you? There are some Nazis over here, and they ain't too friendly. I have no backup. Think today might be a good one to back off some. Can you come over and pick me up where you dropped me off? Please hurry!" Yelling and static were all that remained at the end.

Her heart raced. Could he have been the target in the drive-by? He was in his thirties, just like the guy who had been shot. But that guy was dead.

"Oh no. Please. God, no. No. No!" she screamed as she honked her horn incessantly.

Sophia-Emma could feel Amanda's anxiety and fear. Naturally, she started to cry, as well.

Predictably, in no time, Amanda saw a policeman on a motorcycle, his blue light flashing. He motioned her over, out of the flow of traffic. When he approached, Amanda grabbed her cell and asked him to play Peter's message. The cop noticed the baby crying on the floorboard in front of the passenger seat, but that wasn't what was on either of their minds at the time. The cop clicked on the voicemail and listened. Amanda studied his face as Peter's voice spoke fearfully of impending doom. He then radioed another policeman in a nearby car. Together, they formed an escort so that Amanda could get to wherever Peter was now.

Sophia-Emma continued to cry, but Amanda had to follow the escort that was weaving through the traffic. She was now almost positive that the man who had been shot was Peter, but there was also a slim thread of hope that he'd escaped, that the victim was someone else. It had to be someone else—someone who deserved to be shot, not someone who had dedicated his life to helping the oppressed. This time, life had to be fair.

Chapter 7

Amanda followed the police through a maze of back streets and alleys, living in what seemed like the worst nightmare of her life. With the baby crying from the floorboard, her nerves were being pinched and tugged from all directions. What's more, she herself was sobbing uncontrollably, alternating between praying, cursing, crying out in pain, and trying to soothe Sophia-Emma. A perfectly wonderful day in heaven was being replaced by a nightmare from a fiery hell.

The sirens stopped, and one of the policemen came to her car door. Amanda didn't know where she would be going, but she knew that little Sophia-Emma had to come with them. While she was worried about whether Peter was dead or alive, she was also concerned about the infant. She needed to stay with her. They needed each other.

When they arrived at the county morgue, the police told her that they had a safe place where the baby could be taken until after they were finished, but Amanda wouldn't let go of Sophia-Emma, even when, for a moment, she thought the baby would be harmed as Corporal Barnes, the policeman, tried to take her from her arms. He finally gave up and let her carry Sophia-Emma.

They were led down a number of institutional corridors that smelled of sweat and room disinfectant. Echoes bounced from one wall to the other and back again. Some doors opened automatically after Corporal Barnes put his card into a slot. When they went through the final door, before her was a body covered with a white sheet. The coroner and a policeman nodded to her. Corporal Barnes moved to her side, ready to intervene if she lost it after seeing the deceased.

Amanda stood, clutching little Sophia-Emma tighter by the second, as the technician slowly pulled the sheet down, first revealing the victim's head. As soon as the sheet reached his chin, she made a positive identification. That was Peter's intricately braided, copper-colored goatee. She handed Sophia-Emma to the policeman and bent down to kiss her lover, who was now cold, inexpressive, and dead. His eyes had been closed by the coroner before her arrival, or maybe they had closed when he died. Amanda didn't know. She knew this was her man, but it also wasn't. Peter would've been complaining about the room being too cold. He would've been smiling at her with his crooked smile, surveying her body from the corner of his eye.

Amanda now wanted little Sophia-Emma back. She asked the three men if they could have some time alone, and they nodded and left the room. She looked down at his perfect body, which seemed, at the moment, to hardly be harmed at all other than a reddish mark and torn skin on his chest. She showed Peter to Sophia-Emma, knowing that everything was probably just blurred shapes in dull grays to her. And perhaps that was for the best.

"Peter, I was going to let our baby go this afternoon, but now I don't think so," she whispered. "This baby is ours. You helped name her. I know you don't believe in God, but I believe that someone special knew we would need each other soon. Without you, I'll have to have Sophia-Emma to make me want to live. Goodbye my dear, sweet, wonderful lover."

Amanda pulled the sheet up to Peter's lips. She leaned over and kissed him one final time. Then she turned and walked to the door, aware that the policemen and coroner had been watching her, maybe even listening to her every word. She didn't care. She just knew she had to buy a car seat before Goodwill closed.

Chapter 8

Outside the county morgue, Amanda pondered over what dire event would happen next. Although she was Peter's partner and loved him more than any man alive, she couldn't get bogged down with all the bureaucracy that went with investigations, trials, and media spinning. Not to mention the controversy that would be caused by those who couldn't wait to incriminate the victim instead of the real culprits. After all, Peter was an avowed anarchist. He had participated in his share of civil disobedience, going as far as destroying property and calling police "pigs." He'd hampered police work and had probably cost local and state governments thousands, maybe millions, of dollars by disrupting meetings, vandalizing buildings, and causing havoc wherever he could.

The police who'd brought her to this place already knew the victim. They also knew her and realized that she was an embarrassment to genteel Alabamians. Their purpose today had been to show her the error of her ways, to let her see the consequences of messing with the status quo.

She did want to see the culprits brought to justice, but not with the death penalty. She just wanted them to rot in jail forever. Well, maybe not rot. Long ago, she had taken a vow of nonviolence. A better punishment would be to destroy all that they held dear—their money, their flags, their slogans, their websites, and their meeting grounds. Send their kids to schools that taught nonviolence. Stuff like that. Destroy the evil, but not the people who had become victims of evil.

As Amanda got into her van, she knew she had made her mind up. She wouldn't give up Sophia-Emma. Over her dead body.

Her first goal was to get her baby everything she needed, especially a car seat. Then she would get the documentation. She knew some guys who were good at falsifying documents. She would contact them tomorrow. Before Christmas came with carols and peace to all, Sophia-Emma would be her real baby. Even the Alabama Health Department would find a record of her birth, with Amanda listed as her mama. And both would live happily ever after.

She would need to find a place with a roof and front door, but not on wheels. She needed to secure a job that would help her support her baby, and she would check on the small trust fund she was currently living on. And she would even try to reconcile with her mother. All of it would be worth it if Sophia-Emma became her real daughter, if they could share memories and grow together.

Amanda had often thought about how she could have been brought up better. Most of what she'd learned about life was taught to her by her anarchist friends. The boarding schools and private college, the nannies and nurses, had only taught her what she needed to know in order to become the oppressor, the supremacist, the bigot. Perhaps someone like the one who'd killed her lover. But her daughter would learn love and truth and would have a passion for life, nature, and justice for all. Maybe a little idealistic, but so what? She was the mom, and she was going to give it a try. She couldn't do any worse than her mama had done.

Then her heart tore apart again. Her Peter wouldn't be around to share these hopes and dreams. He wouldn't be around to hold her hand around the campfire, to chase her with a sticky marshmallow, to kiss her, to make love to her, to hold her. Was there life after Peter?

Chapter 9

After purchasing the car seat, more Similac, and some real diapers, Amanda called Chaos, a friend she'd made in the anarchist movement in 2003—back when they were getting their feet wet in social-change work, raising hell at the Miami Free Trade Zone during a protest. Today, Chaos insisted on meeting Amanda in her van at Bud's. Really, Amanda felt like being alone with Sophia-Emma, so she could hold her close and simply watch her breathe life in and out, but she knew that Chaos would give her space and also company when she needed to scream.

Few knew Chaos's real name, but Amanda had always thought that her alias fit her perfectly. She was a superb organizer who inspired others by having principles she only bent when the ends justified the means. A gal with some meat on her bones, her enemies would say. Those in her bloc knew she was tough, and many on the other side had literally felt her strength. Like Amanda, her dishwater blond dreads went down to the middle of her back.

Chaos drove her ailing, little red Saturn, which she called Moose, to Amanda's campsite. The two hugged for a long time. Chaos felt Amanda's tears wetting her shoulder. She herself was crying near Amanda's armpit, and the smell brought back memories from when showers were quick and rare. *Not much different from current times*, Chaos reminded herself.

Eventually, Sophia-Emma broke up the pair's embrace with a cry from the back of Amanda's van. Chaos got to her first and said, "Oh, girl, where in the devil did you scrounge this little diamond morsel from?"

Amanda tenderly looked down at her little girl, who seemed to realize that this strange lady wasn't her mama. She smiled and motioned for Chaos to join her on the stump next to the chair where Peter had typed his letters yesterday.

"She's my lifesaver, Chaos," Amanda explained between sobs. "I found her at my mama's place yesterday. She was the future dinner for an eagle out in the pasture. She was abandoned out there. No other human was around. Just a neighbor's dog hightailing it back down the road. Don't matter, though. She's now mine. We need each other now that Peter's gone. Was going to turn her over to the State, but not now. Not now."

Together, they called other cell members and social activists. Most had heard about the murder and were ready to create havoc on Saturday. Peter had been the blood and guts of the People's Global Action in Alabama. White supremacy groups, along with the Church of the National Knights of the Ku Klux Klan, had recently partnered with the Neo Nazis in the state. The killing of Peter was a major accomplishment for these groups—a cowardly accomplishment, but major, nonetheless.

Amanda looked over at Chaos as she finished her last call. "I don't know what I'm going to do from here on out, girl. With a baby to care for, I have to reassess my involvement in our revolution. In many ways, we fight violence with violence, even if it is for the right causes, like human rights and equality. I love both. But both need the other. My baby will one day be someone the Supremacists go after. And she might also be part of a new generation of people who'll use nonviolence to be victorious and win people's hearts in the process."

"Holy shit, Manda, for someone who's just lost her lover, you talk a good line. This baby, as pretty as she is, isn't yours. Let some middle-class family raise her. You can still hand her over to the State and continue as you always have. After a little grieving time, of course," Chaos suggested.

"I know, I know," Amanda responded. "But my gut tells me I have to strike out on a new path. Don't know where it'll lead me, but my baby here is part of the journey. Don't try to talk me out of it. Please, Chaos.

"For now, we need to talk about what'll happen this Saturday in Montgomery. I understand that some activists are planning a big memorial event in front of the Governor's Mansion. No requests for permission. No, the Black Bloc isn't about asking for permission. They'll show up, masks and all. Don't get me wrong, I want them to mourn for their leader and to recommit to the cause, opposing fascism and white supremacism through direct action," Amanda said between sobs.

She went on to clarify that there would be no body or ashes, as the authorities wouldn't release the body while the investigation was ongoing. She insisted that she wouldn't be at the Governor's Mansion. She was concerned about the safety of Sophia-Emma. Maybe she would hang out on the fringes of the gathering, where she would be able to leave quickly if violence erupted. Chaos insisted that she would be there to cover for her and would be available to help with the baby.

That night, as she fed Sophia-Emma, Amanda explained the vision she had of her life and asked Chaos questions. She knew that Chaos wouldn't understand anything she said and that she wouldn't receive the answers she so desperately needed. But Amanda had to talk to Chaos, to let her know how important little Sophia-Emma was for the future. Since viewing Peter's body, the infant had been particularly quiet and cooperative, giving her new mama time to consider all that had happened in the last couple of days. Amanda began to think her baby was also thinking about their future.

"Sweetie, I don't know why I found you out in that pasture. At first, I thought I was protecting you from the eagle soaring over you. Now

I don't know what to think. Do you have a real mama mourning your absence right now? I hope not. I can't express how honored I feel to have found you at a time when I have no one else to love. I hope you'll help me move on. And if some woman someday claims you're her baby and I can see the resemblance, I'll pass you back. But not tonight. I hope not ever."

Amanda once again mourned the loss of Peter, burying her sobs in her pillow, hoping she wouldn't wake Chaos, who had fallen asleep nearby. She eventually continued her talk with Sophia-Emma outside the van.

"Today is unbearably sad for me. I do believe that Peter would have made the job ahead possible. But maybe his spirit can help us in ways his human body can't. Sophia-Emma, all I can promise is that I will do my best. Remember, becoming a mama was the furthest thing from my mind three days ago. Now it's the only thing on my mind. That in itself is a miracle. And someday, I'm confident we'll see a miracle happening in my mama. When she comes to know you, there's no way she'll be able to hold on to her outdated ideas of family exceptionalism. Patience, child. Patience. And love." She gave the baby kisses on both of her delicate little cheeks.

"And by the way, my trust fund's about gone. Your grandma won't let us move to Promised Land. I can't raise you in the back of my van. Homelessness is not an option. I promise you, we'll find a way. I just need a little time. Speak to me with your eyes if you can lend me some ideas. I'm open to anything."

Later, little Sophia-Emma was fast asleep beside Amanda in the back of the van, which was once again parked in a quiet spot under a couple of oaks. Their branches extended out over the Alabama River. Amanda couldn't help but think of the last time she'd lain there with Peter, making love. Even though he had so often been consumed by plans to fight the enemy, she'd been able to bring him into a zone of pure love every so often—during nights when the moon was full, when spring dawned and the birds serenaded them, when thunder and lightning filled the sky, and in the evenings after big turnouts and disruptive, direct actions. There were so many times when their bodies were linked, almost as if through magnetism. Their hearts had pounded as one, their bodies on fire yet cool and soothing to the touch. Eyes told stories, and lips spoke romance. When the energy depleted in their tired bodies, simple touches in tender places could ignite flames of erotic love that eventually wound down into agape love, togetherness, resolve, and loyalty to the end. But the end was now.

With such thoughts, Amanda drifted off into a deep sleep, dreaming of loss and hope for the future.

Chapter 10

The next couple of days were long days of mourning for Amanda, and she clung to Sophia-Emma even tighter. Chaos left to help plan Peter's memorial demonstration, but she made Amanda promise to call at any moment if she needed help or someone to yell at.

Even though Amanda missed Peter, in his absence she was developing some structure in her new life of caring for a baby—learning the routine of boiling water, cooling it, and mixing it with powdered formula; learning to change diapers and wash them; and learning to do other baby chores.

She had even discovered why Sophia-Emma's bowel movements were so dark and tar-like. She had picked up a paperback book about babies at Moses's and had discovered that this was normal for newborns. It was meconium, the waste that came from ingested amniotic fluids during the infant's time in the womb. It was usually out of the baby's system by the second or third day. So that, along with the ugly belly button, told her that Sophia-Emma was a very recently born baby. Sophia-Emma's bowels were now yellowish, like they should be, and her umbilical cord was becoming less gross by the hour. That little book answered so many questions about babies. But of course, it couldn't locate an absent mother. Amanda was almost grateful for that.

On Saturday morning, she got up early. (It was as if she never slept these days.) Today was the day that, out of respect for Peter and their relationship, she planned to attend the memorial honoring his life. She would leave early, get some breakfast on the way, put Sophia-Emma in the stroller, and spend the day a few blocks away from the Governor's Mansion. The weather looked like it would cooperate, and Sophia-Emma loved being in her stroller during their walks.

A few of Peter's friends had called, urging her to at least say a few words during the memorial. But she insisted that she would remain silent this time. No way would she get mixed up in the mess that was bound to be made. The other side had won some recent battles, fighting against homosexuals' right to marry. Her side needed a victory. Maybe if there wasn't a baby in her life, she would join them, but not now.

She had also received some calls from the Montgomery police since Peter's death. They wanted to know more about the groups her lover had been part of, where other members hung out, what their plans were, and who she suspected may have killed him. In her eyes, all of the questions were a farce. There was no way they were going to pursue this case and find Peter's killers. No, all they wanted was to blame the victim himself. They wanted to depict him as a troublemaker who got what he deserved.

Today, she would keep her cell phone off, only checking occasionally for messages. She would show Sophia-Emma the mansions and the ambiance around the governor's residence, then take her over to the Old Cloverdale neighborhood and Huntington College. But during their tour, she would tell Sophie-Emma a different story than the one told to her by her own mama.

On such walks, Amanda's mama would tell her about the refinement of "their" people and their innate ability to bring beauty into the world. According to her, some neighborhoods needed to be only white, as they were carrying on a tradition of southern gentility. Beautiful, chaste white ladies and their little princes and princesses. Marvelous parties that had colored servants who were appropriately attired, who knew their place in polite society, and who waited on the white people's every desire. A life of garden parties, cocktail gatherings, bridge nights, and debutante balls was an ordered life. Why would anyone want to be negative in a city of such godly grace and love, where men were men and women were beautiful, graceful ladies?

Last night, Amanda had rehearsed the story she would share with Sophia-Emma today. She would use the beautiful homes as examples of the artistic skills of the slaves and craftsmen who built them. The colorful, well-sculpted lawns were beautiful because of the constant care of talented landscapers, who were mostly people of color. She would also tell stories from before the big houses were built, like how the Alabama and Coushatta nations formed the first confederacy, called the Muscogee Creek Confederacy, which was made up of autonomous towns before white and black people came to the area. The memorable, pretty parties were made possible because of the work of black slaves and hard-working servants. Little white children were attached to their black nannies and maids, whose own children often saw tired-out remnants of their mamas.

But no matter which story was told, Amanda felt sure that her afternoon with Sophia-Emma would be surrounded by beauty—colorful leaves and flowers, clear blue skies, and lots of love. Could anyone ask for more?

Chapter 11

The day started as planned. Little Sophia-Emma seemed to now be focusing on Amanda's face, even smiling ever so slightly. Amanda knew the day would soon come when she would dress her in a beautiful white christening gown, take her home to her mama, and declare that her baby would be baptized as a Foster. But there would be stipulations. She hadn't yet decided if they would be verbalized. Some things were better left unsaid.

She stopped at a truck stop with a restaurant on the way to Montgomery. Little Sophia-Emma watched her eat every bite of pancake and sausage, almost as if she wanted to ask for something other than formula. Amanda empathized and wondered what it must be like to eat the same thing up to twelve times a day. She concluded that life as a baby must be very mundane.

In Montgomery, Amanda could feel the tension mounting as she headed downtown. There were more state patrol cars on the road, but there were just as many vehicles bearing bumper stickers with slogans like *Fuck the Police*; *Adam and Eve, not Adam and Steve*; *Power to the People*; and the anarchist logo, which was an A with a ring around it. As soon as she saw the opportunity, she veered off on a side street that appeared to be serene.

First, she took Sophia-Emma on a stroll along the sidewalks around and through Huntington College. She reminded her little girl that the landscaping in the fifty-eight acres was done by Frederick Law Olmsted, who also designed Central Park in New York City. She talked as if Sophie-Emma really cared, though she was sleeping at the time. From there, Amanda ventured into other parts of the Old Cloverdale neighborhood, where she gave her little speech that she'd rehearsed the night before.

Upon finding a bench by a bus stop, she fed Sophia-Emma her bottle, changed her, and then ate a sandwich she had packed for herself. As people arrived for or left from the bus, she received some curious looks, especially when she was putting a real diaper on Sophia-Emma. Amanda wished she could breastfeed so she could shock them even more. Maybe someday. Some mamas had made it happen. She made a mental note to buy a breast pump so she could stimulate her mammary glands in order to produce milk. *Aww, that would make the whole mamahood thing complete*, she thought.

They both rested, and then she once again nestled Sophia-Emma into the stroller and headed to the Garden District, where the Governor's Mansion was. She knew there was a fence all around the grounds, and there was even a guard house in the front. If a big crowd showed up, they would fill the sidewalks and the grass before expanding into the street. She envisioned streets filled with angry mobs and angrier, better-armed police. And if the other side showed, the whole scene would not be pretty.

Old Cloverdale morphed into the Garden District. Amanda's steps became more deliberate. Her ears and eyes were on alert. She felt like a mama bear bringing her cub into Dumpster Land for the first time. She had no fear for herself, but for the child—the innocent, unscathed baby—she was afraid. Sophia-Emma hadn't taken sides in this conflict, yet she was being taken into a place of danger. But her mother was determined not to take her too close. Amanda would avoid this modern-day Roman colosseum of lions, hungry for the blood of the Christians. She was going to stand on the distant edge of this disruption and show her baby that people loved the man who would have become her father. She would be safe. She had to be.

The small, faraway sounds became not so far away. They grew louder, more passionate. Amanda heard profanity, passion, remorse, and out-right mourning. Demands for justice, heads, blood, and revenge. On the fringes, where Amanda had wanted to stand, were the peaceful people. They were holding signs and being silent. Some—mostly old hippies from a time long ago—lit candles and asked the universe to heal the pain on this Earth. They asked for opposites to come together and just get along.

Mostly, there were angry people. They were after revenge, ready to slash tires, bust windows, and throw flammables. Young men and women, as she often did on days like today, wore black with masks of the same color.

But most frightening of all were those across the street, separated from the mourning and mad. They stood behind the police, dressed like characters from *Star Wars*. They stood with signs that said, *Peter is Deader*; *One down, 1,000 to go*; *The South is Rising Again*; and *Your Back: Our Target*. Plus, there were scores of swastikas, confederate bars and stars, and crosses. She saw agitated people armed with guns, knives, and even a few machetes.

Amanda had seen enough. She turned away and slowly walked to her van, planning to go back to her peaceful riverside campsite. She hadn't taken ten steps before six of her old friends surrounded her, demanding she say something in honor of Peter.

"No, I can't do that. Peter wouldn't want me to." Amanda kept looking straight ahead as she tried to walk through them.

"Amanda, this is your chance to bring some sense to this crowd," Chaos said as she grabbed her arm, stopping her in her tracks. "You know you owe it to Peter to say a few words. I'll watch the baby here. Why in the world would you bring a baby to something like this?"

Then the other five—three men and two women—literally picked her up and carried her to a stack of pallets that had become a temporary stage.

The rally speaker saw her and interrupted his call to action so he could turn his megaphone over to Amanda. This wasn't in the plan. Amanda had played second fiddle in the movement, and it was a place where she had always felt comfortable. She wasn't a motivator of people, a cheer-leader. Now she was expected to be a speaker at a memorial. She wanted to get off the stage, but she was hemmed in. So, she simply opened her mouth and let her feelings out. She cried. And the longer she cried, the harder she cried. She wasn't looking at those who were waiting for her words. She didn't care what they thought. She just knew she was devastated.

Finally, she spoke. "Y'all know what? I hate hate. Hate killed the man I love. But I don't want his murderer to be killed, too. Someone loves him or her as much as I loved Peter. Peter was kind and generous and even funny. He didn't have a drop of hate inside him. He did, however, hate hate. He hated racism, fascism, bigotry, corporate greed, oppression, injustice, poverty, and inequality. If you want to hate, hate what needs to be hated. Hate this damn system that makes us want to kill each other. Hate the powers that divide us.

"What would he say to y'all if he was on this beautiful stage today? He wouldn't tell you to hate anyone. He would say to forgive the human who has done wrong. Hate what was done, but love the hater. Love the guy who thinks he'll find happiness if he can just feel a little bigger than the black guy, the woman, the homosexual or lesbian, the immigrant, or the poor person. Peter and I both knew that only love could fuel love. Build a fire that doesn't destroy. Build one that purifies and molds love itself into an image we can all emulate.

"Thank you all for coming today. Let's quit the fighting and hating and try to talk a little. Just a little. My Peter would like that."

With that, a space on the tiny stage opened up, and she stepped down. She looked once more at the crowd of folk standing out there. They weren't clapping. They weren't booing her, either. She assumed they were simply stunned. Both sides. The police were ready to react, but there was nothing for them to do.

Amanda, for a moment, identified with Moses of the Old Testament. As she stepped through the crowd and went back to her baby, it felt like she was stepping into the Red Sea. The waters were splitting as she was reunited with her daughter. Even though her day hadn't gone exactly as planned, that was okay. Both she and Sophia-Emma were safe.

Chaos gave Amanda a long and silent hug. "You go, girl," she said as she walked back to the crowd.

Chapter 12

The sun was dipping lower behind the feathery gray sky as Amanda drove back to her camp at Bud's Place. She felt a deep sense of peace, but at the same time she was quite aware that her life was in the process of falling apart. She would soon have to find a place to live and work. She still wasn't on good terms with her mama. There was no sweet little grandma who begged to babysit her granddaughter.

That evening, with new eyes she saw the peaceful haven where she and Peter had spent the last few months. Not long ago, they had been on the run from a direct-action organization that had turned violent in New Orleans before Katrina hit. Like so many times before, once back in Alabama, they had attempted to blend in with the surroundings and had successfully avoided being found by people on their trail. Nevertheless, they'd known there were targets on their backs. They'd had to go into hiding for a while. In the long run, what they'd taught residents there was worth the "disappearance" they'd had to endure. Even her mama didn't know. Oh, the dozens of things about which she knew nothing.

She pulled into her regular parking spot and unbuckled little Sophia-Emma. She lifted the sleeping baby ever so gently out of her used car seat. For a moment, all she could do was stare down at this special tiny human. She realized she knew nothing about raising a child. All she could give was love. From there, she was confident the rest would come.

The September air had a slight nip to it, making Amanda realize that this life she was living would have to be changed soon. For tonight, she would put up with the chill, but tomorrow she'd look for real shelter. First of all, she'd hit her mama up for a loan so she could pay the deposit and the first month's rent somewhere. Then she needed some furniture, food, and utilities. She could manage some of these expenses, but not all.

Amanda dug into her ice chest in the back of her van. There, she found a generic brand of vegetable soup and a box of crackers. It would be enough to get through the night. She found her hot plate and plugged it into the old cigarette lighter socket so she could warm up the soup. When she crushed a layer of soda crackers over the soup, Sophia-Emma woke up.

"Well, hello, little sleepy head," she greeted her baby. "Just wait a minute while I inhale this soup, and then I'm all yours tonight."

And that's what she did. Sophia-Emma seemed to follow her mama's every move, watching the spoon move from the hot plate to her mama's mouth over and over. Another little smile made Amanda set aside the remainder of the soup and pick up Sophia-Emma.

"We're going to make it, babe," she whispered to her daughter. "You don't know how much your mommy can do when she sets her mind to it. But tonight, we're just going to lie here, watch the stars appear and sparkle, and then cuddle up together and have sweet dreams." She gently touched Sophia-Emma's nose with her index finger.

Sophia-Emma was fine with all of that, but she was also hungry and wet. She let Amanda know by letting out a few baby cries and wiggling around in her small nest, which Amanda had made for her in what had been Peter's favorite chair. The new mother made another bottle using some boiled water she'd put into an insulated coffee cup from a convenience store. She added the soiled diaper to the big black garbage bag, where the other diapers were being stored until they could be washed at the Wash and Dry laundromat the next morning. In the meantime, the two of them would have to put up with a slight sewer smell through the night.

After Sophia-Emma had once again fallen asleep, Amanda checked her phone. She waded through a number of texts that updated her on how Peter's memorial had gone after she left. Chaos wrote that the supremacists had made movements to agitate the mourners. A few from her side had reacted, but for once the police had been able to calm both sides. Traffic had been shut down, and the media had made a bigger deal of it than they'd needed to, but no one was sent to the hospital or jail, no bystanders were harmed, and by dark all was quiet at the Governor's Mansion.

But the struggle isn't finished, Chaos had texted. *Long way from it. Thanks for doing your part to help us mourn your man, our leader, and your love, Peter.*

After she'd gotten caught up with all the news about the struggle, she found the nerve to call her mother.

"Hey, Mama, how're you doing?" she quietly said in greeting after her mother answered the phone at Promised Land.

"Well, you're getting back in touch at last, are you?" she responded. "I was watching the news tonight, and I see, like usual, you're out there making a fool of yourself."

"Mama, to be truthful, we were mourning Peter's death. He was shot in the back the other day, or didn't you hear?"

"Well, if he'd had a real job and hadn't stuck his nose into places where it didn't belong, he would still be here. I hope you've learned your lesson."

"Thanks for all your sympathy, Mama. The last couple days could have gone a little smoother if you'd been at my side, guiding me through this ordeal."

Amanda heard a noise outside her van and lost her train of thought. "Hey, Mama, can you keep the door unlocked tonight? I hear something going on outside my van. Probably just some raccoons going through the garbage, but if it's more than that, I need a place to crash."

She heard no response. She could only imagine her mother shaking her head in disgust and pondering over whether she'd practice tough love tonight or give shelter to her only surviving child.

"You know I'm not leaving Promised Land unlocked overnight," she warned her daughter. "I go to bed at nine o'clock and will lock the doors at that time. Come after that, and forget about getting in."

Amanda could imagine the satisfied look on her mother's face as she laid down the law, only leaving a tiny opening in case her daughter really needed a place to sleep.

"Okay, Mama. I know your concerns about your fine antiques and well-being. Believe me, I won't bother you unless I absolutely have to."

With that, she hung up, then listened closely for any additional noise outside her van. She checked to see if all her doors were locked. No noise. A good sign. How she wished she still had the protective presence of Peter next to her.

Amanda laid down close to Sophia-Emma and was about to drift off when a jagged rock flew into her rear window. She abruptly sat up, transferred Sophia-Emma into her car seat, and slid herself into the driver's seat. She put her van into reverse, then shifted low, moving into second and third gear before squealing out of the park. She kept checking for vehicles following her on the dark, curving road, but saw none. She assumed this was a warning for her to get out of town. Her heart was pumping frantically.

Less than half an hour later, before 9:00 PM, she wrapped Sophia-Emma up in one of her new receiving blankets, grabbed some clean diapers and formula, and walked up to her mother's back door. She'd decided as soon as she started thinking clearly that until her mother accepted Sophia-Emma, she would no longer use the front door.

Louise heard the commotion on the back porch and yelled for Tillie, who was now upstairs preparing for bed, to go see what was going on.

"Tillie, hurry," she yelled five minutes later.

The old servant, in her long nightgown, muttered under her breath and made her way down the spiral staircase.

"You're no help up there. I think I'll have you move back down to the servants' quarters tomorrow," Louise complained as Tillie shuffled by her.

In the kitchen, Tillie found Amanda holding her baby...if that bundle cradled in her arms *was* a baby. "Oh no! Mrs. Foster ain't gonna be happy at all," she told Amanda, then yelled to her boss, "It's just Amanda, ma'am. I'll lock up and see if she wants a bite to eat. Why don't you get ready for bed? I'll check on you before I go to bed."

"Well, tell her I'm tired but that I want to see her bright and early tomorrow. Goodnight, Tillie."

Tillie peeped into the bundle Amanda cradled in her arms. "Let me see the little darling, Amanda," she insisted as she stood on her tiptoes to peer between the blankets. She saw wide-awake little black eyes looking back at her. "Well, I'll be," she whispered. "What a little beauty!" The old lady shook her head and pointed her finger at Amanda. "Now, you sit down here with me and tell me why you still have this baby. I know she's a charmer, but you know your mama. She's no Foster. Wrong color and wrong breed to be a blue blood."

"I've adopted her, Tillie," Amanda said to the old woman. "I decided that, with the death of Peter, I need someone to live for. I decided to keep her as my own. And just think, no pregnancy and no labor pains." She gave Tillie a pleading half-smile, her tears ruining her joke.

"Talk about pains, you're going to get plenty of them from your mama. May I suggest we keep her our little secret?"

"Can't do, Tillie," Amanda insisted. "This baby—her name is Sophia-Emma Foster—is going to be a part of this family long after Mama and I are gone. I can't hide her the rest of my life."

"How you able to adopt her so soon, Ms. Amanda? I thought somethin' like that took years, or at least months."

"Let's just say I have my ways, and some good contacts." Amanda checked Sophia-Emma's diaper. "After all, you know us Fosters. We find friends in all kinds of places."

Tillie knew there was more to this story than she cared to pursue. "Well, I'll leave the battle up to you, Ms. Amanda. I just want to say that you need to be aware of what that old lady can do to you and that baby. For your own good, talk a smooth line tomorrow, or she'll make your life miserable."

"You think I don't already know my own mama, Tillie? But thanks for the advice. Sometimes I think you're the only one with any common sense in this house."

Tillie pointed to the room off the kitchen, where she would probably be sleeping from now on, and suggested that Amanda sleep there tonight so the baby wouldn't disturb Louise. Amanda agreed and started to prepare Sophia-Emma for the night.

"Goodnight, Ms. Tillie," she said as the servant left to lock the house up and go back upstairs, presumably checking on Louise one more time before retiring herself.

Amanda wasn't disappointed that she wouldn't be sleeping in her old room tonight, as she preferred this room instead. The bed upstairs was out of her league. It belonged to the capitalist oppressors and racists who'd purchased all the furnishings from others just like them. In the servants' quarters, she would be sleeping on a lumpy mattress and would be surrounded by cast-off furnishings that were more suitable for homeless centers. But no matter what condition the surroundings were in, she now felt secure, at least for the night.

No one on the other side knew her last name. In the anarchist world, she traveled with one name only. Both sides knew her as Gonzo, a name Peter had jokingly given her. Everyone except Chaos, that was. And she trusted her with the secret as much as she had trusted Peter with it.

Though the air in the old pipes squealed through the night, Amanda and Sophia-Emma slept soundly until sometime in the early morning.

Then Amanda heard the crying and the voices again. Although still half-asleep, her eyes glued shut, the baby squirmed beside her, almost like she understood the voices. Then all was quiet once more.

Tillie was up at daylight, preparing one of her full breakfasts—bacon, eggs, pancakes, fresh fruit, and freshly ground coffee. For Amanda, the aroma brought back so many memories of sitting around the kitchen table, not the formal dining table that was off in the more ornate part of the house. She and a younger Tillie would discuss the garden—what was coming in, what was blooming, and what would be eaten for dinner that night. Her mama would be off in the dining room with her daddy, going over the estate's finances and pestering him to be tougher on the field crews, including docking them when they fell behind. Amanda didn't like all that fuss.

This morning, she heard her mama calling for Tillie to help her dress upstairs.

"Go on up, Tillie. I can finish here. Besides, I want to dress Sophia-Emma in one of her newer outfits so she'll impress her grandma."

Tillie just nodded and gave her a strange look, like she wanted to tell her how naïve she was for expecting Mrs. Foster to love Sophia-Emma, regardless of how cute she was.

Amanda had no trouble feeding and dressing the baby while also watching breakfast and setting the table. When she heard the stair-lift bring her mama down to her waiting wheelchair, she decided to pour the coffee and put on the best fake smile she had for the Promised Land matriarch.

Louise was in her normal grumpy mood as she entered the kitchen, yelling at Tillie for making such a big meal on a Sunday morning, therefore meaning Louise would have to rush to get to church on time.

When Tillie swung open the kitchen door so Louise could wheel herself in, Louise saw her daughter and the baby and warned, "I hope you don't have a baby wrapped up in that blanket. Didn't I tell you not to keep that mixed-blood baby. I don't want it in this house. And you can leave with her right now if you intend to keep her." She then gulped down her first cup of coffee and motioned for Tillie to give her a refill.

"Mama, I really think that if you just look at little Sophia-Emma, you'll love her. She's such a good baby. She would be an asset to our family." Amanda was trying, for once, to be respectful. She wanted to give her mother one more chance to reconcile so they could all live here at Promised Land in peace.

Amanda told her about how she could make plans for a nursery for Sophia-Emma, order heirloom seeds for next year's garden, turn Promised Land into an organic farm, and maybe even offer cow shares for neighbors who preferred raw milk. But Louise turned a deaf ear to all of Amanda's proposals.

"Get that baby out of here, and then we'll talk," Louise insisted. "Didn't I tell you that her type didn't belong in this family? Look at her! Coal-black hair and eyes. Dark, dirty skin. She belongs out in our fields as a day worker, not as my heir. Who do you think I am? Why do you disgust me with this piece of pasture shit?"

That did it. Amanda gathered the dirty and clean diapers, the clothes and formula, and her baby, then ran out of the house, too mad to eat or cry and too sad to yell back. She revved up her van's engine and barreled from the manicured driveway out onto the road, heading north. Sophia-Emma was crying. After all, this had been her first home, too. Were ancestors refusing to let go of her? Too bad. Amanda was determined to get away to Anywhere Else, USA, beginning now.

Chapter 13

Amanda found her way over to I-65, which took her northeast, then got on I-85 in Montgomery. Soon, she'd be out of the state. As she kept making her way as far away as she could, she realized that both she and her mama had blown it. Her mother had thrown out her only living heir, and Amanda had separated herself from any source of support or security. Yep, the women in her family weren't too smart, she concluded.

She didn't like being alone in a world where white nationalists were on a roll with getting folk like her out of the way. And people seeing a baby of color with her wouldn't help either of them.

And then there was the money issue. She had a baby in this van with her. This baby had no one to depend on other than Amanda. She hadn't asked to be left in that pasture, a bird circling her, waiting for her to die so she could become meat. Amanda shuddered at the thought.

But all wasn't lost. If she had learned one thing while running with anarchists for the last three years, it was that there were groups doing what she had been doing—fighting white nationalism and fascism—throughout the US. Part of the agreement was that they would provide shelter for members of the movement who were passing through. Maybe they would help a mother and baby, especially since they had a connection to Peter. Everyone knew him.

Peter. That word. That man. For a few moments, she again remembered their lovemaking, their first and last times. If only she'd known earlier in the week that the wild and intimate caresses would be their last. But her sorrow was deeper than that. She remembered the jokes they had played on each other and the glances at each other during important strategy sessions. She reminisced about the birthmark on his neck and the peace sign tattoo with her name etched around it. He had been the love of her life. No one would ever measure up. She was sure of that.

"I can't believe you're really gone, Peter Pan," she said, using the name he preferred among Anarchist groups.

Sophia-Emma stirred behind her, disrupting her sweet memories and bringing her back to the now. She sat up straighter and soothingly assured the baby that all would be fine. She would figure something out.

"Patience, baby. Mama's thinking our future out," she told Sophia-Emma.

Time to make some contacts, she decided. Chaos first.

"Hey, Chaos?" she said when Chaos answered the phone.

"Where are you, woman? We've been looking for you. Saw that your van and most of your goodies were gone from Bud's," Chaos noted. "We thought maybe you'd been kidnapped, or worse! Are you traveling or at your mother's? Where are you?"

"I have to get out of Alabama." Amanda started to cry again. "Last night, after Peter's memorial, some screwballs threw a rock into my van. I spent the night at Mama's. She kicked me out a little bit ago because Sophia-Emma wasn't white enough. So now I'm on the road, heading north. Any ideas where we can crash? Or where I can pick up food for us? I'm really low on the green stuff."

"Where do you think you are right now?" Chaos asked.

"I'm on eighty-five, heading out of Alabama. Soon, I hope. Never want to see this 'Roll Tide' shit again."

"Stay on eighty-five," Chaos instructed her. "I'll try to get you into Virginia. There're some great intentional communities up there where you can crash for a couple weeks, sort things out, and decide what you want to do from there."

"Hey, I don't know if I'm ready for one of those commune-type places, where you have to get a consensus just to go to the outhouse." Amanda was once more thinking like her old self.

"Amanda, I don't like to boss you around, but you got a baby with you who isn't really your baby. Yeah, we got Amigo and Sorrell working on putting together an ID for her, and they're hacking into the state offices' computers, documenting her as yours. But that takes time. You can't be all over the place while all this is going on. You need a place where you'll get some R and R while you wait for documentation."

Chaos talked like she knew what to do. Amanda was impressed. A place where she could rest, feel safe, really grieve, and be a good mama. It sounded so much better than hanging out in Very Wicked the rest of her life.

"Now, all you have to do is drive, my girl. Turn your phone off. Knowing you, you didn't charge it recently. Check in with me every couple hours. As you get farther away from home, you may have to put it on roaming. With as much as you've moved around, you know that. In the meantime, I'll be calling some communities I know of that might be able to give you some safety."

Amanda was relieved. She checked the time and turned off her phone. She kept driving north on I-85, just as Chaos had advised, stopping every other hour to feed and change Sophia-Emma, to stretch her own weary body, to check her phone, and to rest.

Meanwhile, Chaos was on the phone with Triple Trees, Sanctuary, and Off-the-Grid communities. Two of them wouldn't take a chance on Amanda and her baby, and one gave her the runaround. The last said she could spend two weeks with them on a probationary basis, and from there they would discuss whether membership was for her. The last place was Sanctuary, which wasn't far from Beaverville, VA., just a little bit of a jaunt off 85.

Amanda breathed a sigh of relief when Chaos gave her the report. "What did you tell them about my situation?"

"I told them everything. After all, they're the closest to an anti-capitalist community I could find. They are used to situations as weird or weirder than yours. I told them that you are still grieving Peter's death, that you have a baby who you literally found on your mama's farm, and that this information is not to be shared with any outsiders. They'll only tell a few insiders. Lastly, your income is almost non-existent, so this is the only place you can crash safely for the time being. Anything I forgot or should have kept to myself?" Chaos sounded like a spy making plans for a comrade to disappear.

"You were fair. I figured I would have to level with them eventually anyway. Thanks for leveling with them and me. What should I do now? We're both extremely tired here. I need to get some shut eye, like, in the next hour. Is there any place, like a park or a parking lot, where I can sleep tonight? I'll go over to this Sanctuary place tomorrow."

Chaos said, "I have my Virginia map out now. You said you're on eighty-five, right? I see a rest stop at mile fifty-five. That might be relatively safe. Did you say that one of your windows is damaged because of those bastards who threw a rock through it last night?"

"That's right," Amanda admitted as she looked at the jagged edges of glass that remained in the rear window of her van.

"You know that I can't assure your safety anywhere with that situation. Why don't you make a stab at getting to Sanctuary tonight? Delay all the paperwork crap and just go to bed when you arrive."

"This place is probably on a narrow dirt road out in the middle of nowhere. I can't be driving in that neck of the woods the way I feel right now. No way." Amanda was close to tears.

"C'mon, Amanda. The folks at Sanctuary are cool folks," Chaos reassured her friend. "What if I get you to that rest stop? You feed and change the baby, and I'll see if two members can meet you there and take you to their place. You can let one of them drive your van with you and the baby in it."

Amanda wasn't in any mood to argue the fine points. All she wanted to do was sleep. "I think I can live with that," she said.

"Okay. Keep moving on to mile marker fifty-five. Get off at the rest stop there and park close to the bathrooms. I'll be contacting Sanctuary. Don't worry. I'll get two of 'em there to drive the rest of the way." Chaos, the master of organizing, spoke as though she was sure everything would work out just fine.

"You're a real angel," Amanda's tired voice managed to mumble. "I don't know how I'll repay you for all you've done. Much better than a casserole brought to me, the grieving lover."

"Just be a good mommy and don't piss anyone off right away," Chaos answered.

"Oh, I'll behave myself. I'm looking for some normalcy, at least for a little while. But don't count me out of the movement forever. I'm still with y'all."

"Okay, I'm on it. Call me back in about half an hour, and I'll tell you if they're on board with my agenda. Goodbye."

Amanda looked in the backseat and saw Sophia-Emma sound asleep, as if she were at perfect peace. *At least half the humans in the van are worriless,* Amanda thought. Now it was up to her to follow suit. She turned on the van's ignition, looked for any oncoming traffic, and pulled out onto the now-dark highway.

After a few minutes, her eyelids felt like elephants were stomping on them. She lowered her speed but discovered she grew even more tired at the slower speed. Amanda pushed down on the gas pedal to speed up. She turned the radio's volume up and switched to a hard-rock station. There was only one more thing she could do to remain awake. She got off the interstate at the next exit so she could take a water break and put just enough gas in Very Wicked to hopefully get them to the resting place tonight.

When she was pulling the gas hose from the van's tank, she noticed her daughter beginning to fidget. Amanda went over to Sophia-Emma's car seat. When she opened the car door, a rush of Virginia's cool October air hit the baby's face and tiny fingers. Her eyes opened, and her little body, full of fear, suddenly shook. Amanda reached over to calm the infant.

She realized that she would have to mix Sophia-Emma's formula powder with cold boiled water. *Will she take it?* she wondered How Amanda wanted to take her into her tired arms and breastfeed her now. She climbed over and sat in the seat next to Sophia-Emma. Gently, she removed Sophia-Emma from her seat and cuddled her tightly. She lifted her sweater and put Sophia-Emma to her warm breast. This was completely new to both of them. They fumbled around, but finally the hungry baby latched on. Amanda relaxed and felt love flowing from her heart into her baby. Such a moment of exhilaration, but calmness, as well. It permeated her entire being. She knew no milk was flowing from Mama to baby. That would come later. But for now, both needed skin-to-skin, Mama to daughter. Both givers, both receivers.

While baby and Mama were sharing this special moment, Amanda turned her phone back on and called Chaos. While the phone rang, she broke the baby's latch on her nipple and nestled her back down in her seat again so she could concentrate on what Chaos had to say.

"Hello, Chaos," she whispered into the phone.

Chaos asked, "You okay?"

"I'm trying not to upset Sophia-Emma," Amanda whispered back. "I'm at a gas station and have been trying to settle her down by nursing her."

"You're kidding! You don't have milk, do you? But that aside, I want to tell you what I found out."

"I'm listening. What's going to happen?" Amanda asked.

"A couple members are on their way right now to pick you up. I described your van to them. It's one man and one woman. I understand that they're in a purple van with a bad muffler. Their names are Jupiter and Zhen Bang. They'll be dressed in black."

"Any idea how much longer?" Amanda asked.

"Really hard to say since they live out on a dark dirt road off the interstate. As a guess, I wouldn't expect them for another forty minutes or so."

"Well, guess I'll feed Sophia-Emma some formula, change her, and check in my ice chest to see if I have anything to munch on," Amanda drowsily uttered. "If you talk to them again, tell them I have a broken window. Or if you want, you can give them my mobile number."

"I think everything's okay, Manda. Take it easy. Before you know it, you'll be safe and sleeping in a real bed, with only raccoons and opossums to worry about."

"I hate to let you go, Chaos. I'm so scared. Living in a community. Making room for others. Not being out in the dirty, egotistic world. I wonder if I can adapt," Amanda said to her friend. "Can you just stay on the line with me? Talk to me, please. Keep me awake. What else is going on in Alabama today? Any leads on who killed Peter? You're not going to tell anyone how to get in touch with me, are you? Especially don't say anything to my mama, okay? Better get on with what I have to do before getting back on the road," Amanda concluded when she realized she was just asking questions that didn't require answers.

After Amanda hung up, she refocused on Sophia-Emma. She started removing the baby's dirty diaper and the little onesie that fit over it. The idea of living in a real building for at least two weeks was a good reason to get into new clothes. One of the first things she would do in the morning would be washing the clothes so that the horrible, shitty odor would be scrubbed away, along with the bad memories of the last few days.

She made some formula for Sophia-Emma, who by this time was so hungry that she didn't seem to care if it was cold or hot. It was substance, and that was what mattered.

Sophia-Emma fell asleep with a milk-drunk look on her face, giving Amanda some time to scrounge up something to put in her mouth, as well. She found some kombucha, peanut butter, and old flour tortillas, which would be enough to stop the growling in her stomach.

Within fifteen minutes, the two of them were on the road again, heading toward Exit 55. Amanda checked her rear-view mirror and noticed an old black, beat-up pickup following closely behind her. She focused her weary eyes even more and noticed at least three men with shaved heads crowded into the cab. A Confederate flag waved from the pickup's bed. She knew they saw her bumper stickers, which were not compatible with the Confederate flag. Her imagination ran wild as the pickup sped up. She sped up, too, staying ahead just enough so they couldn't pass her. She prayed for the first time in years. Now the driver behind her was honking, edging up to her and coming within inches of her rear bumper.

She saw the sign for Exit 55 on her right and screamed in excitement. Quickly, she pulled into the rest area without using her turn signal. The pickup guys seemed to have been caught off guard and missed the turn. Amanda suspected they would be back to harass her, though. Perhaps they would even kill both her and the baby.

As she drew closer to the restrooms, she saw a purple van like the one Chaos had described earlier. She quickly put Very Wicked into park and ran over to the purple van. She didn't ask who they were or why they were parked there.

"Let's go now," she shouted to the two in the van. "Some skinheads were on my tail and missed the turn into this place, but they'll be back. One of you will drive my van, right? My baby's in there right now. We need to get out of here this minute."

The woman in the passenger seat of the purple van gathered her bag and got into the driver's seat of Amanda's van. She introduced herself as Zhen Bang when both she and Amanda were seated.

"The driver in Purple People Eater is Jupiter," the petite brunette with black eyes noted as she put Amanda's van into reverse and merged back onto the interstate.

In the deep blackness of the night, Amanda looked at the vehicles heading south. One was the black pickup, now traveling at top speed. She hoped they hadn't noticed her van again. Jupiter was driving Sanctuary's van directly on her left, hopefully hiding Amanda's vehicle from the eager eyes of the skinheads.

"How much farther till our exit?" Amanda asked. "Can you go faster? We need to get off this road. Someone like these men just killed my partner in Alabama. I can't bear to also lose my daughter to those bastards."

"Another two or three miles, ma'am," Zhen Bang answered. "Where we're goin', they'll never find you. My feeling is that they'll go back to the rest stop first, then get behind us. By then, we'll be long lost. They'll have to go bug some other lone woman driver. Now, you relax. Everything's under control. We're going to get you to our place, help unload your van, and put you in a guest room where you can sleep tonight. Tomorrow, we'll take care of all the paperwork for your stay here."

All Amanda could do was nod. She tried to lose her tension and relax in the passenger seat. She let herself sleep, not even trying to stay awake even though she might need to know where she would be staying for the next few weeks. In her light sleep, she heard Zhen Bang talking to Jupiter on her cell. They were arguing about what guest-room to put Amanda and Sophia-Emma in. Apparently, someone named Robust had cleaned one, but he always did a sloppy job. The room Jessie Jane cleaned would be a better choice. Zhen Bang also insisted that she would count this pick-up as at least three hours of her work requirement for the week.

Amanda briefly wondered if these were the mundane things people talked about at this place she was going. She was ready for the mundane, but was she ready for this long-term? She never answered her question. She was back asleep and making love to Peter.

In spots of her journey, Amanda felt bumps and swerves. Other times, she was breezing up and down hills, like she was on a roller coaster. Another time, the van came to a quick stop while Zhen Bang cussed at some type of animal staring into her headlights. Amanda felt like this was the wildest love session she had ever had. Peter was looking into her eyes and smiling when at last Zhen Bang pulled Amanda's van into a driveway in an area that looked like a cow pasture. Jupiter opened the gate and closed it after both passed through. Now awake, Amanda looked in all directions around the van. Complete blackness everywhere. But she heard the familiar sound of night frogs croaking off in a lake somewhere, and locusts were singing. There were no human-made signs to welcome guests.

"Based on what's out here, I think I can feel safe here," Amanda said to Zhen Bang, who was busy avoiding the ruts in the never-ending mile-long driveway.

Between the three of them, they were able to get everything into her guest room at Eagle's Landing dorm. Amanda glanced around the clean room, which was furnished with the bare essentials. No computer, TV, or radio. What really caught her eye was the freshly made bed with a hand-stitched quilt on it. She lay down on it while still dressed, then put her baby on her stomach. They were glued together this way until the early morning, at which time Sophia-Emma wanted an early breakfast.

Chapter 14

Both baby and Mom slept like they hadn't found a bed in weeks. Sophia-Emma woke first, kicking her mama with her tiny feet, nudging around for some milk from this human body near her. Amanda woke as the little one searched for her nipple. She got the message. She reminded herself that she would need to search for a breast pump today, but in the meantime she would have to make some formula for the hungry little bugger.

Not having any boiled water left, Amanda had to leave her guest room and find a kitchen. Upon opening her bedroom door, she noticed a long hall with doors every ten feet or so on both sides. She turned to her left and walked softly in the direction where the most light was. She got lucky. When the hallway ended, she found the kitchen, along with people she assumed were members of Sanctuary. First light was making itself known through the window facing east. Some of the early risers gave her puzzled yet friendly smiles. The others looked like they hadn't really woken up yet.

"Hello, I'm Amanda." She sleepily reached out her hand to the nearest friendly face.

"Oh, hi," the guy with the friendly face answered. "I guess you're in one of our guest rooms? I thought I heard something going on last night."

"Sorry if we woke you," Amanda responded. "It was a long day. Hey, I've got a baby back there with me. Mind if I boil some water for formula?"

"Sure. There's the teapot. It probably already has some recently boiled water in it. We like our tea around here," the friendliest guy—a stocky, bearded blond—offered.

"That's great," she said. "Any women here who can advise me about breast pumping?"

Since there were no women in the kitchen yet, all she saw were blank stares and reddening faces. Complete avoidance.

"Okay, thanks for the water," she said, breaking the silence. "Hope to get to know y'all better later."

Amanda traipsed back down the hall, now with warm water in the formula bottle. As she drew closer to her room, she saw a couple more tired folk in robes, with towels wrapped around their heads, coming out of one of the rooms. She peeped in and saw that she had found the bathroom; it was as big as those found in college dorms. She realized that she was basically living communal life again.

She could hear Sophia-Emma's wailing, hungry cries as she hurried toward their room. When she went inside, she saw on a small bedside clock that it was seven o'clock. She'd have to try to keep her baby quieter in the early mornings, she decided, out of respect for the late sleepers around her. As soon as Sophia-Emma was nestled in her arm, drinking the warm formula, she quietened down. She took long and strong drinks. In no time, the small bottle was empty. Once more, the two of them fell into a deep sleep.

The next thing Amanda heard was a knock on her door. She woke up abruptly, looked at the little clock, and noticed it was ten o'clock. When she opened the door, she saw Zhen Bang. Amanda was now able to fully see the woman who was only a rescuing shadow the night before.

"Have you had enough sleep yet?" Zhen Bang asked.

Amanda groggily nodded and said, "Oh sure. I didn't think I would sleep this long, but I fell asleep while feeding my baby."

"Don't worry about it," Zhen Bang assured her. "But I wanted to get you checked in before I go on my lunch duty in about an hour. I have some papers we can fill out together, and then I'll leave this other material for you to read over. We can both sign the papers later today. Work for you?"

"Yeah, seems to," Amanda said.

"Okay, here are the papers. We ask the normal who, where, what, why, when, and how. You can be as brief or expansive as the paper will allow."

Zhen Bang seems to have her director's hat on, Amanda thought.

"If you decide to stay here for the two-week probationary period, we'll expect you to be a part of the community. That means involving yourself in the many tasks we do around here. You'll have some say in what you want to do, but everyone takes at least one turn in meal preparation or cleanup.

"Someone will give you a thorough tour of our little hideaway tomorrow. Today, complete the paperwork, look over our rules, and get yourself settled in. You've missed breakfast, but lunch starts at noon, and dinner is served at five-thirty tonight. If you have any questions, don't hesitate to ask any of the members you see around our grounds. Also, we ask that you don't leave our little compound here unless you're with another member and have a specific task to do. In short, we keep as low a profile in this region as possible. We like to think we're a true sanctuary for those who need to hide themselves from those on the prowl for them. Many have a history like yours. Don't give anyone on the outside any details about how to find us, or you'll be exiled as soon as we find out."

Amanda shook her head in agreement. She immediately liked this tall, slim Asian woman who looked to be about thirty. Besides being decisive in the midst of danger, Zhen Bang also exuded empathy with her smile, and she was poised. *Why in the world would such a woman hide out in this place!* Amanda wondered.

"I understand, Zhen Bang," Amanda said as she scanned the forms. Then she looked up and asked, "Do you know of anyone from whom I can borrow a breast pump?"

"Check with the commie store," Zhen Bang answered, then left as abruptly as she'd shown up.

Chapter 15

After finding just the right outfit for little Sophia-Emma, bathing her in the bathroom sink, and showering herself, Amanda put her baby in her special stroller and asked where lunch was being served. A Latino-looking short lady with a couple of kids—who scampered after her like baby chicks following a mother hen—pointed left, where the biggest building in the compound was. It was a huge lodge. (In other circumstances, it could be for a males-only club in the Northern Alabama mountains.)

Since she was starving, she hurried up the ramp for those on wheels and followed the smells. Noticing the similarities between this lunch-room and a dorm cafeteria, she picked up a plate and silverware and took whatever entrées she wanted. There were only salad greens, veggies, and rice with a tofu sauce. No meat in sight. She didn't care, but it told her that this was a vegetarian commune. She hoped they would at least have french fries once in a while.

She pushed Sophia-Emma over to a table where some women, who seemed to be about Amanda's age, were chatting over their meals. They all looked her way as she approached.

"Well, who do we have here?" One of the women slid over on the bench and patted a place next to her.

Again, the confused newbie introduced herself with, "Hello, I'm Amanda," and put her hand out. All but one lady, who was engrossed in her meal, shook her hand. Amanda then sat down and introduced her baby. "And this is the love of my life, little Sophia-Emma."

One of the blondes with an Afro curl got excited. "Oh, I love her name. Sophia for the goddess of wisdom. Is Emma after Emma Goldman?"

"You win the prize," Amanda responded as she dug into the tofu and rice.

She wondered why no one identified themselves, but she figured that would come later.

The women resumed their conversations while she ate her meal. Just as they were all getting up to leave, Amanda yelled over at them, "Can any of you help me get started using a breast pump?"

They looked at one another, and then all eyes settled on the woman who hadn't acknowledged Amanda when she'd come over to the table.

A stocky woman who had pink and black hair piled on top of her head pointed to the quiet woman. "Crevice does that every day, don't you, Crevice?"

The shy woman nodded, briefly looked at Amanda, and resumed eating her apple cobbler.

"Thanks. If Crevice doesn't mind, I'll stay here and talk to her. Hope I run into y'all again soon. Any of you play Bridge or Scrabble?"

They simply returned her smile, some of them nodding, and walked back to the garden.

Amanda drew closer to Crevice and waited for her to finish her dessert. Between bites of cobbler, Crevice said something Amanda didn't quite catch, but she knew it was something about always being hungry and dealing with sore breasts. Amanda couldn't help but see a very unhappy woman sitting next to her. Her ear-length brown hair needed a good shampoo, and her clothes looked like they'd been pulled out of a dumpster. Amanda had done the same herself, so she knew the smell.

"Could you repeat what you just said, Crevice? I just got here from way down south, and I don't quite understand talk from most northerners."

"I'm no Yankee, smart aleck!" Evidently, Amanda had said the wrong thing.

"I'm sorry, but, Crevice, do you see my baby over there? She wants my milk, and I don't have any. From one mama to another, can you help me give her some?"

Crevice picked her plate up and licked it. She then got up from the bench and said, "Follow me. I ain't got time to talk to little southern belles."

Amanda felt like she was on a treasure hunt, and this woman had the clues. All of them. She knew she had to follow her, regardless of her mood and where she went. They went out the back entrance of the huge building, which members called Opossum Lodge, and then walked through an orchard and went by some outhouses. Eventually, they came to a small building decorated with picket signs that said, *We love You!*, *Mary's Little Lamb is Safe!*, and *We Even Love Pigs and Cops!* She noticed some toddlers playing in a small play area behind the building.

Crevice walked into the building and took the first right. A lady met her and gave her some contraption with little plastic suction things on it. It reminded Amanda of the pumps she'd seen the farm workers use to milk the cows. She must be on the right track. As she watched, Crevice methodically hooked herself up and turned on the machine. After a few seconds, she started to see a clear but whitish liquid come from Crevice's breast and go into the bottles at the end of tubes. Amanda observed it all, hoping she would remember all the steps.

"Crevice, how does all this feel?" Amanda asked.

"Oh, not so bad," Crevice responded. "I guess there's a little pull, something like the baby or your man sucking on you. Sometimes, though, I just feel like a cow, not a real human being."

"Really?" Amanda asked. "I had assumed it would make you feel special, to have that milk flowing out of you for your baby."

"I would much rather lie down with my baby and hold her, look her in her eyes, and touch her, but this...well, I feel like I'm industrialized."

"Why aren't you doing all the stuff you would rather do?"

"Because I have to work, stupid. And I don't want my baby to have dirty cow milk. That's for baby cows, not my baby."

"How old is your baby?" Amanda asked.

"Nine months. I was with her full-time for six months, but the rules here say that mamas have to work at least twenty hours a week when their babies are older than six months. So here I am. My baby is with the other young'uns. Oh, I like my job working with the janitorial crew, but no babies allowed in that job."

"Gotcha," Amanda said. "If they have another machine over in the commie store, will you help me get started?"

She didn't want to tell Crevice much about her situation, especially that Sophia-Emma wasn't born to her. But she felt like she had to share a little bit about her situation. "You see, I've never breastfed Sophia-Emma, but I want to start by pumping regularly. Do you think I can get my milk to come in at this late date?"

"I suppose so, if that's what you's really want."

"Oh, I really do," Amanda said, glancing over at Sophia-Emma, who was squirming for another meal.

Crevice turned off the machine and screwed lids on the two baby bottles, which, along with the machine, she gave to another worker in the childcare building. She buttoned her flowery blouse and said to Amanda, "Follow me to the commie store, and we'll see if they have one."

Again, Amanda followed Crevice to the commie store, which wasn't far from Opossum Lodge. Amanda almost forgot what she went in for when she saw rack after rack of bright flowing skirts, loose sexy blouses, and furry coats. Crevice was the one who spotted the breast pump first.

"How much?" Amanda asked.

"You're borrowing it, stupid," Crevice impatiently answered. "Has no one told you nothin' about this place yet? We don't use money much unless we go into town. They say we're all equal here. We borrow about everything we use or wear. We work. We have a little room. It's not perfect, but sometimes it's not bad, either. Plus, some of us...well, there are no other options in the middle of nowhere."

Chapter 16

Amanda checked out the cleanest breast pump she could find, along with more baby clothes, diapers, and a few of those awesome skirts. Then she headed back to her room at Eagle's Landing. (She figured the name was a sign that she was in the right place at this time in her life.) On her way back to her room, she couldn't help but notice that there were so many people doing a variety of activities. Some were mowing, others were mulching the garden, a few were hanging out laundry, and some gentle women were working with the community's children. She noticed, as well, the wide diversity of people and age. Was she really in the United States of America?

Sophia-Emma was getting irritable and wanted to be fed, so Amanda quickened her steps, hoping she wouldn't disturb too many people while they worked. She wasn't very familiar with where her building was, so she followed her intuition, remembering her walk to Opossum Lodge earlier. In no time, she found herself at Eagle's Landing.

Inside, she found spring water in a big ceramic container. She hurriedly boiled some of it for Sophia-Emma's formula. She knew it would be too hot for the infant for a half hour or more, so she decided this would be a good time to put her to the breast again. She felt sorry for her baby and wished she could explain why she was putting her to the breast even though there was no milk in there. That discussion would have to come later, perhaps fifteen years from now. Sophia-Emma needed the sucking, however, whether the milk came or not. So, they both relaxed and let nature take its course. Amanda felt the strong pull on her breasts and couldn't help but think that every suck was toughening her nipple and telling her mammary glands to start producing milk. She assumed the constant pumping, and having Sophia-Emma at her breast, was all she had to do, and then she would wait for that special day when the milk came. She wished she would predict when that day would be.

At long last, the bottle had cooled enough for Sophia-Emma to drink it. Once again, she devoured the mixture without stopping. Amanda had learned from reading the baby book that burping was a necessary next step. Before moving to Sanctuary, she had never been able to simply relax and enjoy the entire process of feeding, burping, and then putting the baby to sleep. Today, though, the whole experience made her sure she could be a damn good mama if she was given half a chance in this new environment.

As Sophia-Emma slept in the middle of her mama's queen-size bed, Amanda completed the paperwork she would hand in later. Then she read over the information that went with the questionnaire. It answered a number of questions about this place.

The community had about a hundred members and was founded by Christian anarchists about twenty years ago. One of its founders was Monica Garcia, who had grown up in and out of Dorothy Day Hospitality Houses around the country while her entire family was on the run from both El Salvador's right-wing military and the US Immigration and Customs Enforcement (ICE). The land for the community was donated by a wealthy left-wing family whose name had never been revealed.

The mission of the group was to provide safety and camaraderie to all who found it difficult to survive in the general population. *Sounds good*, Amanda thought, but she wasn't sure the Christian focus would be something she could tolerate. *Time will tell*, she thought. Her Christian family's hypocrisy had turned her off religion long ago.

Having unpacked the few items that she'd brought in from the van, her thoughts turned to Very Wicked, which had been her home on wheels for the last few years. She wondered if she would have to forfeit it when and if she became a member of Sanctuary. She jotted the question down, along with a question regarding the requirements of members who didn't consider themselves Christians.

She quietly wandered out of her room and looked to see if there were any members around who lived there full-time. She saw only a stocky elderly lady who was straightening up the kitchen with one hand and pushing her hair behind her ear with the other. Amanda extended her hand to this lady, who was humming a snappy tune under her breath as she stacked dishes in the cupboard.

"Pardon me, ma'am. I'd like to introduce myself." Amanda realized that the lady hadn't heard a word she said. She spoke louder and waited for the woman to face her. Still no response. Amanda tapped her on the shoulder and finally got her attention. "Hello, I'm Amanda. I'm staying down the hall with my baby," she said.

Most of the old lady's pearly white hair was gathered into a donut on top of her head. Her complexion was ruddy red, and her nose was the most prominent feature on her smiling face. "Buenos días, señorita," she replied. "No hablo inglés."

Amanda smiled, wishing she had paid more attention in Spanish class ten years ago, and the lady returned to her humming and continued to wipe down the kitchen counters.

Amanda returned to her room. The only thing left to do now was to take a nap alongside Sophia-Emma. She wondered why Chaos hadn't called to check on her. Here she was in this strange place where everything was beautiful and serene, yet she was scared to death.

Sometime between admitting she was scared to death and waking as Sophia-Emma used her as a pacifier, there was a knock on her door. Standing at her half-open door was Zhen Bang.

"Can I come in, Amanda?" Zhen Bang asked.

Amanda sleepily nodded in the affirmative.

"Have you settled in?" Zhen Bang asked.

Amanda detected a little judgment in her tone, but she tried to ignore it. "Sure," she answered as she pulled Sophia-Emma from the breast. "We appreciate all Sanctuary has done to help us. I've filled out the paperwork. It's over there on the windowsill. Also, I read the info sheets. Quite an interesting place."

"Glad you like it." Zhen Bang, now in holey jeans and a UVA sweatshirt, softened a little. "Let me look at your application while you nurse your baby and change her. Then I'll take you on a tour of our home."

"It could take a little while," Amanda warned. "She has to have a diaper change, and I need to make her another bottle."

"That's right. You bottle feed, don't you? But you *want* to breast-feed, God willing."

There she said it: *God willing.*

"That's something I need to talk to you about." Amanda was mul-titasking, changing a dirty diaper while preparing to ask about practic-ing Christianity.

"You mean that you aren't religious. Is that right?" Zhen Bang questioned.

"'Fraid so," Amanda acknowledged. "But it's important for me to know."

"I don't want you to get your feathers up for a fight. We don't force anything here except a designated number of hours of work."

"Whew, that's a relief. I've not had good vibes from most Chris-tians. Hated to go to church with so many hypocrites when I was a kid." Amanda used the rest of her boiled water to make a new bottle, then started to feed Sophia-Emma. "I'm not religious...not anything."

"And we're not here to convert you," Zhen Bang assured her. "Now, what else can I discuss with you?"

"What's the status on my van? That's been my home for the last few years, and I may want to get it back sometime. Kinda sentimental, you know."

"It's parked behind this place, where it will stay for your first two weeks here. If you decide to become a member, and if we like you, we'll move it to our motor pool garage. For the time you're living here, it will be ours to use as needed, but we'll also take care of all its routine maintenance. You do know that your tires are bare, don't you? Wondered if we would make it here last night."

"Well, I'm done with— No, I'm not," Amanda interrupted herself. "One more thing: I need someone to help me get some herbs or hormones that will help me produce milk for Sophia-Emma. And where are your washing machines? Can you smell her dirty diapers?"

"My, you're full of questions, aren't you? I'll introduce you to our midwife here. If anyone knows about medications and herbs, she will. Her name is Medie. She lives over at Day's Light, which I'll show you on our tour. Laundry has its own building. Small loads, just down the hall. But you'll have to hang them out."

"Okay, I promise that's it. Your questions now." Amanda zipped her lips.

"First of all, let me get your story straight. You're here because your mother doesn't want to have anything to do with you now that you've brought this baby into your life. She wants you to turn it over to Alabama Human Services, God forbid, and you refuse. Also, your boyfriend may have been killed by some white supremacists. You feel you need to get away from all that. Is that right?"

"You've put it about as simply as it can be put," Amanda admitted. "One thing you left out, though, is that I'm about broke and need to have a roof over little Sophia-Emma's head."

"And you don't want us to share any of this information with anyone, right?"

"Better believe it."

"I need to let you know, as I may have already told you, that almost everyone here has secrets only they know. If anyone finds out about you, it will be because you tell them. The information you have put on these pages will be locked up, and only a few trusted individuals will ever see them. Sometimes it's best not to ask other people about their past, and they won't ask you about yours," Zhen Bang explained. "An unwritten motto we have here is, 'Practice the here and now. Not where you used to be, but here in Sanctuary. Not yesterday or tomorrow, but this minute."

"Sounds okay with me. And about my little girl? I want people here to think she's mine, not a baby I found out in a field. I think Chaos told you that, right?"

"Not me, but I won't let your secret out. You can just say she looks like her father, which she probably does? A little advice: Try not to lie. For one, because it's wrong. And secondly, because you'll get yourself into some deep shit. You'll tell more and more lies, till nothing seems real anymore. I suggest you become a woman of mystery. People like that, and you'll not have to stack lie after lie on top of each other."

Zhen Bang continued, "Since you're on a probationary visit here, and because you have what looks like a newborn with you, we won't require you to work normal hours during these two weeks, plus five months more if you decide to stay. But we don't want you moping around sleeping all day, either. Baby comes first, then you and the community. Offer to help out here and there. That will be the best way to fit in."

Amanda smiled and agreed she would try to do just that.

"Now, let's drop these papers off in our locked files, and then I'll guide you through our home and most of its one hundred and fifty acres."

Amanda put Sophia-Emma in her stroller and followed Zhen Bang to the office in Raccoon's Den, which was next door. They walked past four other dorms: Raven's Nest, Crow's Quarters, Haymarket Square, and Day's Light, named after Dorothy Day. The fifth dorm, Legacy Place, was specifically for older members. It had wheelchair ramps, one floor, and lots of rocking chairs.

"That's something you might want to do. You could visit our older members, offer to run some errands for them. We believe in honoring our older mentors here," Zhen Bang suggested as she waved at the old lady Amanda had seen in the kitchen earlier.

After the dorms, they walked past the childcare center, the orchard, the huge gardens, the commie store, and Opossum Lodge, where she'd visited earlier. Then it was on to the farm creatures, including chickens pecking around their coops. Zhen Bang told her that the coops were moved from place to place every other day in order to fertilize the pastures. They saw the milk cows and sheep in the milking barn built above the lake. A few ducks were roaming around the lake. Amanda's eyes twinkled when she saw horses being ridden by a couple teens. They also saw corn and soybean fields, which would eventually provide tofu and cornmeal for the community.

As they headed back toward the lodge, they walked by a few big buildings that provided at least a portion of the employment for all community members. One was the lamp shop, where members made and sold lamps to individuals. Another was a rug shop, where hand-braided rag rugs were made.

"These shops are where the community gets its funds, which we use to buy necessary items outside the community and to pay members a stipend that they can use as they please. And that's about it. As you can see, we try to be self-sustaining and environmentally responsible in all we do, but sadly we still need at least a little of that green stuff. But we use less."

Zhen Bang asked Amanda what else she would like to know.

"I saw a few outhouses, but I also noticed bathrooms in Eagle's Landing. What's up?"

"I meant to address that, Amanda," Zhen Bang said, laughing. "Most of our toilets in this community are non-flushable types. After you go to the bathroom, you sprinkle sawdust on top of your poop or pee, whether you use toilets inside or outside. It cuts the smell somewhat. Always put the lid down after you use a toilet. That also helps. They're cleaned out regularly, and the refuse is dumped in various places on the farm, where it can age and be changed by microbes and worms. If you're outside and want to pee, just squat anywhere and do it, understand? No one will look at you strangely."

"I see." Amanda pondered all that for a while, telling herself this was really a weird place.

"And may I suggest one more thing, Amanda? We've all changed our names here. Think about what you want to be called, and it can't be Amanda. Nothing wrong with the name. But you, as an anarchist, surely know by now that having an alias is preferable in some circumstances."

Amanda thought about it. What name should she give herself? One that would last this time. *Gonzo* and *Amanda* would soon become history. Maybe then she could heal.

Chapter 17

After feeding Sophia-Emma, Amanda sought out the midwife, Medie, over at Day's Light. On her way, she noticed the quiet beauty surrounding her. She saw winter pansies planted along the path to the dorm's side entrance. The bushes around it were well trimmed, and the yard around it was asleep under a thick layer of recently fallen leaves. She concluded then that if she survived her two-week probationary period, this would be her choice for a permanent home.

As she struggled to pull the stroller up Day Light's four steps, she heard women and men in the kitchen. She was greeted by some tantalizing smells, such as nutmeg, ginger, and cloves. *What's the occasion?* she wondered.

One of the laughing women opened the kitchen door for Amanda. She was short and middle-aged. Her body was covered with freckles, and her wooly red hair didn't seem to trust a comb. Her apron hung like a long bib from her neck, as if she hadn't gotten around to tying it in the back all day.

"Can I help you, young lady? Oh my, what a darling little baby! You must be new. I know I didn't deliver this baby."

"You must be Medie, the midwife." Amanda smiled and put her hand out to shake Medie's.

The midwife would have nothing to do with that. She spread out both of her arms, as if she were about to take flight, and wrapped them around Amanda. And she didn't stop until Amanda had relaxed into her embrace.

"My, that was some hug," Amanda managed to say after a second or two of simply catching her breath. "I'm glad to meet you. You see—"

"Let's go back into my little room down the hall and talk," Medie interrupted her. "Too many people trotting back and forth through here."

Amanda wheeled the baby down the short hall. Medie turned into a room that had a small sign on the door. The sign dangled from a chain and said, *The Baby Lady*. Amanda followed Medie into the small bedroom-sized room and sat down on a huge green ball.

"You have a healthy-looking baby here, Amanda. How old is she?"

Amanda was tongue-tied, not wanting to tell the truth but also not wanting to make up Sophia-Emma's age, either. Then she remembered the telltale meconium stains on Sophia-Emma's first diapers and said, "Oh, she's about a week now."

"And her weight at birth?" Medie had started writing in a small notebook that was simply labeled *Babies*.

"Ah, about seven and a half," Amanda guessed.

Medie reached down to pick up Sophia-Emma, who was startled and let everyone know it with a bloody yell.

"Looks like her lungs are good," Medie said as she laid the baby on a scale like the ones Amanda had seen at farmers' markets. The needle settled on eight and a quarter.

"Not bad weight gain," Medie noted as she again wrote in her book. "Did you give birth at home or in a birth center?"

"At home. Did we do okay with the umbilical cord?"

"Who was your midwife? The cord is healing fine, but the little clamp here at the end seems kind of strange, maybe even primitive."

"Well, to tell you the truth, everything went so fast that I had to take the first midwife I could get. Then she left for another patient as soon as she delivered Sophia-Emma."

Now Medie just stared at her and gave her an inquisitive look. "Young lady, midwives don't do that. I have a feeling you're not wanting to tell me the truth about this baby's birth. If that's so, say so. But don't lie to me, please."

"I wasn't really lying. Well, I guess I was. Can we just skip all this? You say she looks healthy. Isn't that all you need to know?"

"Lady, if you have to hide a few details from me, I'll understand. We fill in lots of blanks here at Sanctuary. I try to fill in the blanks the best I can, but sometimes it helps if you share information that won't reveal your secrets. So from now on, when that happens, just say, 'I can't say,' and I'll understand."

"Good. Now for the real reason I've come to visit you. I want to breastfeed my baby. Do you know of any hormones or herbs I can take?"

"Why didn't you say this earlier?" Medie laughed. "Sure. First, I need to tell you that I don't recommend hormones to anyone around here. I specialize in herbal therapy. Let me give you some fenugreek. Make strong tea from these leaves three times a day. Pump as much as you can stand, but don't do it so much that your breasts hurt. You can do both sides at the same time. Probably start with just five minutes. Then go up to ten. Then work up to twenty minutes. Don't expect to see results right away. Patience, my child, patience."

"I just got a pump at the commie store," Amanda volunteered.

"Okay, that's fine to use right now, but when you start actually producing milk, let me know, and I'll make sure it's clean enough that your baby can actually drink the milk. If not, I have a couple here that I can lend you."

"How long do you think it'll take to see results?" Amanda asked.

"Anywhere from a week to six. Most will start producing by a month's time. I hope you weren't in any rush to start lactating."

"Shit. The formula I bought is getting low. Do you have any here that you could give me until my milk comes in?"

"I have a better solution," Medie said with a smile. "We have mamas here who produce too much milk. So, to help moms without enough, we share their milk. It's really much better for the babies. And get this, we can set up a system for you that lets little Sophia-Emma suck from your breast while getting the milk from the mama who produced it. Let me show you how it works."

She showed Amanda some diagrams of a tube that attached a small bag to a mother's chest. The tube would transport the bag's milk to the area slightly above the mama's nipple, and as the baby sucked, she would think the milk was coming from her mama.

"Pretty cool, huh?" Medie said. "Want to get involved in this? Won't cost you a cent, either. Go for it!"

"I don't know if I like the idea of my baby getting milk from a strange mama, someone I don't know."

"Okay. I'll partner you up with one of our newest moms. She's a fanatic about cleanliness. Do you think you feel the way you do because you resent the idea of some other mom nourishing your baby instead of you?"

Amanda responded, "No," almost immediately. But then she became pensive and said, "Well, maybe a little bit. I can't help it."

"Recognizing that you feel this way is a good start. Don't get me started on mamas helping mamas. That's the only way, in my opinion. It's no fun being a loner. Other mamas want to share more than their milk so that motherhood can be an experience full of loving memories and maternal bonding. Sorry for the soapbox talk.

"Now, what else can I do for you? Is there a daddy in little Sophia-Emma's life, by the way?"

Amanda shook her head no.

Medie didn't ask any other questions, but she did give Amanda one more hug before passing on the fenugreek and saying, "Now, go work on making Mommy milk for little Sophia-Emma."

Chapter 18

"I don't know what to do next," Amanda told her daughter as they headed back to Eagle's Landing.

Amanda smelled dinner as she walked by Opossum Lodge. She wanted to stop and eat, but Sophia needed a diaper change. She wondered if she could get over to her dorm, change her, and still have time to head back to the lodge for dinner. She started to push the stroller faster. When she arrived at her dorm, she was out of breath. She parked the stroller outside, carried Sophia-Emma into Eagle's Landing, laid her on the bed, got a fresh diaper, and stirred up a fresh bottle.

"Damn," she yelled when she noticed that all the water she had boiled earlier was gone. She would have to boil some more, let it cool, and then make the bottle. "This sucks," she yelled out again, then headed to the kitchen.

Before she could scream again, someone showed up in the kitchen and stared at her.

"What do you want?" she yelled at the strange man in a red, plaid, flannel shirt and overalls.

"I heard you yelling like something was wrong. I don't like it when people yell while I'm trying to pray. I wanted to yell back, but I decided that wouldn't be the right response. So I decided to stop by and ask you if you needed any help."

Amanda couldn't decide if this man was a pain or a life saver. She decided to come to a conclusion about that later.

"Let me tell you what's going on. I'm new here, and it's been a rather busy day. They're serving dinner this minute at the lodge, and I have a hungry, wet baby. Then I notice I have no boiled water, which I need to make my baby's bottle. So, tell me what I should do. Skip dinner, or take a hungry baby to the lodge so I can eat, therefore letting the whole dinner crowd know that I don't know how to raise my baby. But if I don't eat now, I won't eat until tomorrow at breakfast, which means I'll have consumed one meal all day. This kind of shit sucks."

"It's not such a serious problem, ma'am. I have another idea. You can go eat and leave your baby here for me to watch and feed."

"Forget that option. I'm not leaving my baby with a stranger," Amanda insisted.

"Other option," the young man offered. "Send me over to get some food for you while you tend to your baby."

"That, I like," Amanda said cheerfully. "Can you really do that? You won't get in trouble, will you? By the way, sorry I disturbed your praying."

"Young lady, I don't know your name. I assume that you're either a guest or new. Many of us here pray, but don't worry. We won't make you. And I won't get in trouble if I bring you a meal. This isn't a reform school or any other kind of rule-filled institution. We're more like a family of people who watch out for each other. Relax." The neighbor smiled and seemed to be proud of his little speech.

"Okay, gotcha. I'll forever be grateful if you can bring me a nice hot dinner with iced tea, sweetened. Meanwhile, I'll boil some water, make some formula, and the two of us will go on to dreamland. Promise we won't bother you the rest of the night. By the way, I'm Amanda, a guest for now. But soon I'll be going by another name. Got any good ideas?"

"Nope. Don't know you well enough yet. I'm Pardner. Been here for six years, and that's about all I can tell you. I run the dairy."

"Well, Pardner, good to meet you. Thanks for putting me in my place and teaching me to cool it. When you come back with my food, if I'm feeding my baby, just put the food on the chest of drawers near the doorway of my bedroom, and I'll get to it later."

As Amanda directed her attention to the stove, Pardner went over to the lodge. As she waited for the tea kettle to let out its telltale whistle, she pondered over just how weird this place was. This time, she boiled extra water to set aside for the future. She fingered the bottle of fenugreek. Since she was already boiling water anyway, she decided to start taking the herbs for milk production. She searched for some honey, as it would most likely taste horrible.

Pardner was back sooner than she'd expected, and he came with a plate full of salad greens, baked potatoes, and a seitan concoction, along with an iced tea.

"Thanks very much," Amanda enthusiastically told Pardner. "I'm about ready to go back to my room. When you pass my room, can you look in to see if my baby is still in the center of the bed?"

"Sure," he said as he walked out. He gave her a thumbs up as he went by her room, then went to his room.

"Oh shucks," Amanda yelled out when she remembered that she had parked her stroller outside. She would have to bring it in before retiring tonight. In her bare feet, she rushed outside, picked up her stroller, and rushed back in. When she opened the kitchen door, there was Pardner again, shaking his finger at her. They both laughed.

"Did I tell you that I'm a slow learner?" she joked, then took her first sip of the fenugreek tea. Just as she feared, it did taste awful, even with honey.

That night, as Amanda lay in bed, Sophia-Emma skin-to-skin near her breast, she thought of new aliases. When she'd joined the anarchists a few years ago, she had chosen to call herself Gonzo, but that didn't stick, so she remained Amanda to most people. This time, she needed a name that would stick. She loved her baby. She missed her lover, Peter. She was on the run. She was scared, sad, and in love. Maybe she could become Loving.

"Can your mommy be called Loving?" she asked Sophia-Emma, and she could have sworn her baby smiled in her sleep.

So, Amanda became Loving that night.

"But what if someone already has that name, Sophia-Emma? What then?"

This time, her baby opened her big eyes and ever so slightly nodded her head. And they smiled at one another.

Chapter 19

The next morning, Amanda couldn't believe that only a week ago she'd saved Sophia-Emma from the claws of a preying eagle. This thought mingled with the sad memories of Peter's death and her horrible fight with her mama later. *Enough changes for a year*, she thought. *Certainly, way too many for one week.* And why hadn't she heard from Chaos yet? She promised herself that she would call her best friend soon.

Too much thinking going on, she told herself. From what she had heard so far about Sanctuary, living in the present was what really mattered. Back in Alabama, when she'd felt this way, she'd go sit by Peter and use him as a sounding board. That was out of the question now, though. Would she ever stop missing that man who would always listen and offer solutions?

Loving, formerly Amanda, looked down at little Sophia-Emma, who now used her breast as a pacifier through the nights. She reminded herself to brew more fenugreek tea before breakfast. The sun was rising over the lake, warming the golden and scarlet trees around it. She longed to stay in the moment, gazing out her bedroom window. Within minutes, though, her eyes shifted back to her daughter, who was now bobbing her little head from side to side, searching for Amanda's warm skin. Amanda rushed out to the kitchen to warm some boiled water for Sophia-Emma's bottle. Today, she'd make it to breakfast, she told herself. Then she would do laundry down the hall. The weather was perfect for hanging out diapers.

After hurriedly heating up Sophia-Emma's water, she went in her room before her baby's hungry cry could reach its highest decibel. Formula powder dissolved into a bottle, and she was feeding Sophia-Emma within minutes.

"What a starving child you are," she teased. "This is your third bottle since last night."

No wonder her diapers were soaked every time she checked.

Amanda could now see how Tillie must have been a lifesaver to Louise while they cared for Amanda as a baby. It was hard and sleep-depriving work, no doubt. At Sanctuary, however, Sophia-Emma would have a real mama taking care of her, and that person would be Loving, if the name was available.

Despite her early awakening, Amanda and Sophia-Emma made it to the breakfast line just as workers were closing it down. She stood behind a barefoot woman about her age. She looked around the room and noticed that hardly anyone had put on socks. A few were wearing flip-flops and sandals, but most were barefoot. Amanda was wearing a long-sleeved undershirt, a bulky sweater, a long skirt, socks, and Natural Balance walking shoes. She was overdressed. She wondered if the vegetarian diet made everyone less sensitive to cold weather. Or maybe Amanda had become too used to the weather in Alabama.

One good thing about being last in line, she realized, was that her plate was piled with the rest of the scrambled eggs, oatmeal, and buttered toast. Amanda could hardly wait to dig in. She noticed Crevice eating alone at the table where she'd had lunch yesterday. She strolled Sophia-Emma over to the table so she could sit across from her. Today, Crevice also had her baby with her. She was a cute little blue-eyed, curly-haired blonde with strawberry jam painted on her chubby face.

"Hi, Crevice. How're you doing today?" Amanda asked, trying to get her to talk.

"So-so. Dorothy-Fire has her nights and days mixed up. My only hope is that childcare will keep her up as much as possible today. A few more nights of this, and I might resign from motherhood."

Dorothy-Fire splattered more jam on her face and giggled.

"So I can't expect to get a good night's sleep for months?" Amanda took her first bite of eggs. "Babies sure are hard work, ain't they?"

Crevice seemed to agree, but she was now busy wiping Dorothy-Fire's hands and face with a wet rag.

"I met Medie yesterday. She's going to help me produce my own milk for Sophia-Emma. She also suggested I find a mom to partner with. Someone who could share breast milk with me until mine comes in. You wouldn't be someone who could do that, would you? Or maybe you know someone else? I'm so tired of making formula all day long, and I'm running out."

Crevice turned her attention to Amanda. "Sorry, but this little girl takes all I have to give. If I were you, I'd stay on Medie's back. Tell her you need someone, like, yesterday. She'll find you one if you don't let her rest."

"Thanks, Crevice. I'm disappointed but will try to follow through. One more thing. I've heard that I should change my name here. I'm thinking of having an alias of Loving. Do we have any folks here who are using that name?"

Crevice acted as if she hadn't heard a word Amanda said. She shook all the crumbs from her baby's lap, then put her into her little umbrella stroller. Just as she was about to walk away, barefoot, of course, she answered Amanda's question. "Don't know anyone with that name. But I've got other stuff to think about other than what your name should be."

"See you at lunch?" Amanda yelled as Crevice hurried out the door. She received no response.

Amanda finished her breakfast in silence, most of the time staring into the eyes of Sophia-Emma, watching her little eyeballs bounce from side to side. She was slightly cross-eyed, but the baby book had assured Amanda that this was perfectly normal for newborns.

Once again, Amanda felt like the new girl in school, trying to fit in with the other girls, who just wanted to be left alone. They needed no more friends to complicate their lives. And since there were so many things about her life that she couldn't share—and because the people here didn't seem to carry the anger many of her old friends carried around, anger about oppression, white supremacy, capitalism, sexism, and so many other injustices—what was left to share? As she smiled down at her baby, the answer came. At least 50 percent of the people here were women, and at least 30 percent of them were most likely mothers of babies and children. Another 15 percent were probably older women who might want to mentor her. Maybe that was the connection she should strive for.

Zhen Bang caught Amanda's eye as she was leaving the cafeteria. She stopped by to check on her guests. "So, how're things going, my friend?" she asked.

"We're still trying to get settled, thank you," Amanda answered between bites of toast. "Good food, by the way. As soon as I leave here, I'm washing diapers and baby clothes, and then I'll go to the office and tell them that from now on, my name will be Loving. How does that sound to you?"

"Nice, but let's not get formal about it. If it catches on, I'll go ahead and give you an alias on your application."

Amanda talked about her visit with Medie the previous day. She told Zhen Bang about how one of her priorities from now on would be giving breast milk to Sophia-Emma, first from another lactating mama and then, hopefully, from her own breasts.

Zhen Bang thought for a few minutes, then offered an idea. "We have a mother in Haymarket Square who lost her baby a few days ago. Check with Medie and see if she's a possible match for you in the milk department."

"Aw, that's really sad," Amanda commented. "I'm afraid that if she ever sees my baby, she may feel even worse."

"Don't go there, Loving," Zhen Bang warned. "Go talk to Medie and let her handle the rest."

And that's what Loving did. She took a detour over to Day's Light to check with Medie. To her disappointment, the people there said she was out checking on a patient and had no idea when she'd return. Loving wanted to leave her number but was told to come back later. She got the impression that phones weren't the preferred way to communicate at Sanctuary. Of course, most wouldn't be able to pay the fees with their $50 monthly stipends anyway.

Back at Eagle's Landing, she gathered two cardboard boxes of laundry items—diapers, baby clothes, blankets, and her own stuff. The washing machine there was insanely small, so the task took up most of her day. She got the stinky diapers in the machine first, knowing she would have to get them hung outside so they would be dry by evening. In October, days were short. The job would have gone smoother if she hadn't needed to feed Sophia-Emma every couple of hours. But she was able to squeeze in a warm and fun bath for the baby. That alone made her third day at Sanctuary one that echoed her new name.

A few hours later, Loving was bringing in dry diapers off the clothesline. At her bedroom door was Medie. Yes, this was better than a text or phone call. And Medie's hugs were fantastic.

"Well, imagine seeing you here! Come in. Want to have some tea?" Loving was basically lost for words. "And I haven't even made my bed yet."

Medie laughed. "I've seen lots of unmade beds, sweetie. Most likely, even mine is still unmade. So, no judgments there."

"My mama would have been devastated," Loving muttered. "But then, we also had help."

"Well, not your mother, am I?" Medie said. "To tell you the truth, I was somewhat confused when I heard that Loving needed to see me. Are you Loving now?"

"I hope. Do you like my alias?"

"Yes, I do. And it fits you perfectly."

Loving smiled and carefully folded one of the clean diapers. "I stopped by earlier to ask you about securing a lactating mother who can help me feed Sophia-Emma until my milk comes in. My formula supply is direly low. Hope I can make it through the night."

"Yes, I've been thinking about that. First of all, how's your freezer here? I have a few bags of frozen breast milk in our freezer at Day's Light. And I know a young woman who I think can be of assistance. I've mentioned it to her, and she wants to remain anonymous. I will be the middle person. She'll deliver plastic bags of milk daily. I'll store them in my office freezer after I put your name on the labels. Feel free to drop by daily and pick up the ones I have."

"Wow, I can't believe it! Can you tell me anything about the mama? Does she have good hygiene? Does she have a living baby herself?"

"You know we don't infringe on others' secrets here," Medie stressed. "But I assure you, she is a clean person and has told me she will be on a lactating diet during this time for you. Now, do you have time to come over to my place and get the milk bags I have?"

"Sure. What's the best way to thaw them out?"

"Run warm water over the closed bag until the milk reaches room temperature. Keep the others frozen until you need them. No more boiled water, gal."

As the three of them went over to Day's Light, Loving found herself making up for all the quiet time she'd experienced. "I've started the fenugreek. Not that bad, but not anywhere as good as coffee in taste. I hope I can do more pumping in the days and weeks ahead. Here I'm not working, but it seems I'm busy every minute. What goes on here? If I stay and also have to work, I don't know how I'll be able to manage."

Medie gave her another long hug, relaxing Loving once more. Then she gave her some more advice. "That laundry you did today, send it out to our laundry workers. Yes, they do diapers."

"What, my dirty diapers? Why didn't anyone tell me I had that option?"

"Did you ask?" Medie joked.

Chapter 20

On Loving's third day at Sanctuary, she wore Sophia-Emma in a wrap she had found at the commie store, leaving the stroller in her room. As she walked the path to Opossum Lodge, she savored the feeling of her baby between her two breasts. She had just finished feeding her some real breast milk, which she seemed to love at least as much as the formula. Loving did notice, however, that due to the fact that the breast milk was more like skim milk, Sophia-Emma wanted more than usual. She hoped that sooner rather than later, she would have her own to satisfy her.

Surprisingly, Loving arrived for dinner early. The line hadn't even formed for the meal yet. She noticed that some people were sitting at tables with drinks, either raw milk, tea, or juice. Forget about soft drinks or alcoholic beverages. Through the grapevine, she had heard that some of the members were discussing brewing beer or fermenting wine from a vineyard yet to be planted. They would most likely only be able to mass-produce kombucha and kefir. Plenty of milk to make the kefir. Sweetened tea and time were all that was needed to make kombucha.

After choosing a tall glass of milk from the community's own cows, Loving sat by some women who were probably forty-five years and up. Most likely, their childbearing years were well behind them by now. They smiled as she sat at the end of the long table.

"Move in closer, doll," said one of the women. She dressed rather professionally compared to the other barefoot hippies. This Latina woman looked like she had just stepped out of a stockholders meeting. She even wore hose and heels. Her red lips accentuated her short curly hair, which flirted with her small ears.

Instead of confidently reaching out to shake hands and introducing herself, Loving simply smiled and slid in closer.

The lady with the hose and shoes started a conversation, saying, "Do you mind if I take a peek at your little sweetheart here?"

"Oh, sure. Her name is Sophia-Emma, and she's just over a week old."

The lady moved the flowery wrap away from Sophia-Emma's face. Her sweat-wet hair was in coal-black ringlets all around her dark skin.

"She's absolutely preciosa," the lady marveled. "You must be so proud. Was her birth difficult?"

"Really, I don't want to talk about it." Loving was trying another approach so she wouldn't have to lie.

"We understand, don't we, ladies? Sometimes we get a little snoopy around here. By the way, my name is Navidad. I'll let the other girls introduce themselves."

"Glory here. Good to meet you," a lady with braided purple hair and emerald eyes said in an English accent.

"I'm Party Girl. Welcome," said a heavy-set woman whose mousy-brown hair seemed to be thinning.

"And me, I'm Barbie Doll," said the last lady, who seemed to be lost behind a big nose and bushy silver hair.

"My name's Loving. Thrilled to meet y'all." She somehow felt good about these older women. She imagined they might be mentors in the future. Even though they were around the same age as her mama's friends, she told herself that was no reason to write them off.

"I bet you're new here," Party Girl remarked. "We usually get here early so we can, as they say, 'harvest the first fruits.'"

"Yep, I'm the newbie on the block," Loving admitted. "Have y'all been here long?"

Suddenly, they all spoke up at once, but Barbie Girl was loud enough to drown out the others, saying, "We all moved here in the early days, before there were all these living options. I don't know about the rest of you gals, but I really had fun back then. Then there was after nine-eleven, and I personally wanted to get away from civilization. Our country was about to go into Afghanistan and Iraq, making more enemies. Bush was president, and I saw no hope out there in the unreal world. To me, this became the real world."

The others shook their heads in agreement.

Party Girl then addressed Loving. "I was like you, I'm guessing. My life out there was getting unmanageable. Folks knew more about me than I wanted 'em to know. And they were invading my boundaries. Through the grapevine, I heard about this place off in the Virginia woods that was looking for new members. After a little research, I found it, and this was in the days before GPS. Been here ever since. I'll probably be buried here. I love it so much."

"I was a good friend of Party Girl," Glory remarked the first chance she had. "My family was big-time dysfunctional. I could see I's going to end up like my ma. Anything was better than that, so I wrote my old buddy Party Girl, and here I is today."

Navidad, seeing that her friends had all had their say, finished the story. Tears began to roll down her cheeks. "Believe it or not, I was one of the founders of this place. I was sick of what our leaders were doing to my brothers and sisters in Central America. I surprise lots of people because I don't seem like your regular commune-type person, but I did this for others more than for myself. I took a chance, and now look at how far we've come." She wiped away a few more tears. "There have been some tough spots, but we're still here to talk about it. So I guess we're doing something right. Now, what do you want to tell us about yourself?"

Loving felt put on the spot again. "Just that I'm new here. I've only been here a couple days. And so far, it's a little unbelievable. I've come from some traumatic stuff myself, and it looks like Sanctuary might be a good place to hang out." She hoped that she hadn't said too much. "For now, I'm a guest for a couple weeks. I have to know more about what goes on here before I'm ready to make any commitments."

Navidad patted her hand. "That's fine, friend. I like cautious people. One thing you might want to know is that although this is an anarchist community, we are quite organized within. For now, with little Sophia-Emma, no pressure on you. But for others without newborns, they all have to bring their talents and use them here. And as far as decision-making, we use the consensus method. No hierarchy or elections. We just use a long, messy process to make decisions we can all live with. We're somewhat like the Quakers in that sense."

"Yep, I kind of consider myself an anarchist, but I've never heard of Christian anarchists." Loving took a gulp of milk. "I always thought those two terms were almost the opposite of each other."

Navidad was now on a roll. "Lots of folks think like you, Loving. But look at the name you carry. What's sad is that many anarchists have adopted the description others have unfairly put upon them. I don't know what issues your group worked on, but I wouldn't be surprised if they were poverty, oppression, white supremacy, preserving the environment, and gay rights. Do those sound familiar?"

"Sorta. Are those issues ones you work on, too?" Loving asked.

"Hey, I came here not knowing what an anarchist was," Party Girl added. "I've since taken the word apart, and I see that it means something like 'against government.' Works for me."

The line for dinner was getting longer, and Loving was hungry. "Excuse me, ladies. I've got to eat. Sure enjoyed talking to you tonight." To her surprise, she found the troupe of middle-aged women getting up with her.

Macaroni and cheese, squash, mustard greens, and coleslaw were on the menu, with chocolate pudding for dessert. Loving salivated just looking at everything stretched out before her. Much better than the hamburgers and canned beans she used to eat around the campfire outside her van. At the time, however, Peter himself had made up for the lack of variety in food. With him gone now, food was beginning to fill the gap he left. *Nothing to worry about*, she thought, *since soon I'll be a lactating mom.*

Loving chatted with the ladies between bites. She discovered that even though they had lived here for a long time, they seemed to be excited about a number of things, such as upcoming bridge tournaments, new designs for another rag rug line, and some gossip about who was dating whom. They even discussed recipes. She had promised herself as a teen that when she was among a group of women discussing recipes, it would be time to leave. She found an excuse to do just that.

"Ladies, I've enjoyed talking with y'all. But duty calls, and Sophia-Emma isn't very patient." She looked down at the little body inside her wrap.

"Now, don't you hole yourself up in your room, young lady," Navidad advised.

"Oh, I won't," Loving said as she lifted her tray and wedged it against her body. "Hey, before I leave, are there any good hiking trails around? Also, I have to convince my milk to come in. Advice in that area would certainly be appreciated. I'm staying at Eagle's Landing."

"My girl, you sure are leaving us with a lot of conversation topics for next time," Navidad joked.

Chapter 21

While Loving was wondering why her best friend wasn't inquiring about her safety, Chaos was missing her buddy, as well. Amanda had been at that place for close to a week now, and Chaos hadn't heard a word from her. No phone calls. No emails. Not even a letter. She had taken to biting her nails again as she tried repeatedly, without success, to call Amanda. Sometimes Amanda's phone didn't even ring. She began to think that Sanctuary was so far out in the uncivilized area of Virginia that maybe cell service there was nonexistent. She worried that her friend might be a prisoner of a cult, but she reminded herself of the conversation she'd had with the folk there, when she'd convinced them to pick Amanda up. Evidently, they had. Still no follow-up, though.

"Someone should have called her to let her know everything was fine," she complained to her other anarchist friends.

Amanda would want to know how the investigation into Peter's murder was going, and she'd want to know what the Black Bloc was up to these days. She would be interested in knowing that a white skinhead was sitting in jail now, mostly because of the investigation Peter's friends had done themselves. They'd found the gun that fired bullets like those found in Peter's body. They were in a cabin known to be the supremacists' meeting place. The gun had someone's initials etched onto it. They'd guided the police there and dared them to arrest the man they had found drinking homemade moonshine among newspaper articles describing the murder.

Chaos decided to take a chance and visit Amanda's mama over at Promised Land. The woman, still living as though Jim Crow was her best friend, wasn't crazy about Amanda's friends, but this was the only option Chaos could think of. Most likely, someone at Sanctuary had contacted Louise about one thing or another. Within a couple of hours, she was knocking on Louise Foster's front door.

It was Tillie's job to welcome guests...if they were sensible people. Tillie wasn't sure that Chaos would be included in that category.

Chaos had dressed in what were the most conservative clothes she could find—a mid-thigh denim skirt and a white t-shirt with *How about them Dawgs?* scrolled across it. She had even showered, slicked down her dreads, and put on some men's deodorant.

"Hello, Tillie," she greeted the old woman, who had aged some twenty years in the last eight. "Do you remember me? I'm Amanda's good friend."

"Why yes, I remember you, sweetheart," Tillie said with a smile. "You're looking good these days. Let's just sit out here on the front porch awhile. Mrs. Foster is taking an afternoon nap and ain't to be disturbed."

"I see," Chaos said as she sat down and nervously rocked back and forth in a big white rocking chair.

Tillie went in the house and then brought out some sweet iced tea and cookies. They both looked at the long, circular driveway. It was lined with azalea bushes that were not blooming now, but the ginkgo trees along the long road were at the height of their yellow splendor.

"I'm so glad you came by today, Miss, uh..."

"Chaos."

"You girls are ridiculous. What mama would name her daughter Chaos? But we don't have time to discuss that right now. Do you know where Mrs. Foster's daughter is? She's worried sick, and so am I considering I've been more like a mama to her than Mrs. Foster. I know that sometimes in the past, Amanda would stay away for weeks or months, but this time...well, it's different."

"I know," Chaos agreed. "She told me about the fight they had. She's in a safe place now, and I'm sure that when she gets her act together, and when she is confident that her mama will accept her baby, she'll come back and make amends. But she needs some time away. Things are not good for her these days."

"What ya mean by that?" Tillie asked, the wrinkles on her forehead deepening.

"You know that someone killed her boyfriend, don't you?" Chaos answered. "Both Amanda and Peter were not liked by these KKK-type people roaming around the state. They're like roaches in dirty cupboards at night. She had to go into hiding. That was one reason she came here a couple weeks ago. She thought no one would look for her way out here. But Mrs. Foster made that impossible."

Tillie wiped her sweaty hands on her apron. "Oh, I know. But they've had some good fights before. Deep down, they really love each other."

"But, Miss Tillie, this time her baby was involved. Sure, she didn't bear that baby herself. She had no great desire to have a baby or to find one, but she did. She found her out in that shit-filled cow pasture. The eagle was about to take her home for dinner. When Amanda picked her up, she and that baby almost immediately bonded. No way she was going to let the state of Alabama get that baby and put it in a maze of bureaucracy." Chaos found herself becoming as passionate as her friend.

The discussion was interrupted by a yell from inside the house. "Tillie, where in the hell are you? It's three and time for my mid-afternoon sherry. You know, there are a lot of little Mexican girls out there begging for your job."

Tillie sprang to her feet.

"Let me go in, Tillie," Chaos pleaded. "I came to talk to her anyway. I promise I'll try to respect the old hag."

Tillie tried to hold her back, but Chaos's youth and strength proved too much for Tillie, who stepped aside and let Chaos make her way into the parlor unannounced.

"You aren't Tillie," Mrs. Foster snapped. "Are you that little tramp who turned my daughter into a no-good whore? How dare you stand in my house, you nasty witch."

"Now calm down, Mrs. Foster. Your daughter doesn't let anyone, especially you, lead her down a path of damnation." Chaos stood as close to her wheelchair as she could without tripping over it.

"Now that you've forced your way into my house, sit down. We've got to talk," Mrs. Foster insisted. "Doesn't she have any idea the worry she's put me through? I assume she's still alive, isn't she?"

"I'm sure she's fine." Chaos tried not to show her worry. "She's staying at a place where she's safe. Surely you'll agree that things weren't going well for her here. You know her partner, Peter, was killed by some right-wing homophobes in Montgomery. And while she was camping at the park after Peter was killed, some thugs threw a rock into her van. She couldn't stay there any longer. And sadly, after you two fought the next morning, she figured she couldn't stay here, either," Chaos explained. She saw Amanda's mama reach for a tissue and blow her nose. "Do you have a message you want me to take to her when I visit her soon?"

Mrs. Foster remained quiet for what seemed like minutes. "No, just tell her not to come back here as long as she has that baby with her."

"That's the message you want me to give your only daughter, who doubts you ever loved her?" Chaos gasped. "Here Amanda's lover has been taken from her, and her life has been threatened, and all you can do is threaten her, too?"

The old lady, refusing to look at Chaos, stared out into the courtyard, and ordered, "Tillie, put this piece of trash out with the rest of our garbage, will you?"

"I can find my own way out, Mrs. Foster," Chaos shouted as she rushed to the front door and slammed it shut behind her.

In her car, Chaos realized that her trip had been a waste of time. Mrs. Foster knew nothing about what was going on in her daughter's life.

"So glad I got Amanda out of this shithole," Chaos yelled as she barreled out of Promised Land.

Chapter 22

"That fat trash bag," Louise yelled as she wheeled herself out into the courtyard, leaving the sherry on the little round table by the piano.

Louise didn't know when she would ever feel alive again. Life wasn't treating her well these days. *So unfair*, she told herself. Even Tillie seemed to be losing respect for her lately. When she entered her room every morning to wake her up, she was failing to greet her with a cheerful, "Good Morning," like she had until a few months ago. She also wouldn't raise the bedroom blinds in the morning, so Louise usually had no idea what kind of day to dress for.

Didn't people have some sympathy for her condition anymore? She used to get so many invitations to tea, shopping sprees, bridge parties, and luncheons. She hadn't seen invitations like that for more than six months now. Of course, a good number of her old friends had moved away, were now in care centers, or, worse, were dead. Out of her circle of friends, she estimated there were only about half a dozen of the originals left. She would tell Tillie to call them and set up a date for them to gather at her estate and catch up. Maybe a gathering before Christmas. They could decorate the parlor like they used to during the holidays—put up the nativity scene and add lots of greenery. It would give a fresh and festive glow to this old house. Each of them could bring their favorite Christmas cookies and eat them with tea or brandy. For a few moments, these thoughts brought a smile to her face.

Louise looked down at her cigarette, now mostly ashes about to fall onto her lap. The Marlboro man was about the only true friend she had left these days. He never complained when she lit him up, crushed him out, or threw him into the bushes. Amanda repeatedly warned her that he'd eventually assault her. But until that day, he was the only constant, non-arguing friend she had.

"Mrs. Foster, aren't you going to take your afternoon drink? You know it makes you feel so much better. Why don't you come in now?" Tillie coaxed.

Louise would show that dumb old woman who was boss of this household. She didn't even bother to answer her. Let her worry. She was getting paid to worry. Shit, Tillie had no idea what worry was. Had she ever paid for servants or farmhands, let alone landscapers and gardeners? Did she ever oversee the budget for an estate larger than Selma itself, maybe even Montgomery? Had she planned for what would happen to the estate once she was gone? No, that lady went to bed every night without a care in the world. Even her cooking had become mediocre. No wonder Louise was losing weight.

Then Louise's thoughts turned to her sweet boys. Why did she have to lose two sons as they fought for their country in Afghanistan? She was so proud of her men-children. Only two years apart in age, they'd often worn the little sailor outfits, specially ordered from Bloomingdale's in New York City, when they were kids. And in school, the girls had swooned over them. And she could see why. They had both been captains of the football and soccer teams. Matthew was the oldest, with hazel eyes and sandy hair, a tall boy. Lawrence, however, had blue eyes to match the sky after a spring rain. He was chunky, was somewhat serious, and had light-brown hair. They both would have been perfect managers of this old plantation. She clicked her tongue and shook her head, feeling remorse as she thought of her predicament, of her boys under the ground up there under the old oak tree.

Why she had ever approved of letting both her sons serve at the same time, she'd never know. Losing Matthew and then Lawrence Jr. within a year of each other was about as much as she could take. She still mourned their deaths and dreamed of them constantly. One of the few comforts she still had was wheeling herself into their bedrooms, which were kept just as the boys had left them three years ago.

And now she felt one more nail in her coffin. A daughter, her only remaining child, was avoiding her, hiding from her. Didn't she realize it was all up to her now? She would one day be the matriarch of the Foster dynasty, a dynasty dating back to the days before the Revolutionary War. Most young women—she could name at least twenty that she personally knew—would give every hair on their head to be the most important woman in this region. *Oh well. Amanda will give in one day,* Louise thought. Her little girl would come back, begging to reconcile. She would eventually realize that this baby, which she carried around with her like a pet kitten, would be a blight on her name. That child was probably a half-breed. One of those Lunds had probably abandoned the little Melungeon half-breed in that pasture. If only that eagle had put the baby out of its misery before Amanda had gotten to her.

Louise coughed. She looked at her cigarette again and realized she should have thrown it into the bush much sooner. Someone had told her that the most toxins were present close to the filter. But occasionally, she'd get lost in her wandering thoughts.

Louise took one more panoramic view of the land she loved—its rolling hills, the old oak trees, and the romantic pecan grove where she used to walk with Lawrence Sr. in their courting days. He was always so gentle in the days before they married. No one would have predicted that he would abuse her countless times after they married. She remembered trying to cover her body's bruises and scratches with makeup. She assumed no one ever noticed, as no one called attention to them.

Women today expected too much from their husbands. She hoped Amanda would eventually realize that herself. Status was the greatest gift a man could give a woman. So what if he drank a little, beat on you some, or found other women once in a while?

"Tillie, I'm coming in now," she yelled in her commanding voice. "Please bring me an extra sherry."

Chapter 23

C haos needed a drink. But first, she sped out of Promised Land as if she had robbed a bank and the cops were charging after her. She'd tried. But at this moment, she felt like she'd fallen flat on her face.

Amanda's mama was an impossible bitch.

If she hadn't learned anything else, at least she was fairly certain that neither Mrs. Foster nor Tillie had any new information about Amanda. She could now either stop her pursuit and wait for Amanda to call her, or she could do whatever it would take to find out if her friend was indeed safe.

Once more, she tried to call Amanda. Again, the call wouldn't go through. She then tried to call one of the members who'd picked her friend up at the rest stop. This time, there was an answer, but it was only a recorded message promising to call back as soon as possible.

"Hello, I'm Chaos, the woman who sought your community out to help my friend Amanda. I'm calling to make sure she arrived at Sanctuary safely, and I'd like to know if she needs anything else from me. Please call me back at 334-220-3892 or have her call me. My calls aren't going through to her cell phone."

A couple of days went by, and still no return calls. Chaos wondered why she'd been able to contact the community the first time since they now seemed uncommunicative. The next step was to drive up there herself. She had no idea how to find this Shangri-La-type place called

Sanctuary, though. First, she decided to call the two sister communities she'd looked into as safe spaces for Amanda. While she wasn't able to get through to Triple Trees, she did reach a human at Off the Grid.

"Hello," Chaos began. "I'm planning to visit my best friend at Sanctuary, which I understand isn't too far from your community. I don't even know its address, and phone service there seems to be down. Could you help me with directions from anywhere in Virginia?"

"Ma'am, I'm new here, and I'm also directionally challenged."

"Don't hang up on me, please," Chaos begged. "For days, I've been trying to get ahold of my friend. There has been a family emergency, and it's imperative that I talk to her immediately. I'm even willing to drive there if I can simply get the directions. How about letting me talk to someone else in the office? Maybe they can help me."

The shy voice responded, "I'm just serving a shift here. There's no one but me right now. I can leave a note for someone to call you, if you want."

"Just wait a minute." Chaos wouldn't give up. "Tell me how to get to your community. From there, I'll find my friend."

"We have a secret location that we share with no one. There are too many freaks out there who would love to destroy us. All I can do is take your number and have an elder call you."

By now, Chaos had given up. She left her number and hung up, knowing no one would call her back. For half an hour, she sat in her rented room and pondered her next steps. She decided to do some research at the public library. Surely, she could get some needed hints there.

At the library, she got on one of their computers. There were no communities anywhere listed as Sanctuary. There were no sites for Off the Grid or Triple Trees, either. She was dumbfounded. How had it been so easy to reach these places a couple weeks ago when now they all seemed to be incognito? Surely, all three couldn't be cults. Or maybe each was a front organization for one major sinister group. What had she done to a friend who'd really needed her?

Finally, she did word searches for each group. On some sites, former members told about their experiences at Sanctuary, Off the Grid, and Triple Trees. She contacted each site, begging for directions to any of the communities, or all of them.

She was visiting the Fellowship for Intentional Community website when her phone beeped. She didn't know the texter, but she opened it, hoping it was a response to one of the emails she'd just sent out.

Got your message. Glad to hear your friend is at Sanctuary. I'm sure she'll be safe there. I left three years ago because I felt strong enough to go out on my own. Let's meet at that same rest stop where your friend was picked up, and I'll take you there. I still visit occasionally, so no big deal. Craig.

Chaos immediately texted back to set up a date. She then ran over to Harry's Pub and celebrated with a pint of dark ale. One of her favorite bartenders was working.

"Hey, Joe. You know, sometimes life isn't quite as bad as we make it out to be, right?"

"But I leave it up to you to find the bads and fight 'em." Joe gave her one of his winning smiles, like the one he'd given her a couple months ago, when she'd gone home with him for some hanky-panky.

Chapter 24

Loving wished she could talk to Chaos, if only for a couple minutes. She wanted to tell her that she wanted her old life back. She was sick of the fenugreek tea she was forcing down her throat three times a day, and she was sick of pumping her breasts at least four times a day. All of this to coax her body into producing milk. She had wanted to be more involved at Sanctuary, not to just eat, sleep, and pump. She decided to give the tea and pump one more week, and if by then she hadn't produced her own milk, she'd forget it.

But she also wanted to share some good things with Chaos, too. Using the other Sanctuary woman's milk was going well. All Loving had to do was nestle the little bag of milk between her breasts; stick a clean, skinny tube into it; bring it over to one of her breasts; and let Sophia-Emma suck away. Not quite as good as her own milk, but it would do until the better stuff came in. She wanted to tell her about how Medie constantly encouraged her to keep up the routine. According to Medie, eventually they would see miraculous results.

While Loving was remembering the last hug Medie had given her— something she'd always wanted from her own mama—she felt her left breast get heavier, a warmth spreading all through it. She had never felt anything like this before. She knew her milk was on its way.

Sophia-Emma looked up at her mommy and smiled. She seemed to understand something different was happening. Milk was coming into her mouth directly from the breast, and it tasted the way her mama's breast smelled.

Loving smiled back. Then she did more than smile. She broke out into a big laugh-cry, nearly shaking Sophia-Emma from her breast. She couldn't wait any longer. She gently pushed her nipple, releasing her baby's latch, and squeezed the nipple herself. A white milky liquid came out. She did the same to the other breast, and sure enough, both had milk.

"Whoopee-do," she screamed, knowing that Pardner was at work now and she wouldn't disturb anyone. She had forgotten about Sophia-Emma, whose little body jerked when Loving let out her high-pitched yell.

Earlier, Loving had rushed Sophia-Emma back to their room after she had let the entire lodge know how hungry she was. She'd demanded her breakfast right then. From now on, though, no matter where they were, Loving would just have to pull out a boob and give it to Sophia-Emma. She wouldn't have to run back to her room, warm up the breast milk, and hook up the Lact-Aid contraption before actually feeding her baby. Plus, Sophia-Emma would at last be a part of her. Her nutrients would flow into her baby as if Loving had really birthed her. She couldn't wait to tell Medie, Navidad, and any woman who'd listen next time she saw them.

All of a sudden, Loving was hungry again. She knew this gnawing hunger was mostly her imagination. Eventually, everything would settle down, and she would adjust her eating habits, eating to feed two instead of one.

As she sat in her rocking chair, letting Sophia-Emma nurse, she thought of Chaos again. Why hadn't she called? Why hadn't she been able to call her? She felt at home here at Sanctuary, but she also felt cut off from the world. If someone were to ask to visit her, she wouldn't even know how to get them here. She hadn't left the grounds in four weeks, not since she'd shuffled in during the middle of the night, alone, scared, and tired. Chaos had accomplished so much by finding this place for her, and Loving hadn't even thanked her yet. It didn't seem right.

Loving drew Sophia-Emma up to her shoulder and started to burp her. She looked out her window and saw that the trees around the lake were now leafless, except for a few coniferous trees interspersed here and there. The sun was out, as were all of her housemates. Loving assumed this would be a good day for her and Sophia-Emma to get out, too.

Now that the community laundry was doing her diapers and other clothes, Loving found that her day was wide open. She would bundle both of them up and start walking. Maybe she'd walk down the long driveway and see if she could make out some landmarks. That way, she could describe them in case Chaos ever decided to visit. She doubled up the diapers on Sophia-Emma, then went over to Opossum Lodge for some staples to take on their walk.

Party Girl was still hanging around, scrubbing down some tables and ordering the other workers around. Loving strolled over to her and shared the good news that she was now a breastfeeding mama.

"You're joshing me," Party Girl said as she stared at Loving's boobs. "I've heard that very few women have been able to succeed at that."

Loving unbuttoned the top buttons of her blouse, took out her left breast, and squirted it onto Party Girl's perfectly clean table.

"Well, I'll be!" Party Girl congratulated her new friend. "So how you gonna celebrate? They say a beer a day helps increase the milk. Want one?"

"I haven't had a beer since before Sophia-Emma came along. That sounds so good. Where are they?"

"I got some over at my place on Haymarket Square. Let's go!" Party Girl threw her wet washing cloth into the kitchen, where it landed in the sink.

Party Girl seemed to be in great shape for her age, which Loving estimated to be around forty-five, maybe even fifty. Loving had to take two steps for every one of hers just to keep up.

In her dorm's kitchen, Party Girl opened the refrigerator and took a couple of local brews out of it. Both bottles had her name taped across them.

"My running order every week when our drivers go into town. Considering the small stipends we make here, it's one of my major line items."

"Well, I promise I won't beg for more in the future," Loving assured her.

"No problem. You're a lactating mom. We like people like you. You keep us all young."

"No children of your own?" Loving asked.

"I had a couple, but their dad got 'em. He convinced some judge in Delaware that this was a no-good place for kids to grow up. I couldn't afford a decent lawyer, so he won. For a number of years, they spent their summers with me here, but eventually their visits got shorter and shorter. One year, they just decided not to come and haven't been back...yet." Party Girl looked like she would literally cry in her beer.

"Well, you're welcome to play with little Sophia-Emma anytime you want. I'll never let any man or woman take her away from me."

"Atta girl." Party Girl patted her hand. "Let's drink to that, huh?"

"Are you in charge of any work groups here?" Loving asked her. "I know you like to wipe down tables, but how else do you get your thirty-five hours in each week?"

"My real love is the rag rugs." Party Girl smiled as she talked. "Give me a couple strong, colorful rags, and I can make a gorgeous piece of art. And those outsiders—the world out there—they love them rag rugs. We sell 'em to individuals. No wholesalers. And our customers give them to their grandmothers, cousins, teachers, and neighbors. You name it. We can't keep up with the orders."

"I think I would like to learn how to make those rugs someday. Can I bring my baby with me?"

"Sure. Hey, you're no longer a guest here, are you?"

"I guess you're right," Loving said, a surprised look on her face. "Anyway, I wasn't ready to go anywhere a couple weeks ago. You think they'll want me to stay?"

"I'd say so. You don't cause no trouble. You're a responsible mommy, don't drink...in public, that is."

Party Girl noticed that Loving's beer was gone, too, and said, "Well, I gotta get over to the rug shop."

They threw the empty bottles into the recycle box and walked out on the side porch.

"Now, girl, go out and discover the world today with your little sweetheart," Party Girl yelled as she walked away.

"I plan to, Party Girl, I'll come over in a few days to watch you do your rug thing," Loving yelled back, and then she and Sophia-Emma started their excursion, walking along the winding driveway.

A few lingering leaves fell around Loving's feet. She made a game of dodging deep ruts in the narrow path, crunching lots of acorns under her feet, and sampling a few wild grapes along the way. *Sour with a hint of sweetness*, she thought. Maybe a little like her life. When they got close to the area where the fence opened, she sat down on a big beech log and took out the homemade bread and cheese she'd packed before her walk.

While she ate, she opened her blouse and let Sophia-Emma latch on. She felt the let-down and knew those love hormones, especially oxytocin, were rushing through her entire body. Loving held her baby even closer. She noticed the cardinals looking down on them and smiled back. Sophia-Emma fell asleep at the breast, so her mama buttoned her blouse. Loving then tightly swaddled her baby, just like the baby book had instructed.

Loving learned the hard way, with a simple touch, that an electric current was running through the barbed wire atop the fence. All she could do was look left and right beyond it. And in both directions, all she saw were weeds, gravel, and a long, narrow, bumpy road that seemingly led nowhere.

"Time to turn around," she said softly to Sophia-Emma. "At least we tried."

On her way back to Eagle's Landing, Loving couldn't help but wonder if she was in Utopia or a compound that would one day imprison her. Where was Chaos at a time like this, when she really needed to talk to someone?

Chapter 25

Chaos arranged to meet Craig a couple Saturdays after his first text. This would be a long trip for her. She was up with her car, Moose, before dawn. By nine o'clock, her little compact was already huffing and puffing. Some of her anarchist friends had raised some dough to help pay for her gas there and back. She remembered her exit was number 55. She tried to send out good vibes as she attempted to keep up with the hundreds of semis creeping up on her and whizzing past Moose (he was more mouse than moose). She counted the states with excitement—Alabama, Georgia, South Carolina, North Carolina, and, at long last, Virginia. Now she understood why Amanda had been so tired by the time she got to the rest stop at exit 55.

Chaos texted Craig upon arrival. He told her he was running a little late but should be there within the hour. While she waited, she decided to take another chance and see if she could reach Amanda. She glanced in the backseat and imagined little Sophia-Emma wearing the miniature camouflage fatigues she'd found at the Army Surplus Store. Once again, there was no answer. If Amanda wasn't using her phone anymore, it probably wasn't charged. Chaos was completely wiped out, so she leaned her head back and fell asleep. The next thing she knew, a short, rugged guy with ginger hair and perfect teeth was tapping on her window.

Chaos rolled down her window immediately and, still half asleep, apologized for being so out of it. "Can we take your car?" she asked the handsome man named Craig. "Mine's like me, all tuckered out."

Craig's car was a Subaru Outback all-wheel drive and seemed to like rough roads. She knew immediately when they got off the interstate that she had done Moose a favor by letting him rest in the rest stop's parking lot.

"So, tell me more about the culture of this place." Chaos was making an effort to make small talk while they drove on the wicked roads. "Why do they make it so hard to communicate with anyone who lives there?"

"It's basically a good place, but like its name says, it's a sanctuary. Lots of wanted people living there, running away from abusive relationships, from ICE, from the prison system. You name it, and someone there probably did it or had it done to them. I was wanted by my uncle, who liked to abuse me every time he got around me. My parents wouldn't believe a word I told them. I ran away when I was twelve, and to this day I don't think anyone knows I'm still alive. Okay with me!" He maneuvered his way over a narrow wooden bridge, then breathed a sigh of relief once on the other side.

"That sounds like a miserable childhood. Was it hard for Sanctuary to accept you since you were underage and all?" Chaos asked.

"Nah. Like I said, we were all on the run from something or someone. Squeal on me, and I could squeal on lots of other folks."

"Why did you decide to leave?" Chaos wanted to know.

"Isolation, I guess. In a way, this little piece of land was as close to Utopia as one could get. I loved it. But eventually, I was on the crew that drove into town to ship orders, purchase groceries, and make doctor's appointments for the real sick. Well, when we got into Charlottesville and Richmond and saw all the action there—imperfection, stuff that didn't fit into Utopia—well, I decided I would rather have the imperfections."

Chaos pondered what Craig had just said, then asked, "Even the poverty, the capitalist oppression out there, the right wing, the environmental degradation, the murders, the racism, and all that crap? You liked that kind of shit?"

"I guess so. Can you believe it? But I did try to bring about some good in a small way after I left."

"You're kidding! Are you part of a group trying to bring about justice, or do you work for a bank or something?"

"Hell no! And I don't even have a bank account, would you believe?"

"More power to you, man." Chaos decided that this man was a cool dude. She wondered what he thought of her and whether he had the hots for someone already.

"You know, I'm with an anarchist group working down in Alabama for a while. We're fighting the KKK, the white supremacists, the homophobes, and the politicians in both the right and left wings. Want to join us as we defend the immigrants, the poor whites, and the African Americans who are kept enslaved in prison their whole lives?"

"Sounds like you're doing lots of good things, Chaos. But I've got a little farm here, and I've made a commitment to it," Craig said. "You want to stay a couple days after our visit at Sanctuary and see it?"

Chaos thought about it. "I'll tell you later. We have some big direct actions coming up down there."

"Sure, that's fine. But I think you'd like it."

Chaos smiled and felt something warm circulating throughout her body. She felt something for this man who seemed to have no anger or desire for revenge in his heart.

She looked him straight in the eye and said, "Yeah, maybe I would."

Chapter 26

Loving's whole body jumped when she heard a knock on her door. She had fallen asleep while breastfeeding Sophia-Emma.

"Enter at your own risk," she muttered, still dreaming that she was hiding out with Peter.

Zhen Bang stepped in and sat on the edge of Loving's bed. "Well, I'm somewhat behind schedule, ain't I? I'm here to discuss your plans here at Sanctuary."

Loving sat up straight and blinked a number of times, trying to wake herself and focus on the important conversation. "I wondered when you'd come see me," she said, now wide awake.

"As you may know, this is a busy time of year for us. Members here are putting in extra time trying to fulfill orders on lamps and rugs for the holidays." Zhen Bang fingered the little piles of thread that formed a circular pattern on Loving's chenille bedspread, which she'd borrowed from the commie store. "We had to find time for members to vote on whether they wanted to invite you to be a regular member."

"And I didn't even know it?" Loving asked.

"No guests ever do," Zhen Bang explained. "Now it's your turn. You want to be a member here?"

"Does this mean they like me?" Loving's heart was pumping harder than usual.

"We like you, and we've decided to offer you membership," Zhen Bang said.

"Whew!" Loving let out a big breath. "I don't know what I would've done if these folks had decided against me."

"So, your answer is that you do want to be a member?" Zhen Bang wanted a clear-cut answer. It was like she was recording the conversation.

"You bet! This place is great. I do miss some of the activism I used to be involved in, my van, and some long-time friends. But all in all, I do want to be a member of Sanctuary."

"That's good," Zhen Bang said, and she checked off a box on the paper she held in her hand. "Now, one more time, let me review what's expected of you and what you can expect of us. As I said earlier, we don't expect you to work until your baby is six months old. So, I esti-mate that means you have about three or four more months of full-time care of your baby."

"I like that idea," Loving noted as she glanced down at Sophia-Emma, who was cradled in her arms while she nursed at the breast.

"But when she's six months old, you'll be required to work in the community for at least twenty hours a week. This is why we offer child-care, which is run by women in the community. We hope that in the next few months, you'll acquaint yourself with all the work opportu-nities open to you. But even beyond that time, we plan to rotate you through different jobs on the farm. That way, we can see where you fit in best. Whether you're on the twenty-hour work week or the thirty-five-hour one, you will have fifty dollars a month that can be put aside for your personal expenses. If you decide to leave one day, we'll settle with you at six hundred dollars a year, but only if you haven't with-drawn any during that time. One other thing is that you'll be on the twenty-hour work week until Sophia-Emma's five."

"Wow, I've never heard of such a deal," Loving commented.

"Remember, we have everything you need here—clothing, hygiene supplies, medical care, tampons, some snacks, and transportation to and from nearby towns or cities—but the rest you buy, including a phone of your own, a computer of your own, chocolate, or gifts for friends. You get the idea, right?

"Regarding phones, we strongly advise against them. They'll eat up your monthly allowance and distract you from building relationships with the people around you here."

Live without a phone? That will certainly be a strange change, Loving thought.

"What if I want to go on a trip?"

"That's something you'll have to arrange with your own funds," Zhen Bang answered. "Now, there are times when the community will participate in some direct actions, but they have to be a community-wide decision. If you want to go to one on your own, remember that you represent only yourself, not the community. We may give you a ride there if we're going that way anyway, but if not you're on your own. You'll have to catch a ride with someone you know. And in case you hadn't noticed, we're secretive about this place. Your friends would have to meet you somewhere else.

"Lastly, I need to let you know that a former member is coming here today, and he's bringing an old friend of yours. We don't normally allow strangers here, but he assured us that she was instrumental in getting you here. I remember talking to her before you came. Note, please, that she's the exception. If you want to visit old friends, meet them somewhere else. And currently, we aren't taking any new members. We're at our max. Any questions?"

"When do you think my friend will be arriving? It has to be Chaos, right?"

"That's one reason I made a point to come see you now. They're on their way here from the same exit where we picked you up a few weeks ago. And yes, it's Chaos. They could be showing up at any time, by the way."

"What! You mean Chaos is on her way? Here, can you hold Sophia-Emma and change her, too? I've got to take a shower. You don't know how I've missed that girl."

"Hey, I squeezed this visit in. I can't watch your baby for you."

But by then, Loving was already in the shower. She hollered to be heard over the water, saying, "Does she know I go by Loving now?"

Sophia-Emma knew that a new person was holding her, and she was totally confused. This woman held her like she was a bouncy ball, not like she was a baby. So, in order to get the word out to the world, she knew she had to cry boldly, daringly, and loudly.

Loving hurriedly rinsed her hair and ran into her room. There, she found Zhen Bang holding Sophia-Emma as if she were a basketball about to be thrown, a Hail Mary shot. She grabbed her baby out of Zhen Bang's arms and held her skin-to-skin.

"Thank you for your help, Zhen Bang. Couldn't have taken my shower without you. You can go now. And if you see a tanned woman with frizzy hair that goes every which way on her head, who is also dressed in camouflage, that's Chaos. She knows me as Amanda. Don't send her away, please!"

"All right, I get you," Zhen Bang said on her way out the door. "Have a fun time with your friend."

Chapter 27

U nlike Amanda, Chaos kept mental notes on how exactly to get
to Sanctuary from I-85. She felt like she was training to be rein-
carnated as a GPS. Her theory was that whenever you approached an
intersection, a hill, a muddy road, or a steep, winding road, you needed
to take the way you dreaded the most. By the time they arrived, the
directions were etched into her mind.

Craig pulled off the road onto a short rise that had a culvert under
it. Chaos knew the culvert was necessary, as it allowed water to run
through the ditches on both sides of the driveway during the wet season.
Craig grounded the electric barbed wire at the top of the disguised gate
and pushed it open. Chaos would never have found this driveway. No
mailbox stood at the entrance to the place. There was no sign announc-
ing Sanctuary. She looked all around. There were no special trees, no
particular types of plants. Just weeds, a rocky road, and a culvert. If she
ever got back to this spot, she would have to come in the daylight and
focus on every little culvert built into the right side of the road. That
was where the concealed driveway would be.

She wasn't driving this time, so she tried to relax for the moment.
Craig knew what he was doing, so she let him do it. She looked closer
at him as he opened the gate (basically just part of the fence, except
this particular part opened in a miraculous way). Craig had a good butt,
she decided. Farming must be good for the physique. She could see the

muscles in his arms contract as he undid the fence's gate. His hiking shoes were scuffed, and mud still clung to the soles and sides. *This man is all man*, she told herself. He wasn't the perfectly groomed *Gentlemen's Quarterly* type; he was more of a *Farm Journal* type.

After the gate had been opened, Craig returned to his vehicle and drove through, stopping one more time to close the gate behind them. Chaos figured that they were now near the main part of the compound, but Craig continued driving around the gully, up and down a winding hill, and past a lone, primitive corn crib. Eventually, she saw a cluster of wood-stain-colored buildings. This was the place away from the world.

"So, we're here, I see," Chaos said. "Pretty place."

"Yes, it was a lifesaver for me. I doubt I'd be alive without Sanctuary." Craig breathed in and out deeply, smiling, hoping the tears would stay in his eyes. "Let's go to the office first and see if they can tell us where to find your friend."

"Sounds like a good start," Chaos remarked.

Just as they were about to enter, they heard a shout behind them. Chaos immediately knew the voice was Amanda's. Chaos turned around and ran toward her best friend, and her friend, baby wrapped tightly in front of her, ran toward Chaos. Once within reach, they gave each other a hug that was as tight as the hugs Medie gave Loving every time she saw her.

"You won't believe how hard I've worked trying to contact you," Chaos stressed. "What goes on here anyway? It's nice and all, but it's really hidden away…"

"As it should be," Loving said. "One other thing before we get on to other things. Around here, I'm known as Loving. So, try to call me that."

"Fine with me, but I'm not promising that Amanda won't sneak out occasionally."

"Every time you call me Amanda, I'll call you Heather," Loving teased her friend.

"Come on now. Do I look like a Heather?"

"And do I really look like an Amanda? Let's get real here."

"Okay, now that the important stuff is settled," Chaos said, "let's look at your little girl."

Loving lifted the wrap enough to expose Sophia-Emma's chubby face.

"Well, shit! That baby isn't the little turd you brought in here. She's too big," Chaos joked.

"That's my baby. Just ask my boobs."

"What have your boobs got to do with this, hon?" Chaos asked.

"That's the best news I have." Loving couldn't wait to share her news. "The midwife here showed me how to make my milk come in even though I didn't give birth. I did everything just like she told me, and voila. After drinking this awful-tasting tea and pumping my dry breasts for over a month, milk started coming out of these here boobs. Now, isn't that a miracle if there ever was one?"

"Are you going religious on me, Amanda? I mean, Loving?"

"Heather—I mean, Chaos—this is a Christian anarchist community, and I've been assured that they'll never push me into worshiping a god I don't believe in. Lots of folks have lived here since it started a couple decades ago. Everyone believes how they want. I think the main thing is that we treat each other with love, Christian or not."

"Well, all I can say is to keep your head on straight, and if you ever want me to break you out of here, I'll be here in almost the blink of an eye," Chaos assured her.

"Let me show you around, and then we'll go to dinner. What about the man who brought you here?"

Chaos flashed a wicked smile. "Don't you think he's cool? He also used to live here. I was getting so desperate to find you that I asked him to contact me after he mentioned Sanctuary in one of his blogs. He offered to meet me at that exit you stopped at, and then he brought me here with him. He's already asked me to come see his farm sometime. I don't want to rush things, though."

As they walked around the community, Loving couldn't help but ask about the investigation into the murder of Peter.

"We found a cabin in the woods not far from where you were camping out. The cops found a gun there that was likely used to fire the bullet that killed Peter. The guy—a skinhead—is in jail. Can't make bail, maybe because now his cabin is completely smashed. Any idea who would've destroyed his property?"

Loving knew, as did Chaos. They smiled at one another mischievously.

"If this goes to court, do you think you could testify?" Chaos got serious.

"If they subpoena me, don't I have to? I hope you'll keep me up to date on this. Please write me if you want to contact me from now on. Before you go back, I'll give you a PO Box number. They frown on us being glued to our phones all day. Besides, reception around here—I don't know where we are—is almost nil," Loving said.

"Tell me about Mama," Loving said to her friend. "Have you seen her lately?"

"Another reason I had to get up here to see you as soon as possible," Chaos said. "I went by to see her, thinking either she or Tillie would've heard something about you by now. Neither knew more than I did. Tillie, to be fair, seemed to be really concerned about you, but your mom, she was something else. Of course, the woman can't stand me. And I even dressed in my best clothes and tried to act nice when I stopped by. Damn her. She was awful! I tried to let her know you were safe. Have the holy folks here pray for her, because she's a hopeless mess."

Chaos got distracted when she saw the woman ahead of them squat and pee. "Did you see that woman?" she asked.

"Normal here," Loving said. "We're an eco-village. We conserve our water, which comes from a spring up the hill. We grow most of our own food. We milk our own cows and eat our own eggs. We raise a few crops, mostly corn and soybeans. We make cornmeal from the corn and tofu and tempeh from the beans. The cows get some of the corn, too."

"But here you are, isolated out here. Don't you go batty? I would." Chaos was struggling to keep up with Loving's pace as she escorted her by the dorms, the childcare center, the gardens and orchard, the dairy, the chicken coop, the lake, and the work sites. "Okay, that's enough. Wanna rest?"

"We're going to Opossum Lodge, our gathering place. It's where we eat, drink, and socialize. Oh, did I tell you that today I found out I've been approved for membership?"

"Well, it's your life. Maybe when I come up here to see Craig in a few weeks, I'll sneak into your compound and help you escape."

"Hey, sweetheart, you spent a whole day getting me in here, right?"

"True. But it was just supposed to be until things back home settled down some."

"In my mind, things are more settled here than anywhere I've ever lived. I have safety, a roof over my head, food in my belly, new friends, free childcare, and a twenty-hour workweek till Sophia-Emma is five. I think I've got it damn good. And I don't have to deal with my mama's insults."

Loving opened the front door of the lodge and let Chaos lead the way in. A big fire was ablaze in the fireplace. Both went over and warmed their hands in front of it. Loving unwrapped her Moby wrap, then helped Sophia-Emma emerge from it like a butterfly from its cocoon. She held her close to her breast. Chaos noticed two wet marks on her blouse, confirming that Loving had definitely been able to lactate because of magic potions and weird practices. *What in the world is happening to my old friend*, she wondered.

Chaos then saw Craig enter the lodge. "There he is," she whispered as she moved closer to Loving. "Kind of cute. Don't you think?"

He walked over to the two women.

"Craig, this is Loving, aka Amanda. She seems to really like it here." She grabbed the man's arm. "Loving, here is Craig."

"Chaos, hope you don't mind, but we need to get back on the road soon, unless you would rather just wait to go back tomorrow morning. These roads around here can be real headaches after dark," Craig said.

"Let's wait until tomorrow, okay? I don't think anyone will take Moose from the parking lot at the rest stop." Chaos flashed Craig a pleading smile. "Besides, I want to taste all that homegrown food tonight. Can I stay in your room tonight, Loving?"

"Sure, but you have to sleep with Sophia-Emma, too."

"That's okay. If she's like most babies I've seen, she'll take up most of the bed. We'll straddle the edges of the bed, and we can talk all night, just like the old days."

"The line's getting long, Chaos. Let me wrap Sophia-Emma, and I'll join you in line in a few minutes."

By the time Loving joined Chaos in line, her plate was filled to the brim.

"Can't wait till dessert," Chaos said as she shoved the food into her mouth. "Maybe you don't have things so bad here, after all."

Chapter 28

After dinner, Loving proudly introduced her old friend to her new friends at Sanctuary. Though Chaos was more adamant about changing the world by whatever means necessary, the people here also wanted to change the world, mostly by changing themselves first. They knew they couldn't fight every battle out there. There were some battles the people here would have to sit out, at least for a while. Some even admitted they loved the bad guys, or tried to. Most anarchists like Chaos thought such people were naïve in thinking that if they loved evil dudes enough, they could change them. But Loving wondered if it was naïve to think violence would conquer evil.

Chaos saw that most of the Sanctuary members were there because they were running away from violence. Maybe as they began to feel safe again, they could grow in strength and eventually confront the violent world outside of the barbed-wire fences.

Chaos and Loving debated the positives and negatives of the community long into the night. Sometimes their opinions clashed so passionately that Pardner and his partner had to knock on Loving's door and ask them to calm down.

The two friends eventually started talking about memories. Chaos talked about growing up in a right-wing family in the wilds of Idaho, where if one was different in any way, they were treated like an animal. She remembered her tiny town with no stoplights and no Wal-Mart.

The biggest thing to ever happen there was the high school football team winning the state championship back in the '50s.

"One of my best memories after childhood, and after getting out of the hole in the ground where I grew up, was meeting you, Loving." She waited for a laugh from her friend, but Loving just smiled and nodded. "Remember New Orleans? How we came up with ways to get water to folks stranded in the Superdome? That will always rank right up there as one of the biggest highs I ever felt."

Loving didn't have to tell Chaos about her background—a privileged childhood on an antebellum plantation. Such a life carried its share of sorrows. Her father loved her deeply as his only daughter. Perhaps he doted on her too much, leaving her mama to languish in self-pity. And then there was the loss of her brothers. So many hopes had been focused on them. When Lawrence was killed in Afghanistan, Matthew had been determined to avenge his brother's death by fighting in his place. Same place, same war, but Matthew died from friendly fire, a mistake made by a new enlistee who, in the heat of a shoot-out, thought her brother was the enemy. Losing his sons caused her father to drink even more. He drowned his sorrow in bourbon and died from liver failure—one reason her mama was so bitter these days.

Chaos gave Loving a rundown on what the Black Bloc in Alabama had been up to lately. They were destroying Confederate flags wherever they sprouted up, having mock weddings between gay couples in drag, and disrupting religious services at right-wing churches, where white nationalists faked piety. Members were showing up at bank presidents' homes, playing loud music and chanting risqué slogans while blocking traffic before Auburn games. Many were planning to disturb upcoming political conventions and Klan gatherings near old Confederate strongholds. With cold weather coming up, some of the main agenda items were to find places to squat for the winter and to strategize for warmer months down the road. Maybe they'd do some home brewing and smoke a little pot from the hidden fields they'd recently harvested and dried.

All Loving planned to do was nurture the gift who was her daughter, and she also wanted to learn a skill. Maybe she'd learn how to be interdependent. Perhaps she'd release her fear of scarcity and trust that her brothers and sisters here had her back.

"Have you heard anything from Amigo and Sorrell about getting my baby legalized yet?" Loving asked. "I'm afraid to take Sophia-Emma away from here. Someone could take her from me."

"I'll check on that when I get back," Chaos promised.

"Good, because I wouldn't be surprised if my mother reported this to Alabama authorities, and then I'd be a wanted woman for kidnapping. And worse, I'd lose my baby."

The talk became softer, with longer moments of silence, and eventually the only noise in Loving's room was the soft, rhythmic sound of Sophia-Emma nursing.

.

Chapter 29

The spat with Chaos became history to Louise Foster, whose way of dealing with anger and revenge was to prepare for a holiday party. Since everyone she asked was booked in December, she and Tillie hurried to host their party closer to Thanksgiving. They invited as many old friends as possible. As she started making calls, Louise realized that she'd overestimated how many were left in the region. The passage of time had left few of the women who used to be in her circle. Louise actually broke down and cried one day as she counted a dozen who were now deceased. She had Tillie drive her to Selma Memorial Gardens one nice November day so she could leave bouquets of flowers on their graves, all the time wondering why no one had bothered to tell her about their passing. Would she be next?

Getting in touch with mortality prompted her to set up an appointment with Dr. Tanner, her family doctor. If anything was happening to her body, she wanted to catch it early. Promised Land needed her alive, because after her, there was...well, there was no one anymore.

Some of the people she'd invited were suffering from dementia or Alzheimer's. It'd be too depressing to have them at the party, Louise decided.

There were also those who had moved farther south, living in those retirement communities in Florida. Others had moved up north to the mountains. Their houses were built on slopes, and they could look down on all the crazy tourists. She was curious about what had happened to their fine homes and estates. Did some modern-day carpetbaggers move into them and bring their Yankee values with them? Probably people with values like Amanda's friend had. She had spoken so disrespectfully to Louise a few weeks ago. She had to be a Yankee, for sure, and a dirty one at that. She had no idea what feminine charm was.

Even with multiple changes going on around her, Louise got commitments from five fine women. They promised to visit in their finest holiday attire, their favorite cookies in hand. They would enjoy an afternoon of joyful small talk, brandy, and holiday cheer. She couldn't wait to catch up on all the news. Maybe they would even discuss some politics. God knew the country was sinking into the gutter—drug-crazed criminals, uppity minorities and gays, and those prospering on welfare and food stamps. Shameful!

In the last few days, she'd gone over budget. She'd had to call in the landscaper and a couple of cleaning crews. They'd washed the windows, waxed her hardwood floors, and cleaned the drapes throughout the house. Tillie had absolutely refused to take on extra duties. Maybe it was about time to retire the old lady. She was beginning to get too big for her britches. But Louise felt sorry for her. Like her, Tillie had no one else to lean on.

Tillie *did* take her shopping in Montgomery for appropriate party-wear. It'd been years since Louise had stepped into a mall. So many young girls looked like sluts with too much makeup, and they wore short shorts in November. Nevertheless, Louise finally found an adequate party dress. It was silverly blue with navy sequins, but not too many, just enough to be refined. Her new shoes, surprisingly, were very comfortable, and they complemented her dress perfectly.

At last the much-planned day arrived. She had a hair stylist coming later this morning to do her hair. Until then, she decided there was time for one more cigarette. She put a shawl around her shoulders and wheeled out to the courtyard. She looked around her massive estate, most of it brown and deserted because of recent hard frosts.

A few Guernsey attempted to graze in the small pasture near the barn. The neighboring Lunds milked for her; they took most of the milk for their growing families, leaving Mrs. Foster and Tillie with the cream and a few quarts of milk a week. Louise was glad she had been able to write the milk off as a tax deduction and make the IRS happy. The Lunds family also gathered the few eggs the ten hens laid, leaving Promised Land the couple dozen they needed.

The Lunds, despite their meager breeding, were basically honest and dependable people. A little lacking in intelligence, but Louise figured this was good for her. After all, wasn't that what made the world work? Some folk did the sweat work, and others provided the overseeing.

Tillie announced that the stylist had arrived, so Louise added another butt to the pile behind the hydrangea bush. Inside, the hairdresser was setting up her supplies in Louise's favorite spot, the little end table over by the baby grand piano, where the sun flashed a silver streak across the recently polished lid.

"Tillie, remember to sweep up around this spot as soon as Rosie leaves. We don't want anyone getting little hairs in their sherry today. Also, you're baking the cookies, aren't you? Those cinnamon raisin ones? And, Rosie, just do your thing, the regular."

Rosie was a quiet, middle-aged Mexican woman with too-rosy cheeks and turquoise eye shadow. She always wore a light-blue uniform and little white flats when she came by to fashion Mrs. Foster's hair. Today, she had added a green-and-red wreath to her collar, and matching baby wreaths hung from her ears.

"Tillie helped me wash my hair this morning, so all I need is a slight cut and style," the old woman declared. "And can you please do this quickly? I wish you'd come by earlier so I wouldn't be so rushed when you are finished. Oh well. Get on with it."

Rosie did her best to accommodate her customer. She first ran her wet comb through Louise's hair. Then she began to rapidly snip ends off with razor-sharp scissors. She eventually put in some curls and combed it all out. She took her mirror from her big pocket and let Louise look at the final product.

Louise said something under her breath, shook her head from side to side, and said, "Well, guess it'll do. Get on now, Rosie. Tillie'll pay you on your way out."

She wheeled herself over to the staircase and got into the stairlift, which would take her to her wheelchair upstairs. "Tillie, once you deal with Rosie, come upstairs and help me dress. Are the cookies cooling? Oh, *so* much to do on party day."

Upstairs, Louise found her new dress hanging in her closet. Before Tillie could join her, she touched up her makeup and sprayed holiday perfume all over her body.

"Tillie, put some nice Christmas music in the CD player before you come up," she yelled downstairs. "When our guests come, I want them to be greeted with appropriate music for the occasion. Maybe 'Silver Bells' or 'I'll be Home for Christmas.'"

She grew impatient. She looked at the grand old clock near the fireplace in her bedroom. It was 1:30. Guests would be arriving in forty-five minutes. Knowing Hilda Grant, she would be there in half an hour.

"Tillie, put a firecracker under your ass and get up here."

That got her moving. Louise could hear shuffling footsteps moving up the wide, red-carpeted staircase.

"Here, now help me get this dress on and this slip under it. We have to get these knee-high hose on, and the shoes. Move, Tillie, move. We don't have much time!"

The two old women hustled and pushed and pulled until, at last, Louise looked like the true matriarch of Promised Land.

"If I may say so myself, I look nearly perfect." Louise smiled as she added her final touches from her jewelry box, which was normally stored in the family safe. She added dangling diamond earrings, a string of real pearls made haphazardly from unfarmed oysters, and a couple of rings adorned with emeralds and sapphires. "Now, let's go down and have ourselves a party, Tillie. And please comb your hair and put on some deodorant. You smell like a farmer."

Louise was outside in the courtyard admiring her farm when the Christmas music spread cheer. She took a last drag on her Marlboro before going back into the house and popping a mint in her mouth. None too soon, either. The doorbell rang.

Hilda Grant, after a greeting from Tillie, walked into the parlor and saw Louise. She handed a platter of chocolate cookies to the servant. Mrs. Grant and Louise had been friends since their boys were little. Her Michael hadn't served in the military and was now poised to take over their estate. Today, she was wearing a pink, knitted mid-calf dress and dark-colored accessories. Her blue-silver hair, gathered into a bun on top of her head, glowed when she sat down by the fireplace.

Hilda was exuberant, as usual, as she said, "Oh, Louise, darlin', you look as scrumptious as ever. How long has it been? Thank you for inviting me today. But I will have to leave a little on the early side. I have another engagement over at the Barton house at three-thirty."

Louise wondered why she hadn't been invited. But that was something to think about later, she told herself. Besides, Hilda had a habit of always bragging about her popularity.

"Hilda, that will be fine. You look so Christmas-y today. Can't wait to taste one of those cookies you brought. I saw them out of the corner of my eye."

The doorbell rang again. This time, Tillie greeted two women and took two more platters of cookies, one in each hand. Both women shared a look of disgust when Tillie didn't take their wraps.

"Gladys and Maureen," Louise shouted to her two old friends. "Come on in and join Hilda and myself. I'm so glad you could make it on this beautiful day. You both well?"

Nicknamed the Bobsey Twins, both ladies enjoyed each other's company. They had married brothers named Harry and Curtis. Gladys was the tall, slender one. She normally wore a pantsuit, but today she was in a bright-green top and green polka-dotted pants. She wore her hair short, just like her husband, Harry. Maureen, on the other hand, was wearing a holiday dress, a knee-length red dress with little snowmen all over it. And she was sporting a new curly, jet-black hairdo. All streaks of gray had vanished.

Louise was shocked by Maureen's hair, but she snapped out of it and called toward the kitchen, "Can you bring us all a spot of brandy, Tillie? We also have sherry and hot tea, if you prefer, ladies."

No one responded to the alternatives, so Louise told Tillie to just bring the brandy.

The three ladies joined Louise in the parlor and sat in their favorite stuffed chairs. For a moment, there was silence. Louise wished she'd thought of some good small talk to get things moving.

"Are you ladies all ready for Christmas?" she asked. "Unlike years past, I guess we're supposed to say 'holidays' now. Isn't that ridiculous?"

The three other ladies nodded in agreement.

"Louise, how are you feeling these days?" Maureen asked sympathetically, a look of pity in her eyes.

"Oh, I'm doing very fine. I'm sure you all know that when my husband and sons died such tragic deaths within four years of each other, I was devastated. But as they say, time heals even the most gruesome of situations. Maureen, how is your husband?"

"He's losing it, Louise. I've had to hire a full-time nurse, and my children are of no help. I guess you understand that kind of thing."

"What do you mean?" Louise was surprised by where this conversation was going. Didn't Maureen know that one didn't ever ask how the other's children were doing?

"Oh, I just mean that you only have a daughter left, and she has that new baby. Well, you must be going through a lot right now."

Louise decided to end that subject. She just smiled and nodded in agreement.

Fortunately, she was once again saved by the bell. Two more guests—Lisa Cravens and Linda Graham—greeted Tillie and handed their cookies to her. Now Tillie could make up some pretty platters and pass them around as the ladies sat and chatted. The two women walked into the parlor to greet the other four women. Tillie brought in two more goblets of brandy, smiling a smile that Louise hadn't seen in months.

"Oh, my dear friends Lisa and Linda! You both look so beautiful. Welcome to my home," Louise greeted her old friends.

These final guests were relative newbies to Louise's group. They both attended church with her at the St. Peter's Episcopal Church. They took turns kissing Louise, giving her a peck on each cheek. Linda looked down at Louise and seemed to feel pity for her, as well. That wasn't supposed to happen. Louise felt a strong wave of pity emanating from all the women.

After introducing her church friends to her older friends, Louise tried once more to make conversation. "Ladies, tell me what you have been up to these days."

After the church friends seated themselves, Hilda started the conversation again. "Church work is keeping me busy these days. Our congregation is growing so fast, and do you know we are becoming more diverse every day? We even have a few former Catholics attending lately, as their church has been overrun by Mexicans these days."

"Oh my. I suppose they were being forced to start speaking Spanish," Louise commented, then said, "I'm so glad you could make it today, Linda. I hear you have a new grandson. How's he doing?"

Linda looked around at the other ladies before answering Louise. "Oh, he's fine. He's a cute little feller."

Maureen joined in. "Did I hear that they think he might be autistic? I don't know why we don't have more specialists here who can handle such children. He won't have to be put into an institution, will he?"

The other women were silent. Their looks of pity transferred to Linda now.

"Tillie, put on some more spiritual music and bring out the cookies," Louise ordered. "We're hungry in here."

Things weren't going the way she'd planned. She needed another cigarette. But she'd have to endure this catastrophe first. Or maybe they could all get drunk and let their grief, worry, and fear out just this one time. Proper WASP women needed that freedom when their lives weren't as perfect as they deserved.

Chapter 30

As Amanda and Chaos were celebrating their reunion, the matriarch of Promised Land was throwing away every last cookie after the women had filed from her home ahead of schedule. She'd played the sick victim well enough to get them all out of her house.

"Ladies, you know I've been having so many headaches lately. I hate to tell you, but you're all my best friends. I've had such a good time talking with all of you today, catching up and discussing old times during this holy season, but I've got to take my medicine, or this headache will get the best of me. And my headache medicine zonks me out. Would you mind if we continue this pleasurable gathering sometime in January? I hate to have to send you all home so early."

Louise had noticed that her guests almost looked relieved when she'd asked them to leave. Each had made the expected polite remark as they kissed her cheek and wished her Merry Christmas. Louise had had a difficult time keeping a smile on her face, and she couldn't wait for every last one of the old hags to leave. She had some thinking to do.

Still in her hostess dress, she dug in the end table's drawer and took out another cigarette. She would think better out back, though the weather was now down in the low forties. Those ladies had unintentionally given her a truer picture of who she was. She was just like them, and she was tired of it. Here she'd run her daughter off, her only surviving child, because of pride. Outside, she took a long drag to open up the vessels in her head. She coughed and spit out some green stuff. Maybe she didn't have long to be on this earth. Did she want to leave as a despicable old woman who was talked about, laughed at?

This late in the game, could she make up for all of her mistakes? There were the Lunds and Yoders down the road. Maybe she'd invite them over for a Christmas wingding. They'd bring their fiddles, banjos, and guitars. Maybe Tillie could call the butcher in town and have him kill a pig and smoke it over hot hickory wood all day. Maybe she'd even invite that horrible friend of Amanda's, tell her she was sorry, and ask her to help get Amanda back.

But then she thought of that day when Amanda had walked out on her. No, before she'd forgive her, Amanda would have to apologize, turn that baby over to the proper authorities, and accept her responsibility to carry on the Foster line by bearing white children with a respectable young man. Until then, she had no daughter.

With that, she kicked off her new too-tight shoes and threw them over the wall. Life was the pits when two of your children were dead and the other was a terrorist.

"Tillie, can you bring some cough drops out here?"

No lie this time. The old woman was truly feeling weak. When Tillie brought her the cough drops, Louise Foster fell forward out of her chair and landed on the shiny ceramic tiles, like a monk in prayer. Tillie was unable to wake her, so she called 911 and whispered kind words. She held Louise's cold hand and prayed.

Chapter 31

"Why in the world are those emergency workers taking so long to get here?" Tillie muttered to herself as she nursed Mrs. Foster, who was unconscious on the cold tiles outside.

Tillie didn't know what more she could do to keep her boss alive. She put a wool blanket over her and continued speaking softly to the old lady. She checked her eyes. That was what people did on TV when they wondered if someone was dead or alive. She could see a slight movement in her chest area, so Louise had to be alive.

"Hurry up, rescuers. She isn't going to hang on much longer," Tillie muttered. Didn't Mrs. Foster's position in the community make her a higher priority? *If only her daughter were here*, she thought.

"Stay with me, ma'am! You have so much to live for. One breath at a time. C'mon. Breathe in, now out, in and out. That's right," Tillie coached. "Help is on the way. In and out."

Mrs. Foster was a strong old hag. So many times, Tillie had come within an inch of walking out and never coming back. In her younger days, it was the children who kept her coming back. They were why she took the abuse from Mrs. Foster. Little Larry Jr. and Matthew. Such lively little boys. Her boss couldn't brag about them enough to her friends, but around the boys, and even little Amanda, she left much to be desired as a mother. She left the cuddling and nurturing up to Tillie. And Tillie couldn't help but think of each of them as her own.

Tillie had broken up with her fiancée, Cecil, because of her allegiance to those kids. He had wanted her to set up a home with him in Selma, on the colored side. Mrs. Foster had almost fired her when she'd discovered that Cecil was Black. Those arguments with Mrs. Foster were horrible. She'd told him to lie low and wait a few years, at least until Amanda was sent off to boarding school up east. But Cecil couldn't wait. He had an itch to get married. He found a new woman, and that had been the end of Tillie's romantic life.

After Amanda joined the boys at boarding schools, Tillie stayed on during the holidays and summers, when the children were home. They had so much fun making picnic lunches to eat out by the river, and they'd collected bouquets of wildflowers to cheer up their mommy, who cried herself to sleep most nights.

Louise coughed slightly, but she was out again before Tillie could reassure her.

Despite a history of being treated like a slave, Tillie understood Louise Foster. She usually ignored her tirades. She valued the very few tender moments they'd had together through the years. One such moment was the day Mrs. Foster brought baby Amanda home. When Mr. Foster escorted mama and daughter into the parlor, Mrs. Foster had proudly showed her baby daughter to Tillie and said, "We finally did it, Tillie! Thank you for helping me get to this day."

The sound of sirens was getting louder. Yes, they'd soon be here. Tillie left her mistress and rushed to the door to unlock it. Before she knew it, two paramedics were at the door.

"Mrs. Foster is over there." Tillie pointed out to the courtyard.

The paramedics rushed there and started getting Louise's vitals. They pricked her finger to check sugar levels, they checked her pulse and blood pressure, and they shined a light into her eyes. A woman named Ginger asked Tillie a few questions, such as what happened, how long had she been out, had she complained about any physical problems earlier, was she allergic to anything, and who were her next of kin. Tillie hated admitting that no one seemed to know where her only next of kin was. She did know who her family doctor was. She rushed over to the notebook they kept by the landline, then told them to take the whole thing with them.

"Dr. Tanner of Coogan Family Practice in town is her doctor. Be careful with her. She can't walk, you know. Stroke crippled her right leg a couple years ago," she alerted the paramedics as they loaded Mrs. Foster into the ambulance. "Her husband and two sons are dead. Only her daughter's left, but we don't know where she is. I'm about as close as family, but I'm no kin. Where are you taking her?"

"Over to Vaughan," another crew member said.

"Can I ride along? I don't drive much anymore."

"That's against our policies," Ginger said.

"Well, let me get her purse so you can get all her insurance information," Tillie offered.

Ginger quickly got out of the unit and said she'd get her identification information. Tillie wanted to show her where the purse was, but she was too slow to keep up with Ginger.

"Just tell me where she keeps her purse, and I'll get it," Ginger coaxed.

"It's hanging behind her bedroom door. That's the first room on your left upstairs."

"Well, I'll get her ID but leave her purse. We don't want to be responsible for that."

The young woman ran up the stairs two at a time. A few seconds later, she was running down the stairs and to the ambulance.

"What's wrong with her?" Tillie shouted as the ambulance sped off. She received no answer.

All she could do was amble back into the house and cry the hardest she had in years. She needed a miracle. She needed someone to stop and take her to the hospital so she could be by Mrs. Foster's side.

Chapter 32

Chaos had no way of knowing.

She was running on fumes in the late afternoon when she noticed the exit she'd normally take to go to Amanda's place. On a whim, and despite the fact that her last visit at Promised Land had been a disaster, she decided it was her duty to at least tell Amanda's mama that she was safe. She again reminded herself not to disclose where her friend was now living.

"Don't tell. Don't tell," she repeated in a whisper as she stepped up to the front door.

Tillie answered the door. Chaos had never seen her with such red eyes. She looked as though her old boyfriend—was it Cecil?—had died or something.

"Hello, Ms. Chaos. Mrs. Foster isn't in. Can I help you with anything?"

"Well, you can tell me what that old lady did now to get you in such a fix," Chaos replied as she walked right in.

"I'm okay, Ms. Chaos." Tillie sat down in an overstuffed chair near the piano. "It's been a rough day, to say the least."

"So, what happened?" Chaos asked.

"Mrs. Foster passed out, and they've taken her to Vaughan Medical Center in town," Tillie reported between sobs. "They wouldn't tell me what's wrong with her."

"So sorry to hear your sad story." Chaos put her arm around Tillie. "I'm heading that way. Want me to take you to the hospital?"

"I don't know what I should do. Somebody should probably stay here, but I feel so sorry for Mrs. Foster." Tillie wiped her nose and eyes with her apron. "Can you really take me by the hospital?"

"Come with me, Tillie," Chaos urged the old servant. "I think she'd rather see you than me, but I'll give you support. And I can tell you both some news about Amanda. She's safe. I'm not allowed to say where she is, but I can get word to her so she knows what's going on with her mama."

"Oh, that would be so good." Tillie managed a tentative smile. "Why don't you drive Mrs. Foster's car? I don't think I'd fit into that little red wagon that you drove up in. I know where she keeps her keys. Sure you don't mind?"

"I hope no one sees me driving that monstrosity," Chaos whispered under her breath.

Tillie dug through Mrs. Foster's purse and got out the keys, which she handed to Chaos. "Now let me go tidy myself up a bit," she told Chaos. "I don't want anyone to see me like this, especially Mrs. Foster."

While Tillie was in the bathroom making herself presentable, Chaos shouted to her that she was going upstairs to use the bathroom near Amanda's old room.

"That's fine. Be sure you shut off all the lights before you come down. You know Mrs. Foster doesn't like them being left on, and I don't want her to come home with those lights on," Tillie yelled from the half bathroom by the front door.

Chaos ran up the stairs in the same way Ginger had earlier. She walked down the long hall, where there were dozens of pictures of Amanda's family at different stages in their lives. There was one of Amanda cuddling a beat-up doll. Chaos wondered if the doll was beat up because she wouldn't ever let go of it, just as she would never let go of Sophia-Emma.

She stepped into the bathroom and did her thing. There in front of her was a small saying that she assumed Amanda had hung up shortly before she left home, back when she was an idealistic teen. It was a quote from anthropologist Margaret Mead. It read:

"Never doubt that a small group of thoughtful, committed citizens can change the world. Indeed, it is the only thing that ever has."

Chaos missed her friend already, although she had just seen her this morning. Loving had shared her address and had given Chaos some ideas about how to cut through the protective circle and reach her by phone. She might have to do that sooner than she'd thought.

"I'm ready, Ms. Chaos," Tillie bellowed. "Now, don't you go snooping around up there. That there is private property, and you need to keep your nose out of people's personal stuff, you hear?"

"I'm hearing you, Tillie. Coming down in just a minute. I've been storing this stuff up in me all day. It takes a while to clear it all out."

Chaos flushed, washed her hands, and headed downstairs. Tillie had her winter coat on and had combed her hair into a neat bun.

"Do I look all right?" Tillie asked.

"You look very fine. Now, let's get that Cadillac on the road, shall we?"

Chapter 33

Earlier that morning, Loving had gone back to bed after Chaos left, which was before the rooster crowed. She had wondered if she was getting soft while occupying this new role as a full-time mama. But she knew this was only temporary. In a few months, she'd probably have that haggard look she noticed on Crevice almost every day. Today, though, she and Sophia-Emma would stay in, except when they went to eat at the Lodge. She looked out her window and saw dreary winter weather. *All the more reason to hibernate today*, she told herself. This would be her life from now on—one big hibernation, getting fatter and fatter, becoming more matronly and settled. *But all that fat can't go into milk production*, she reminded herself.

Half asleep, Loving imagined hearing her mama come into her room. Even into her teenage years, her mother would take the broom and actually strike her with its brushy end. Amanda would be forced out of bed and would face days of complete boredom on cold, bleak days like today. The Fosters had hired people to do all the work around the estate. She figured her mama woke her because she just wanted some company, so they'd play cards, checkers, or chess. There was something about those times that made her feel nostalgic and needed. Now she was the mama, and little Sophia-Emma was the little girl. Life would be better for her, but this wasn't the time to be lazy and to lie in bed all day.

Even though she didn't have to, Loving decided that today she'd study the Sanctuary. Today, she would watch the chickens, learn their habits. She would study the milk cows' farts and watch their bags grow fuller and fuller as the day progressed. From there, she and Sophia-Emma would study the gracefulness of the horses and whisper to them. Essentially, Loving would learn what to expect from the other animals. She would learn to respect them, honor them, and be in solidarity with them.

If they had time, they'd visit the childcare center. She wanted to watch how Sophia-Emma reacted to the other little ones there. She'd check out the kids and guess which ones would become her child's best friends at Sanctuary.

After breakfast, she hoped she would be able to help clean the tables and sweep the floor. Maybe she could offer to bake cookies for dinner tonight. And if there was still time by the end of the day, they would visit the work sites, find a rag rug or a little lamp that she could purchase with the little money she had left, and send it to Chaos as a reminder of their friendship.

So why was she still in bed? This would be her first full day as a member of Sanctuary. She threw off all her warm blankets. Sophia-Emma had a full tummy and had a milk-drunk look on her face. *How can life be so perfect,* Loving asked herself. She wedged some pillows around Sophia-Emma before going out into the kitchen and making a cup of hot tea. She hadn't gotten a chance to get to know most of the people who lived in her dorm. Today, she'd make a bigger effort.

Three members—two men and a woman—were in the kitchen. They were sitting around the table, drinking tea and coffee to wake up. The smell of morning permeated the room.

"Well, there she is, the new mama," said the redheaded woman, who dipped her tea bag in and out of her cup until it was the rich brown of chestnuts.

"Yep, I've come out of hiding," Loving said as she poured some hot water into a cup. "No one minds if I have one of these bags of tea, do they?"

"Nah, we all share here," the man said. "I'm Muskrat. What's your name?"

"Loving, and you two?"

"I'm Pulsar, and the half-asleep one over here is Sassy," the fully bearded, handsome, young African American man said. He gave her a once-over and then went back to his tea.

"Glad to meet you all," Loving said as she fantasized about what secret had brought each of them there. "I hope my baby hasn't bothered you too much. If so, I'm sorry. For a while, I was like a opossum in the headlights. Frozen. Took me some time to get our act together. But today, I've decided I'm going to try to get acquainted with housemates and other folks here. So, please come and visit sometime."

"Bet you don't play cribbage," Pulsar said, almost as if he was prepared for a negative answer.

"Used to play with my mama. Want to try and teach me again? Remember, though, that I have to take breaks to feed my baby about every three hours or so."

"I'll come by tonight with my board, and we'll get started. Eight o'clock okay? I'm three doors down from you, I think." Pulsar fingered his beard, and Loving imagined it brushing her cheeks. Beards did that to her.

"I'll put the baby in her stroller so she can watch. I've gotta get back to little Sophia-Emma now." Loving took her hot tea back to her room with her.

"I met some new folks out in the kitchen," she told her daughter, who scanned the room as she walked in. Loving closed the door and added, "And you know what? One of them is kind of cute, but he seems to have a little chip on his shoulder. Maybe he's just tired. He has a cool beard."

Just as she'd promised herself, she helped wipe down the tables and sweep the floors after breakfast. The workers who were putting in their required hours in the dining room were surprised to get an offer of help from this woman. To them, she had always been so preoccupied with her new baby and the other burdens she seemed to be carrying.

The rain cleared away, and by mid-morning mommy and baby were out studying the chickens, cows, horses, and ducks. Loving turned Sophia-Emma around in the Moby, and she noticed a genuine smile on the little girl's face, especially when she saw the horses galloping out in the pasture.

Lunch followed, along with conversation with her favorite women—Navidad, Party Girl, Glory, and Barbie Doll. They were taking a break from the lamp shop, where they were under pressure to meet the quota for Christmas orders.

"I swear, we get more orders than we can handle this time of year," complained Glory, who even smelled like she had worked hard all morning.

"Be sure you keep track of your hours," said Navidad. She was in jeans and a sweatshirt, an unusual combination for her. "Come the end of December, we'll party like it's all the holidays molded into one. And it's all on me."

"What have you been up to today, little mama?" Party Girl tickled Sophia-Emma's chin.

"To tell you the truth, I wanted to stay in bed all day," Loving recalled. "My best friend left at dawn this morning. Got me kind of depressed and made me want to sleep away the entire day with Sophia-Emma. But after reconsidering, I decided that no, I was going to make this day special by trying to fit in better with all the folks and critters here. This is my first day as a full-fledged member, and I want to steep myself in Sanctuary."

"I voted for you," said Barbie Doll. "All of us did. We see some promise for you here. Hope you feel the same way."

"Oh, I do. That's why I'm hoping I can help you some in the shop today. Of course, I'll have Sophia-Emma with me, but I can be a gopher if you want. I want her to see where I'll be working someday. Maybe

I'll make it over to where they make the rugs, too. First, though, we're visiting the childcare center to see how many kids are there. I want to see who I can pick as her future best friends."

The ladies got a kick out of that and laughed in unison. Loving noticed people at the other tables glancing their way.

"Child, enjoy this time with your baby. It'll soon be gone and can never be retrieved. Believe me, I know," said Glory. "Crimson over there... See him? The one with the almost-bald head. We had three together, and they're all out in that cruel world. They come home very seldom anymore. Making a living takes up all their time."

"Oh, that's one reason I'm here. This baby is going to get the best, and sometimes the worst, of me." Loving patted her baby's butt, then gobbled up lunch.

At the childcare center, the ladies showed her around. The twenty children there were separated by size and age. The bigger kids were out on the playground chasing, jumping, and raging. One of the nurturers said that they would all tire out and be little angels the rest of the day. In the infant portion of the building, Loving sat in the corner with Sophia-Emma, trying to be as inconspicuous as possible. She wanted to get a general idea of what life in childcare would be like for her child. She picked the youngest, Dorothy-Fire, as the child most likely to be Sophia-Emma's best friend. No surprise, she was Crevice's little girl.

After immersion in the lamp and rug shops—she was interrupted a couple of times by nursing and diaper-changing breaks—dinnertime had come. The sun left a glistening streak across the lake as it said goodbye on the fall day.

When she was on her way back to Eagle's Landing, Zhen Bang tapped on her shoulder and told her that she wanted to speak to her in her room. Loving grew apprehensive and wondered if the members of Sanctuary had changed their minds and wanted her to leave.

"We just got a call from your friend Chaos," Zhen Bang said once Loving had settled on her bed, Sophia-Emma still enclosed in her wrap.

"She said that your mama passed out today and is now in the hospital. She's regained consciousness, but the doctors won't give Chaos or the woman who works at your house any information, as they aren't next of kin. Chaos left a number for the hospital so you can call back."

Loving was stunned. She dreaded deciding what to do next.

Chapter 34

At the Selma hospital in Alabama, Chaos wondered why Loving hadn't called back yet. She and Tillie sat silently in the emergency room's waiting area. They hadn't heard anything in hours. Chaos didn't know how much longer she could wait. At least this time she had been able to get ahold of Zhen Bang, who had told her that she would immediately alert Loving. But that had been at least two hours ago. She wondered if her friend cared about what happened to her mama. She wondered if Loving might someday treat her own daughter the way she'd been treated before she ran off to Sanctuary. Chaos herself had seen Louise Foster's mean streak. Surely Loving wouldn't follow in her mother's footsteps.

A medical technician came through a swinging door that separated the waiting room from the examination rooms. She motioned for them to come over to an area somewhat away from the other waiting folk, then said, "We're about to move Mrs. Foster to the ICU, where she'll be until we see better progress. Has anyone been able to contact her daughter yet?"

"I contacted the place where she's staying, but it's far from here. I expect she'll be calling soon," Chaos told the technician. "Can we visit her now?"

"Let me tell you, Mrs. Foster is very ill. I can't go into detail with you about her condition, though. If you want to visit, stay for just a few minutes and go in one at a time. Visiting hours tonight are between eight and nine."

"Can she communicate at all, or does she have all these contraptions hooked up to her?" Tillie asked.

"She will be hooked up to lots of machines, ma'am. I'm not sure how communicative she'll be. She's also on sedatives."

They went upstairs to the ICU. Tillie visited first. Chaos stood outside and looked in. The patient in the hospital bed looked like a character from a sci-fi movie. She saw Tillie take Louise's hand and stroke it with hers. Tillie seemed to be crying. She laid her head on Mrs. Foster's chest. Her body was heaving up and down. She turned around and walked out.

As soon as she was in the hall, Tillie hugged Chaos and cried even harder. "Oh, poor Mrs. Foster. No family to be with her. So pitiful. So very pitiful. Can you get Amanda here tonight?"

Next, it was Chaos's turn. While Tillie had been visiting, Loving's friend had thought about what she would say. She decided to say she was sorry for the times she hadn't treated her with respect. She would tell her that her daughter was well and safe and was very concerned about her. *Perhaps a small lie, but hopefully it will be true in the future,* she told herself.

She was astonished by the strong medicinal smells coming at her from all directions when she walked in. The noises from the machines keeping Mrs. Foster's body going—they seemed to monitor every eye blink and toe wiggle—combined to remind her of a factory at full force.

"Mrs. Foster, I'm so sorry you had this accident today." Chaos reached for Mrs. Foster's cold, thin hand. Wiggly veins bulged around thin bones and under bluish skin. "I'm sure Amanda will be contacting you soon, so hang in there." She thought she saw a small smile on Louise's face. "And I'm sorry for being a shitass around you. I hope you can forgive me. And don't worry, I'll take Tillie home tonight."

Mrs. Foster looked away and moved her hand away from Chaos.

When she left the ICU, Chaos again checked her cell phone. Still no calls or texts from Amanda, aka Loving. Even Chaos, as uncouth as she was, would call her mother at such a time.

When they were about ready to leave the hospital, Tillie grabbed her hand. "I can't leave Mrs. Foster at a time like this. You go on. I'm spending the night here. As long as it takes, I'll be with her."

"I can't leave you here like this, Tillie. You need to think of your own health. She needs you to be healthy. What if I spend the night in Amanda's room tonight? Tomorrow, bright and early, we'll come see her again. They have your home number in case she gets worse." Chaos needed her to change her mind. "Besides, she'll rest better tonight knowing that you're home safe."

"Okay, but if something happens to her tonight, I'll never forgive myself or you. Keep that in mind," Tillie warned Chaos.

Chapter 35

Because of the news of her mother's collapse and subsequent admittance at the hospital, Loving skipped dinner at Sanctuary. The idea of putting food in her mouth sickened her. She knew what she, the daughter and only surviving child, should do now. She had to make some phone calls to Chaos and the hospital. And she should probably go back home to Selma. The thought of making those moves paralyzed her, though. Here was her baby kicking around on the bed, needing to be changed, but she couldn't make her arms do the job. She was so tired, so confused.

If she and her mama were emotionally close, she would have already made those two calls and would be on the road, heading down the highway at full speed, on her way to reassure and love her mother. But today, she didn't even know if she loved her mama anymore. Deep inside, she actually wished she would hurry up and die. With her mind thinking such horrible things, how could she put on a false face? But then, why couldn't she let herself be vulnerable and give her mother one last chance? A last chance? Would she ever be able to forgive herself if she let her mama die without first reconciling with her?

She heard a knock on her door. "Come in," she commanded, as if by habit.

Pulsar swaggered in with his cribbage board and a deck of cards. "Ready to play?" he demanded more than asked. "I'm ready to teach."

He kept chewing on the toothpick hanging from the corner of his full, soft lips.

"Oh, I'm so sorry, Pulsar, but I can't play tonight. I've received news that my mama's in the hospital down in Selma, and I've got some decision-making to do."

"So why are you sitting here with a baby who obviously has a poopy diaper instead of making that call?"

"It's complicated, Pulsar," Loving tried to explain. "You see, my mama and I are hardly on speaking terms. She's one reason I'm here. She kicked me out of our house at Promised Land." Then she caught herself. She was sharing personal information that she didn't want anyone to know. "Let's just say that I don't want to give her false hope. I don't even want to know what her diagnosis is. Sanctuary has been great so far. It's given me a chance to get away from all the trauma and drama I was experiencing where I used to be. I feel that I'm finally healing. But this news is all about getting sick again. My mama can be a real bitch."

"Ms. Loving, I've been here now for seven years. I came as damaged goods, too, and much of it was because my worn-down family was trying to make it as Blacks in a white world. But don't get me started on that. My father died three years after I moved in here. He never knew where I was or if I was even alive. Didn't bother me then. As far as I was concerned, he deserved every feeling of guilt and bad diagnosis he got because he abused me constantly, making me feel like a worm." Pulsar put the cribbage board on Loving's chest of drawers. "I've never forgiven myself for not forgiving my old man, for not seeing that this system we're immersed in destroyed both of us. I don't want y'all to go through the same thing. Your old lady is your blood, your connection to the blood of Mother Earth. Our circumstances are different, but blood is blood. Make those necessary calls tonight, and tomorrow find a way to get back home so you can settle this crap 'tween y'all."

"That's your experience, Pulsar. I don't think I'll feel that way about my mama. But I'll follow your advice, force myself to make those necessary calls, and sleep on it tonight before I make any more decisions. That's about all I can force myself to do for now."

"Steps in the right direction, girl. Just remember, if folks there don't treat you right, turn around and get the hell out. Or hang up if you're on the phone. Y'all call the shots," Pulsar said. "Take it from me, parents are the pits. But relationships connect you to your tribe, faults and all."

"Well, I'll go down to the office now and make the calls on the land-line. Can I trust you to stay with my baby for a few minutes? I won't be long," Loving said. "I'll change her when I get back."

"Sure, but no way am I changing those shitty diapers," Pulsar insisted. "Change her before I puke."

Loving found herself doing as he commanded. She wasn't completely convinced that Pulsar was right about the phone calls, but at least she would get him out of her hair, and she could continue with her pity party the rest of the night.

At the office, she found a small room marked *Telephone*. It was empty. The note on the wall above the telephones gave specific directions for getting on an outside line. She'd gone by the same directions when she'd had to use the phone at boarding school more than five years ago. First, she called Chaos, who picked up immediately.

"I'm so glad you called, Loving," the voice on the other end said.

"I know. How's Mama?"

"Since I'm not a relative, I don't know exactly what's wrong. She was unconscious for quite a while. She passed out in your courtyard. Tillie called the EMS, and they took her to Vaughan, where she's now in the ICU. She's hooked up to all kinds of monitoring devices and saline and oxygen tubes. You know, Big Medicine and Big Pharma. But to be honest, she looks awful. I think you need to get down here ASAP. Of course, I'm not a professional, but I don't think she'll be around much longer. Tillie's a mess. Can you believe it? She adores your mom."

"She's all Tillie has left," Loving noted.

"Are you going to call the hospital?" Chaos asked. "The emergency folks gave me a general number you can call to get more information. Just say you're her next of kin. You're the only one they can share information about her condition with."

"Chaos, you know you're my best friend, right? And I can tell you anything?" Loving's tears were making her vision blurry. "Well, I don't know if I even want to contact Mama or the hospital. I can't help her, you know that. I may even upset her more."

"Amanda—I mean, Loving—get your ass down here tomorrow and do your duty as your mom's only surviving relative. I visited her in her room tonight. She almost smiled when I told her you were safe," Chaos stressed. "I can come and pick you up if you don't have a way here. I know the way now. I know you like it there. It's a good place to escape to, a place where you can pretend the real world doesn't exist. But this situation ain't going away. Come home. You hear?"

"I'll think about it, Chaos. Thank you for helping Tillie, by the way. And I hope your trip went well today."

"Tell you more when you get here." Chaos then ended the conversation.

"Okay, Chaos," Loving said, not realizing she was talking to herself. "I'll call the hospital."

She slowly dialed the number and waited for an answer.

"Vaughan Regional Medical Center. How can we help you?"

"Hello, I was given this number because my mama, Louise Foster—date of birth, November eighteenth, nineteen-forty-nine—was admitted there today and is in the ICU. I'm her daughter. I need to discuss her condition with a doctor or a person who knows something about her."

"Just a minute, ma'am. I'll transfer you to ICU," the upbeat voice said.

After a long wait, someone on the ICU floor answered. Loving repeated what she'd told the hospital phone operator.

"Her doctor has left for the night, but I can read you what he wrote on her chart," the nurse said. "Seems Mrs. Foster had a coughing spell at home. Your servant, Tillie Andrews, called for the EMS. She was taken to the trauma center at four-thirty PM. Seems she had not taken in adequate oxygen during the time she was unconscious. She has now regained consciousness, but the patient continues to be in critical condition. Did you know she has had COPD for quite a few years? Of course, the condition in her lungs leaves much to be desired."

"I'm out of town," Loving interjected. "Do you think it's necessary that I come home immediately?"

"Well, that's up to you, young lady. At this time, she can't speak. If she were my mama, I would get here soon."

"Will you tell my mother I called inquiring about her? Tell her she's in my prayers, will you, please?"

The nurse replied, "Is that all you care to say? Not, maybe, that you love her? After all, she is your mama."

"Ma'am, I know this is a small hospital in a tiny Christian town, but you're acting completely unprofessional. Tell her whatever you damn want to tell her," Loving screamed into the phone, then hung up.

She had done what she promised Chaos and Pulsar she'd do. Her conscience was free, at least until tomorrow, when she'd decide what she had to do.

On her walk back to Eagle's Landing, her steps became slower and slower. She felt as low as the dirty sole of her shoe. What was she going to do now? Probably no sleeping. That was a given.

Chapter 36

The rest of the night became one of escape. She walked in on Pulsar trying to reason with Sophia-Emma.

"Now, little girl, I told you your old lady would be back. Now just hush your mouth a little," he coaxed.

Sophia-Emma continued to cry frantically. Loving picked her up and brought her close to her breast, shushing her over and over. When the baby had quietened down enough, she laid her on the bed, stripped off her second messy diaper of the night, and looked at her red bottom. As if dealing with her ailing mama in the hospital wasn't enough, now she had to deal with a wailing, sore baby with a red rash all over her bottom.

"Pulsar, can you run some nice warm water into one of the bathroom sinks, then put some of that mild baby wash in it? Then I can give her a soothing bath," Loving requested. "Please?"

Standing, Pulsar protested. "Woman, I came over to play a card game. Now you have me preparin' your baby's bath? I'm goin' back to my room, where there's some peace. You white, and you a woman, meanin' you double nuts. Anyone ever tell you that?"

Loving looked pleadingly at him. Within a few moments, she had Sophia-Emma sitting in the warm sink, splashing and soothing her little bottom. From there, Loving rubbed her bottom down with some coconut oil from the kitchen; diapered her with a soft, dry diaper; and dressed her for bed in a lavender terrycloth onesie. Pulsar looked on in amazement as he watched Loving recline next to her baby and nurse her to sleep.

"Well, I guess I best be going, Ms. Loving. Next time you get all your baggage taken care of, call me. And by the way, your name kinda describes you," he said as he reached for the doorknob.

"Wait a minute before you go," Loving said. "I want to thank you for all the help you were to me tonight, advising me on what to do about my mama, caring for Sophia-Emma while I was gone, and helping me bathe her tonight. I never would have guessed I had such a considerate neighbor."

"Like I said, you got to take care of your drama," Pulsar said as he once more reached for the doorknob.

Loving got up and laid Sophia-Emma in her stroller, then approached Pulsar. "Can I have some drama with you about now?" she asked as she weaved her fingers into his.

Pulsar got the message when her lips touched his ever so softly.

She reached for his belt and began undoing the buckle. Slowly, almost like a dance, she pulled his shirt up over his head and kissed his nipples, brushing his wool-like chest hair with her lips.

"You know, you're some sexy man. Do you ever make love to a woman you hardly know?"

"I've been known to do that once in a while," he answered as saliva poured into his mouth and onto his beckoning lips.

"So, is this one more once in a while?" she asked as she put on her sexy voice.

"Well, I'm hoping it's not just once," he said as he put his hands under her blouse and felt the warmth of her soft, full breasts and hardening nipples. He played with them a little, and Loving began to desire for him to be closer to her.

Both kicked off their shoes and lay on the bed, which was still warm from her recent nursing session. She moved both her hands down to

Pulsar's lean hips and muscular buttocks. She drew him in, and he fit into the curves of her body. He raised himself enough so that he could move his hand down from her smooth and soothing breasts, letting his index finger meander slowly, zig-zagging toward her belly button. Loving surprised herself by giggling. She had been depressed just minutes ago, but now she felt like she wanted to crawl into Pulsar's body. The muscular flesh around it wouldn't let her, but her body didn't seem to comprehend that.

Pulsar was approaching her private parts, and he found moist areas that were prepared to welcome his. But Pulsar was in no rush. He wanted to tease her, to hear her groan, to make her laugh, and to make her beg for more.

Harder. Faster. Deeper. She wanted to be taken fully.

Loving nibbled and bit her lover's ear lobes, explored his abundant lips with the tip of her tongue, kissed the tip of his fascinating nose, and lost herself in his full and tasty beard. Reaching into Pulsar's jeans and then his shorts, she found the erect member. *Much bigger than Peter's was*, she thought. And she was ready for it to be welcomed inside her soft-pink vibrating interior.

Ever so gently, Pulsar removed his clothing below the waist completely, and Loving did the same. Their entire bodies now pulsated in excitement. Their bodies were warm yet cool to the touch. Loving thought of velvet as she fondled every curve of Pulsar's hips, his chest, and his buttocks.

Pulsar's most intimate part peeked inside her to see if all was clear. *Please come in and explore. Make yourself at home. Love me. Love me. Love me*, her vulva begged. He continued to tease her to the point that she thought he would come, but she did instead. Again. And again. Then, the great finale. The great hallelujah from deep inside her holiest of holies. Curtains down. They remained wrapped tightly around each other. They slept. Peaceful at last.

Chapter 37

Before dawn the next morning, Loving woke to Sophia-Emma whimpering in her stroller. This was the first time they had slept separately since Loving had found her nearly three months ago. She carefully crawled out from under Pulsar's bulky arms and legs, then tip-toed over to Sophia-Emma. She heard her baby sucking her fist as she picked her up and put her in bed with them.

Pulsar then awoke. He smiled and seemed to spend the next twenty minutes just watching mama and child. Occasionally, he'd shift his gaze upward and smile with his charcoal-colored eyes. Loving felt embarrassed and somewhat self-conscious.

"I can't believe what I did last night. I won't jump on you again," she whispered.

"Guess I got much more than what I bargained for. Definitely better than cribbage."

Loving giggled. "Well, I'll watch myself from now on. I promise," she said as she played with Pulsar's ample chest hair.

"Aw, shucks! It was fun." Pulsar laughed as he kissed her dreads. "By the way, who ever said you could copy Bob Marley? White folks love our hair but seem to be suspicious of our brains."

There was a long silence, and Loving changed the subject, bringing up her mama. "I talked to my friend who visited my mama yesterday, and then I called the hospital. I guess I need to find a way to go visit her very soon. Any ideas?"

"What possibilities are you considering now?" Pulsar asked.

"Craig, who helped my friend Chaos come here a couple days ago. Or I could take my old van and drive it back. Or I could have Chaos come up here from Alabama and take me there. I could get a bus ticket or plane ticket, or I could hitchhike. What do you recommend?"

"If it were me, I'd try the van idea first. I don't know what the particular rules are about that, but that makes the most sense to me. If you want, I could see if I could accompany you. I've also got some unfinished business not far from where your kin live. Not on a plantation, though."

"Would you really go with me? That would make all this so much better." Loving leaned over to kiss his cheek. "Who do we ask about this since it isn't a hierarchical decision?"

"Maybe the core group could decide. Let's check it out," Pulsar suggested.

"Another possibility would be for Sanctuary to do a direct action to help my friends with something they're doing down there, like investigating the murder of my old lover." Loving looked away from Pulsar and stared at the bare trees outside her window. When she focused back on him, she wiped her eyes on the bedsheet.

Pulsar grasped her hand tightly. "That's probably unlikely," he said. "Doing direct actions as a group means that the entire community has to endorse it, and that takes a long time. I don't think we have a lot of time, do we? Besides, you'll be under a lot of stress dealing with your mother while you're there."

"Maybe you're right. For now, can we just stay here and stare into each other's eyes until folks start moving? It's still early, so you can sleep here until daylight, or you can go back to your own room, if you prefer." Loving rolled over so she could nurse Sophia-Emma.

"I'll stay," Pulsar answered from behind her. "I like lying here with Mommy and baby. Seeing how the other side lives. For a cracker, you're not bad."

"You make love so easy. Thanks for being my friend and an even better lover," she teased. "Someday, I'll tell you more about Peter."

Chapter 38

While Loving snuggled up beside Pulsar, her mother was miserable and conscious in her hospital bed. Everyone in the rural hospital was treating her as if she were an inanimate object. She had a tube going down her throat. Another was delivering oxygen through the nose, and a third tube, this one on top of her hand, delivered saline water and unknown medications into her body. Without success, she tried to complain to an old lady mopping her floor.

If only she'd come to sooner and told Tillie to keep quiet about the whole ordeal. Then she would be sitting out in her courtyard right now, having a cigarette and looking over her Promised Land. Tillie knew she was tired out from that fiasco she hosted yesterday. Why in the hell did she lose it and call the ambulance? Also, Medicare didn't pay for ambulance service. A waste of money.

As she was worrying about money, what she was missing at home, and being treated like a dead object, in walked Tillie and Chaos. She saw that Tillie looked like she hadn't slept all night. How could she be any help when she didn't know how to take care of herself?

Tillie could tell that Mrs. Foster was much better. She bent down to kiss her, but Mrs. Foster turned the other way and spit some mucus into a cup. Tillie still smiled because she now knew that her boss was returning to her old obnoxious self.

"Mrs. Foster, I do believe you're feeling better today. I can't wait till the doctor sees the big improvement you done made overnight. A miracle. Truly a miracle." She squeezed Mrs. Foster's hand and pumped it up and down. All she heard from Mrs. Foster were some guttural noises.

The nurse walked in and smiled at her patient and Tillie.

"Don't you think Mrs. Foster is mighty improved today?" Tillie asked the nurse, who was busy jotting down numbers from the monitors, checking the IV, and taking Louise's blood pressure.

"We'll let the doctor decide that," she answered.

Mrs. Foster was pointing at her tracheal tube, trying to motion for it to be taken out. The nurse ignored her and left the room.

"Amanda's friend is here to see you," Tillie told her boss. "Can she come in and talk to you a bit?"

Mrs. Foster defiantly shook her head left and right.

"I guess that's a no, huh? But Ms. Chaos brought me here last night and today. I don't know what I'd have done without her. After the emergency people took ya to the hospital, she stopped by to tell us that she'd seen Amanda and that she's safe and well. But she noticed you weren't home, so she offered to take me to the hospital," Tillie bragged. "She's really a nice young lady, even if her name is a bit weird. I never liked my name, either."

A nurse stopped by the ICU door and told Tillie that she had stayed in the room longer than her five-minute limit.

"Guess we have to leave, Mrs. Foster," she said as she turned around to exit. "Oh, by the way, Ms. Chaos wanted to know if Amanda should come see you."

The old lady shook her head left and right again.

Tillie joined Chaos, who had watched the entire conversation from the hallway.

"I guess we can just sit here now and wait for the doctor," Tillie said. "Maybe he'll send her home today. She seems just like her sweet old self, don't you think?"

Chapter 39

Loving pushed melancholy and bitter thoughts of her mama to the furthest recesses of her mind as she and Pulsar spent the entire morning together. Pulsar assured her that he would get his hours in later, once all the plans were made for their trip to see her mother in Alabama. The three of them, including Sophia-Emma, went to Zhen Bang's office.

Zhen Bang started the conversation. "Your friend called again about your mama. You might want to talk to her before asking permission to leave. You can call her in our telephone room."

Confused, Loving quickly phoned Chaos. As usual, her friend answered promptly.

"Well, hello, dear Loving," Chaos greeted her. "Before you say anything, let me report to you that your mom is a bitch."

"Okay, what else is new?" Loving joked.

"We went to see your mama first thing this morning. She was conscious and coherent and didn't want to have anything to do with me. She wouldn't even let me come into her ICU unit. Tillie had come to cheer her up, and she even said lots of nice things about me, but Louise was as grouchy as hell," Chaos angrily noted. "Then the doctor came, and he decided to take her tracheal tube out, but they left in the IV and oxygen tube. Since we're not related, he didn't give us any prognosis, but it seems to me that she's regrettably improved. If I were you, I would call Dr. Bellows, the pulmonologist. His number is 334-848-9390. One more thing, and get this, Tillie asked if she wanted to see you, and she said no. Can you believe that?"

Loving's good mood evaporated. Even though she had dreaded the trip, to have her mama, who could be dying, say she didn't want to see her daughter...it was devastating.

"Okay, gotcha," Loving managed to respond. "I'll call the doctor, like you said, but I won't make any definite plans for now. Sorry you've had such an ordeal with my old lady. You're really a friend from heaven."

"Now don't start that Christian talk with me," Chaos warned. "There's not much I won't do for a good friend. I call it the evolution of humankind."

"Okay, let's do stay in touch," Loving said.

"Craig's still after me to come visit his farm," Chaos joked. "He's not much of an activist, but at least he's anti-capitalist. A start, huh?"

"Love you, Chaos," Loving said. "And I think Craig is a keeper. Bye for now!"

She exited the private room after her call, looked at Pulsar, and cried on his shoulder.

"Has she already died?" Pulsar asked.

"No, she's better, and that's not all good," Loving sobbed. "She says she doesn't want to see me, so I guess that's settled."

"I'd be pissed. Sorry she's doing this to you, Loving. I think she's a tough nut to crack and wants you to make the first move. But if you want to wait for her to change her mind, I'll understand. At least we can carry on here just as we would have otherwise. I'm game."

Loving managed a small smile. "Just to be sure that Chaos's intuition is right, I need to call her attending physician and see what he thinks," Loving said. "So, back into the phone room again."

She dialed the number Chaos had given her. Of course, Dr. Bellows wasn't able to talk immediately, but his receptionist said she would have him call as soon as possible. When she left the room this time, she wrote a note in large letters and thumbtacked it above the desk so anyone answering the phones could see it.

Doctor's call expected soon. Please notify Loving at Eagle's Landing as soon as he calls. I won't be leaving to see my mama until I speak with the doctor.

She then left with Pulsar. She would spend the rest of her day waiting for the doctor's call. Pulsar went to work. She clung to little Sophia-Emma more intently than she had since Peter had been killed less than three months earlier.

Chapter 40

That afternoon, Dr. Bellows returned Loving's call. A messenger from Sanctuary's office ran up to Eagle's Landing to get Loving, just as she'd hoped. She hurriedly gathered up Sophia-Emma and took the phone call in the private room. She put Sophia-Emma to the breast so she would be occupied while Loving talked with the doctor.

"This is Amanda Foster here," she said, figuring she'd better use her given name in this circumstance.

"Hello, Ms. Foster. Dr. Bellows here. I understand you're concerned about your mother. First of all, please tell me her birth date."

"It's November eighteenth, nineteen forty-nine," she responded. "Her middle name is Jane, and she is the widow of Lawrence Foster, Sr. Any other information you need?"

"No, that's fine. Let me tell you about your mother's condition. I understand you called the ICU last night, and they gave you some background information about what brought your mother here. At that time, her condition was critical. Today, we've changed that to stable, but we need to keep her here a few more days to run some more tests and to try out some new medications.

"Your mother's x-rays basically show that her lungs are shot. Now, that doesn't mean she's going to die soon, just that she will be living with a condition that won't improve. We're not even sure that oxygen will help that much. Your mother, I understand, is a smoker and has been for most of her adult life. I've spoken to her about this, and she tells me that no one is going to force her to give up smoking. She said something about a friend who has smoked far longer than her, a lady who still does her own gardening and swims every day."

"That would be Hilda," Loving said. She remembered that the two women emptied their shared ashtray half a dozen times whenever they got together to gossip on lazy summer afternoons.

"Well, so be it. I heard that you were wondering if it'd be necessary for you to come visit her at this time. I asked her today if she would like you to be with her. Unfortunately, she was adamant that you don't come, I'm sorry to say. She doesn't think now is a good time."

"Fine with me, Doctor. I don't want to see her, either." Loving was too mad to cry. Instead, she looked down at Sophia-Emma, who was nursing without a care in the world.

"However, Ms. Foster, she does need to set up a living will, and in my opinion, the person to represent her, in case she can't make decisions for herself at a later date, should be a family member. And it seems that the only family she now has is you. Is that correct?"

"'Fraid so," Loving muttered.

"Someday, you'll need to go over this with her. Does she want us to take measures to keep her alive in certain situations, or would she prefer to not be resuscitated? I know this isn't something we like to discuss with our loved ones, but it gives both some peace of mind after everyone knows what to do in such situations."

"I'm aware of the necessity of it. Have her fill out one of those forms you doctors have, and let her maid, Ms. Tillie, witness it. That will suffice for now. After all, they're with each other every day."

Loving swallowed what seemed to be a huge lump in her throat. "Be truthful with me, Doctor. Tell me, how much time does a person have left when they are in my mama's condition?"

Loving heard only silence. She assumed he was thinking about how he could be tactful while answering her question.

"If she improved on her habits, she could live a good number of years. If she changes nothing about her lifestyle, I can't really say how long for sure. If you're wondering if you should rush home today, no, not necessary. But do realize that her health will probably deteriorate in the coming years."

"When do you expect to dismiss my mama?" Loving asked, changing the subject.

"Perhaps in two to three days. I assume this Tillie, who you already mentioned, will be at the house with her?"

"That's right, Doctor. Mama and I had a spat not long ago, so for me to come visit now isn't a good idea. But I do want to keep up with her health. Please keep me as a contact for her, for when and if things get worse."

"I sure will, Ms. Foster. Hang in there. Your mama will probably come around. I've found that time heals, especially when both parties realize that the remaining time is limited."

"Thank you, Doctor. I guess I do love her despite both of our hot tempers. I really ain't sure that time will heal what we're fighting about, not for a long, long time anyway." Again, Loving looked at her innocent baby.

"I know you love her, Ms. Foster. I can do very little from here, but I will do what I can." With that, the phone call ended.

Loving wondered how she was going to deal with her mama from now on. She also wondered if Tillie could help her with the advance directive. Dr. Bellows acted like this was very important. For now, the old hag didn't want to have anything to do with her, and she felt the same. Forget what the doctor had advised. What did she care? She didn't care if she ever saw her mama anymore. So what if she collapsed while smoking another cigarette, or while having a bowel movement? Loving never wanted to own Promised Land either. Not worth it... except that those voices in the old burial grounds wanted rest and respect. Damn, she still cared.

For the moment, she decided to release all of her worries. She had a new life at Sanctuary, and she even had a new man in her life. She tore up the doctor's phone number. In a symbolic gesture, she also took her cell phone from her pocket and deleted her mama's phone number. She didn't know why she had continued to charge the phone and carry it around months after moving here. After today, no more.

Loving remained in the room and cried as hard as she had the day her father died years ago. She lifted Sophia-Emma up to her shoulder and burped her, promising her that she would be a much better mama than the bitter old lady Loving herself had too long endured.

She opened the telephone room's door and saw no one waiting to make a call. Loving knew she had one more person to contact: Amigo. She needed those papers to make Sophia-Emma legally hers. She could wait no longer.

Chapter 41

Louise Foster wasn't thinking of calling anyone, especially not her only daughter, on December fifth, the day she was released from the hospital. Tillie drove her home, and she just stared out the window, looking over quiet brown fields. She was glad that she'd already decorated the house for Christmas when she'd prepared for the failed party. At least all the bright colors and lights would help her get out of this depressed mood that had settled deep inside her gut.

Tillie tried to put a happy spin on their return to Promised Land. "Mrs. Foster, I've got your favorite meal waiting in the oven. Chicken and rice with creamed corn and the biscuits you love. It will still be warm, and it'll bring color to those cheeks of yours in no time."

"I'm not hungry, Tillie. When you get me home, just help me out of these clothes, give me a glass of wine, and let me go to sleep. That hospital bed was like a cement slab," Louise complained.

"But, ma'am, the doctor said—"

"Don't go repeating any of that trash the doctor said. I know how to take care of myself. Why, he can't be any older than my two boys were. He's nothing but a kid himself. It's my life, and I'm living it my way, you hear?"

"Yes, ma'am, I understand. I think you wanna die, and if that's what you want to do, I can't stop you."

"I'm not ready to die yet, Tillie. I've got lots of personal stuff I need to do before I let myself die. First, I've got to report a baby that should

185

be in state custody, and then I need to talk to my lawyer about disinheriting Amanda. Then I'll be ready to go, God willing."

"Oh, Mrs. Foster, why do you want to cause so much trouble?" Tillie scolded her. As soon as she said it, she knew she was in trouble herself.

"And you, Tillie...you're in the same shoes as me, only I have money to keep me company. You got nobody and no home once I'm gone. So shut your mouth. I know what I'm doing."

Chapter 42

Amigo at last answered his phone a week after Loving first called. She knew that her mother was probably home from the hospital and was most likely up to no good. Sophia-Emma needed legit-looking papers immediately.

"I know why you're calling, Amanda. If I were you, I would be calling me now, too."

"Well, okay. You know our little project? How's that coming along?"

"We're at a standstill for the next few weeks. We're under scrutiny from ICE. Some bigwigs are making life difficult for guys like me, though we're providing an important service. We need to lie low for a while. I'm in Oklahoma visiting a friend, doing my best to blend in with the nation near Fort Gibson. But it'll all pass over when these hearings eventually run their course. I promise that after a few months, the G-boys will be on to something else. Trust and patience, mi amiga. You're on my mind."

"Well, this girl is getting anxious herself. I have confidence in your abilities and your judgment of when's a good time and when isn't, but she's all I have in the world. You know that."

"Entiendo mi amiga," he said. "But if we rush things, our chances for failure are higher. You'll be the first to know when we can get back to our services."

"By the way, save the number I'm calling from," Loving said. "My cell doesn't work where I'm at."

"Amanda, remember, I know what I'm doing. I've been doing this work for nearly a decade now. I wish I could say more, but you understand, don't you? I've got a lot on me right now. Bear with me."

It wasn't what Loving wanted to hear today. She hung up without even a goodbye.

Maybe she'd forget the whole matter of legalizing her baby with fake documentation. They'd just live under the radar for the rest of their lives. Then she thought, *Are any children given birth certificates at Sanctuary? I'll check with Medie.*

Getting papers for Sophia-Emma raised the question in her head once more: Who was her little girl? Sure, Sophie-Emma didn't yet have legal documentation, but she was a real human. She cried like a baby, sucked like a baby, and pooped like a baby. But Loving knew in her gut that there was something more to this little girl than what she knew.

To heck with Amigo. Both had their own battles to fight. She had to win hers somehow.

Chapter 43

Once she was able to let thoughts of her mother move down the list of priorities, Loving found something else to worry about. What if Sanctuary wasn't enough of a secret? The thought of losing her baby had been fluttering around in her mind ever since she'd run off with Sophia-Emma nearly three months ago. But now, knowing that her mama seemed to pathologically resent her actions, these thoughts were haunting her. She couldn't imagine a life without Sophia-Emma. She would rather die than give up her daughter.

She needed to talk her fears out. Zhen Bang knew her whole story, but she wasn't in the office at the moment. She had to do something, though. Her worry was eating away at her. Next door, she heard the daycare children singing "Silent Night." She made a conscious effort to sing along in a slow, meditative manner.

"...holy night! All is calm, all is bright."

Loving could feel her pulse slow as she breathed deeply in, then out, over and over. Sophia-Emma, half-asleep, was starting to search for a nipple. Loving helped her hungry daughter out by moving her right breast to the edge of her mouth. The nursing baby at her breast soothed Loving, so much so that she almost dozed off herself. Boots traipsing into the office abruptly woke her. They belonged to Zhen Bang.

"Are you still here? Do you need to arrange a trip to go see your mother?" Zhen Bang asked as she sorted through the mail.

"No, the trip's off. I need to talk to you about something else. I need to be reassured about protection here, my baby's protection, especially. I think my mother's going to report to Alabama Human Services that I took a baby that wasn't mine," Loving shared as tears started running down her cheeks. "She's terribly angry with me. She thinks I'm snubbing the many generations of my ancestors. I'm the only living member of my family besides her. She can't get what she wants by bribing me. I'm not interested in any of her filthy money. But she can have this little girl taken from me. She knows she won't get me back by doing that, but at least she'll have the satisfaction of having punished me. I'm so scared. What should I do?"

Zhen Bang sat in a chair next to Loving, took her hands, and didn't speak right away. She reckoned this young lady needed time to cry, to break open, and to rid herself of all that haunted her spirit so she could live there unafraid. As Loving sobbed, Zhen Bang prepared for what she would say.

"Loving, you are safer here than anywhere else you could go in this country. We use a Post Office Box in town. When we send mail, we use only the PO Box. Our phone number isn't published anywhere. Our location isn't published anywhere. I'm not saying that it would be impossible to find you. Nothing's impossible. You won't be one hundred percent safe living here, but you're far safer here than anywhere else you could hide. And if we do get wind that some authorities or old enemies are coming here, we can hide you even better in one of our underground safe spots. Still not one hundred percent perfect, but close. I suggest you confine yourself inside our property here as much as you can. Don't go into town. Maybe cut your hair. Dress another way. Eventually, all this will blow over."

"Ya really think so?" Loving asked hopefully. "You don't know how powerful my mama is. She's the meanest when she is the maddest. I remember from when I was a little girl that once she set out to ruin someone, she'd succeed and then laugh about it. Need I tell you more?"

Zhen Bang shook her head. "Don't say more. It'll only make you worry more."

"I'm working on getting Sophia-Emma a fake birth certificate that names me as her mother. If I go further with this idea, am I only making things worse? In a sense, raising a red flag? Do we also need to avoid this option?"

"That's a tough one. We've hacked into state computers in the past, created fake certificates and other documents. We haven't been caught yet. But I tend to agree with you. Maybe just make yourself at home for a while. Let your old lady report you. Let her hire a private investigator and call the governor, the highway patrol, and the white nationalists. Let them all get on your tail. They won't find you. I suggest you make no more calls to anywhere outside Sanctuary, including that little pal you had here a couple days ago. Tell your hacker buddy to lay off the fake documentation. If I were you, I'd send a letter to that Chaos woman and have her contact the hacker. Have her destroy the letter you send. She has to be good with this. Tell her not to write back. Throw your cell phone away. And then just trust. Live your life day-to-day. We've got your back. Okay?"

Loving did feel more secure after Zhen Bang's assurances. Maybe she was right. Loving would never be completely safe, but she would probably be safer staying put rather than trying any other option...short of killing her mother. She stunned herself with that thought, but it was a possible option. With her dead, all would be fine. No more worries...ever. She could hire someone to do it for her, keep her hands clean. Maybe one of the Yoders or Lunds. No, that wouldn't work. They talked too much, especially when they saw money waving in front of them. She toyed with the idea of suggesting this option to Zhen Bang, but she knew that would not be an acceptable option with this group. They might even expel her if they thought she was considering such a drastic solution.

"I feel somewhat better now. I'll write the letter and let everything else go. Can we mail it far from here, you think?"

"I'll check to see if any of our tech folks are making any trips soon, or perhaps someone's going to visit family a good distance away. Do you trust anyone around here? I think we would have to give the letter to someone whom you know would do the right thing."

"True. Let's both scout around."

Zhen Bang stood up, still holding Loving's hands. Loving stood up, as well. Sophia-Emma took a break from breastfeeding and gave both of them a smile.

"I've got to go, gal. Why don't you go cut your hair real short? Stop by and pick up some different clothes at the commie store. Once you look at your new self in the mirror, maybe you'll convince yourself that you're now Loving. Amanda is long gone."

Loving decided to do just that.

Chapter 44

Tillie was becoming more worried about Mrs. Foster. Her boss had slept for two days after returning from the hospital. During that time, Tillie prepared meals that only she ate. Soon, she found herself dusting where she had dusted just the day before, sweeping and mopping clean floors, and staring out at the full bird feeder for what seemed like hours. She filled and refilled Mrs. Foster's water glass and helped Mrs. Foster to the bathroom and back. Early on the third day of the long sleep, she called Dr. Bellows to see what she should do.

"Let her sleep. I had reports that she didn't sleep well the entire time she was at the hospital. If this continues, give her some broth, perhaps some Jell-O. Call us back in a couple days if she still doesn't seem like she has any interest in getting up and resuming life," the doctor advised. "Is she also smoking?"

"No, Doctor. She's doesn't even want her cigarettes. Maybe if I go upstairs and light one up, that'll get her out of bed."

Tillie had to take the phone away from her ear when Dr. Bellows responded.

"Okay, I won't do that. Just an idea," Tillie said. "I'll cook up some good chicken broth and push her to drink it. And she likes lime Jell-O. Thanks for givin' me somethin' to do."

When she got off the phone, she took the chicken bones out of the freezer and covered them with water in the crockpot, where they would slowly simmer for the next day. Then she went through her Jell-O drawer to find the lime package.

On the fourth day, Mrs. Foster woke at 6:00 AM. She yelled as loud as her sick lungs would allow. "Tillie, help me dress so I can go have a smoke out in the courtyard. Tillie! Tillie! Get your ass out of bed and get me dressed. I've got a lot to do today."

Finally, after the second yell, Tillie knew she wasn't dreaming. That was the real Mrs. Foster screaming for her. She hurriedly threw her pink robe around her and dragged herself across the hall. There in front of her was Mrs. Foster, sitting erect against her bed's headboard.

Louise reached out to take Tillie's hands, which would guide her into her wheelchair. Though she had only her gown on, Mrs. Foster had Tillie put a wool blanket around her shoulders and slippers on her feet. Out in the hallway, the dedicated servant shifted her boss into the chairlift, which would take her to another wheelchair downstairs. Out in the still-dark courtyard, Louise deeply inhaled the first hits of nicotine. She relaxed and studied the early-morning fog, enjoying the quiet, chilly dignity of morning.

Tillie went inside to brew coffee and make scrambled eggs and toast. She rehearsed what they would talk about as they sat across from one another at the old kitchen table. Should they discuss Amanda or smoking? Or maybe the old days, when the children got into the strawberry patch and when they brought home that ten-pound bass from the river. Oh, those were such happy times. Not like today, with the kids gone and Mrs. Foster herself barely hanging on.

"Tillie, I'm ready to eat breakfast. Bring it out here, and I'll eat it quickly. No time to waste today. I've slept way too long. While I'm eating, call my attorney. Tell him to drive out here today so we can discuss my last will and testimony. And get me the Human Services phone number."

"Oh, Mrs. Foster, don't do what I think you're planning to do. Little Amanda is all you got. Now, don't you think—"

"Do as I said," Louise Foster commanded. "I pay you to obey, not to question my judgment."

Chapter 45

Loving had made up her mind: The dreads had to go. Six years of determined palm rolling and continued weaving and tightening had made each lock dear to her. They represented all that she was. She was scared that little Sophia-Emma would be afraid of her once they were gone. *What a mother will do for her child*, she thought. To make matters even worse, she forced herself to throw the dreads away after cutting them off.

Anything that identified her had to go. Everything in her dresser drawers, the closet, and even her van... She hadn't thought about Very Wicked. It would be a dead giveaway that she was here. But if it were sold, that would create a deed of sale. The van would have to be buried or something like that. Maybe stripped and repainted. She didn't know. She'd never attempted to become a non-person driving a non-vehicle before.

Loving blinked and looked at herself again. *What a mess*, she thought. Her remaining hair was going every which way and was at varying lengths. She looked over at Sophia-Emma in her stroller. Her big dark eyes seemed to grow even bigger. She simply stared at this woman who sounded like her mama but sure didn't look like her. At least she wasn't crying yet.

After a few minutes of trying to get a comb through her wet hair, Loving gave up. The next step would be to dye it. Perhaps red would be good. She could get some glasses, wear some makeup, and ditch the long whirly skirts for more conventional outfits.

Loving checked Sophia-Emma's diaper, changed it quickly to keep the rash at bay, and then took off to the commie store. She would burn her favorite clothes one day soon. A shame, she thought, since over the years her collection had mirrored who she really was.

At the commie store, she zeroed in on the tight jeans, leggings, sweatshirts, and mid-thigh skin-tight skirts.

"Hello, Loving," she whispered to herself. "New name, new hairdo, new face, and different threads to go with it all."

She wished she could just be a true person instead of this pretending.

She stuffed her new wardrobe into a huge old canvas bag that promoted a local food co-op, and when she turned the stroller around to leave, she noticed Christmas decorations off in the corner of the building. It hit her like an asteroid bouncing off the side of her head. This would be Sophia-Emma's first Christmas. She couldn't wait to see her daughter's eyes light up when she saw the blue, white, green, and red lights. Maybe they would find a baby evergreen tree in the woods, put it in a pot, and decorate it.

All of a sudden, her depressed mood changed to one of hope, excitement, and expectation. She told herself to, from now on, only think of the upcoming holidays. She needed to forget her worries and concentrate on her baby. Just like in the first Christmas story, a baby was born and warmed a mother's heart. They were being hunted down, but they were protected, too. She decided there was hope for her and Sophia-Emma, after all.

Chapter 46

Tillie had lost hope that Amanda's mother would eventually come to her senses and make up with her daughter. Could Louise Foster be like Herod, who'd stop at nothing to capture the infant Jesus? She did what Louise told to do, though in her heart she was pulling for Amanda and her darling baby.

She found a number for Alabama Human Services and was able to get Mrs. Foster's attorney on the phone. She gave the phone to her employer, along with the phone number. Those two errands completed, she sat down to her own breakfast, all the while wondering what would happen to her little Amanda.

Tillie could hear the conversation going on in the next room. Just as she'd said she would, the old lady was redoing her will, cutting Amanda out. Amanda wouldn't even get the smallest chicken running in the chicken yard. Tillie assumed that Mr. Perkins, the attorney, was asking Louise who would get the estate. Louise said she was thinking of leaving it to the church and telling them to use it as a conference center. What? Promised Land a church place? *That woman will do anything to keep this place lily white*, Tillie thought.

"Okay, bring the corrected papers to me as soon as possible," Mrs. Foster ordered, concluding the conversation.

Tillie looked at her employer, who had put the phone down and was smiling for the first time in a week. Louise wheeled herself out to the courtyard for another light. Tillie picked up the breakfast dishes and dropped them into the deep kitchen sink, breaking a coffee cup in the process. She delighted in picking up the broken china and throwing the pieces in the trash. Something in this place needed to go into the trash, even if it was only one of the purple-flowered cups she'd always detested.

The phone rang again. Tillie assumed that Mr. Perkins had a few more questions for her boss, but when she answered, a voice she'd never heard before was on the other end. He asked for Mrs. Foster, the owner of Promised Land. Was he with the church, perhaps, or maybe he had some bad news about Amanda? She knew it was none of her business, so she gave the phone to Mrs. Foster. Her curiosity naturally got the better of her, however. Pretending to go upstairs to make Mrs. Foster's bed, she picked up the phone in the bedroom and put her hand over the mouthpiece.

"You say you're with whom?" Mrs. Foster asked. "Yes, I have a daughter named Amanda. How's it any of your business?"

The unfamiliar voice said that he had seen Mrs. Foster's daughter at the memorial for Peter a few months ago. "I noticed she had a little mixed-race baby in a stroller there. Does this concern you, Mrs. Foster? I know your family, all the way back to the founders of Promised Land, has been proud of your pure European heritage. We at the Creativity Alliance have a mission to preserve the white race for the return of our Savior, which is getting nearer. I'm sure you don't want to stand before the Lord on that day with a half-breed granddaughter."

Mrs. Foster answered, "How did you know... Do you know Amanda?"

"We know the leftist, anarchist, Communist-loving crazies she and her boyfriend ran around with. After the lame demonstration they did at the Governor's Mansion, we followed her to where she was camping. The next day, some of our members followed her into Virginia, but we lost her when she made a sharp right turn off the interstate."

"Is that right?" Mrs. Foster asked. "Can you find her?"

"I think we can, with your permission. We will need some documentation, such as a picture of her. You know, stuff that will help us track her better. When we find her, we'd like your permission to scare her a little, just enough so that she'll give the baby to a nice African family, where the child would be happier. Don't you think, Mrs. Foster?"

"How do I know you're who you say you are? I love my daughter. I don't want her hurt. How much do you charge to bring her back to me without that baby?"

"Does ten thousand dollars sound about right to get your daughter once again under your roof and back in the family fold? If we can knock some sense into that commie brain, I may even be able to line up a fine, respectable, pure-white stud—I mean, husband—for her. No charge."

"How do I get these papers—documentation—to you?"

"I'll meet you over at Berry's Drug in Selma. Does Saturday at two work for you?"

There was a long silence as Mrs. Foster most likely thought about how she was going to meet this stranger. She'd have to ask someone to drive her there. Tillie suspected she'd be hearing a fake excuse in about ten minutes.

"Let me get back in touch with you. I still don't even know your name, and I'm trusting you to bring my daughter back if I invest ten thousand dollars in you. Do you have any references?"

"Lady, I'm not your local plumber. My name is Jim Christian. You're just going to have to go with your gut on this one. You don't use me, and you'll probably never see your daughter again, and your only descendent will be this yellow-brown half-breed who will mess up your bloodline forever. I don't think that's a chance you want to take. Friday at two. If I don't see you there, I won't be offering to help you again. And it's five thousand upfront, too."

Tillie heard Jim hang up. After she heard the click on Louise's phone downstairs, she also hung up and busied herself making the bed. Within eight minutes, just as Tillie had suspected, Mrs. Foster asked her to take her to Berry's Drug and to the bank on Friday at one. Apparently, she had some prescriptions to fill and some bills to pay.

Chapter 47

Loving stepped back from the window and surveyed her room, which was now decorated for the holiday season. She'd also swept the floor, dusted the furniture, made the bed, and washed her lone window. She could barely tell she was in the same room she'd been in for the last three months. Then she looked in the mirror and saw the new Loving. She wondered what Sophia-Emma was thinking about all the changes happening before her big baby eyes.

In a few minutes, Pulsar would be coming by to go to dinner with her and Sophia-Emma. Loving tried to relax by thumbing through a fashion magazine she'd picked up at the commie store. She picked up her baby and tried to interest her in breastfeeding, but Sophia-Emma was too stimulated by the new room and her mama's new look. She couldn't relax. Loving turned off the Christmas lights and pulled down the window shade, making the room almost completely dark. The lack of color and bright lights calmed both of them. Breastfeeding calmed them even more, and both fell asleep.

A familiar knock on the door woke Loving from her dreamy world. Pulsar had arrived, and she invited him in, then got back in bed.

"C'mon. Ain't you hungry? The line closes in about ten minutes. Let's move." He snapped his fingers. "If you want, y'all can stay here, and I'll bring you something. Can't believe I'm acting like a puppy dog these days. Don't tell the bros about this." Pulsar took a look at himself in Loving's mirror and scowled at the image he found there.

"I promise not to tell a soul, but only if you get me some food. Not much, though. Gotta fit into my new leggings," Loving whispered as Sophia-Emma lay beside her, still out of it. "I'm so tired. I'll tell you all about it when you get back. You'll never believe it. Never."

"Well, I don't think I can listen to any long stories on an empty stomach. Putting together hundreds of lamps today has done me in. I could eat anything—two legs, four legs, or slimy fins. But I know we'll be settling for brown rice and beans instead," he complained.

Pulsar stooped over to give Loving one of the kisses she'd been so crazy about the night before. But this time, he planted it on a sleepy face instead. Then he saw the new face, the red hair. Was he in the wrong room? Where were the dreads? Wasn't her hair brown earlier that day? She somehow didn't look the same. If it hadn't been for Sophia-Emma, he'd have thought he was in the wrong room. And the room...it'd changed, too. What in the hell was this white woman up to? The scent of the woman in bed told him this was his lover. Maybe it was because of the holidays. Strange things happened this time of year (like lots of lamp orders). But why did Loving have to change, too?

Pulsar finally left, and in what seemed like five minutes, he was back with tofu, rice, creamed corn, yams, and iced tea for two. Before he started to eat, he had his say. "Get your ass out of bed and let me know what the hell is going on here." He talked mean in hopes of getting a rise out of Loving.

She propped her pillows up behind her and sat upright on the bed, stunned by Pulsar's command. It was like a firecracker exploding before her feet. "What in the world?"

"No, that's what I say," he echoed. "Your hair, this room, what you're wearing..."

"Oh yeah, that. I'll tell you as we eat. You know, we breastfeeding mamas are sometimes starving."

Pulsar teased her by moving her plate over to the chest of drawers, forcing her to get out of bed. He got a full view of this new Loving when she followed the food like a bloodhound tracking a rabbit. He sat in a chair near the bed while Loving shoved food into her mouth, chewing very little, as though a vacuum at the back of her mouth was sucking it down her throat. When she at last found a moment to breathe, she decided to talk.

"Zhen Bang and I talked after I found out that my mother didn't want to see me. I know my mama, and I know that she isn't going to just forget me. She's going to punish me by taking that little girl over there away from me," Loving explained as she took another mouthful and chewed. "Zhen Bang suggested I change everything about me. Thus, the hair and my clothing. When I went to the commie store to get these clothes, which were almost repulsive to me, I saw some holiday decorations. I had to do something to bring joy back into our lives. Thus, the lights, the cleaned-up room, and the tired me.

"Anyway, Zhen Bang says I need to sort of disappear, have no contact with anyone outside. And if the state of Alabama does get leads and alerts officials up here to get my baby, Zhen Bang told me they have an even more secret place where they can hide us. I'm going all the way on this, Pulsar. I'm scared." She set her dinner aside and started wiping her eyes on her sheet as she cried.

Pulsar moved out of his chair and sat next to her on the bed. Sophia-Emma was waking up. He picked her up, but she only had eyes for her mama. Pulsar handed her over to Loving, who lifted her sweatshirt so her baby could nurse.

"Well, I guess you've done a decent job changing your looks. I'll miss your dreads and your pretty long, flowery skirts, but I realize it's either this or no you at all." He gave Loving and Sophia-Emma a big hug and took a long drink of his tea. "Let me be a part of your plan, Loving. No matter how you look or dress or even decorate your room, I dig what's inside you. Are we a pair from now on?"

Loving felt tears rolling down her face once again. "I don't know what I would do without you."

Chapter 48

After having a good cry over the loss of her wayward daughter, Louise Foster told Tillie not to disturb her. Apparently, she had to go through some documents that the pharmacist needed before she could pick up her medicine. Of course, Tillie knew that was a lie. She knew the old lady was putting her only descendent in danger in order to get that beautiful baby out of the family line. But Tillie was just the help. She needed to keep her job.

That night, while Mrs. Foster was sleeping, she called Chaos. "Ms. Chaos, I have some information that I think you need to get to Amanda."

"Yes, Ms. Tillie. I'm all ears," Chaos tiredly said.

"Well, Mrs. Foster got a call today from a Jim Christian, who represents some group called Creativity something or other. He told Mrs. Foster that he could find Ms. Amanda, take the baby from her, and bring Amanda back here. He would probably have to scare her a little, but he could find her. He guaranteed it."

"Are you sure of his name, Tillie? Do you think he might have made up that name?"

"Ms. Chaos, I'm just passing on a conversation I heard today. I was upstairs making Mrs. Foster's bed, and I heard her on the phone. I picked the phone up in her room, and that's what I heard. Anyway, she's going to pay this so-called Christian man ten thousand dollars to bring Amanda back home. She'll be giving him some documents about her at two o'clock tomorrow at Berry's Drug. Maybe someone in your group can come around there about that time and get a look at him."

"You're a smart lady, Ms. Tillie. I'll see if I can get word to Amanda about this. She may want to hide out more. She does need to know this, I agree. Please keep me in the loop if you get any more information."

"Oh, I will," Tillie assured Amanda's friend. "I sure don't want anything to happen to my little girl and her baby. It's so sad that Ms. Amanda and her mother can't come to some type of agreement on this. Please call me on my cell after ten at night so Mrs. Foster doesn't know I'm squealing on her. She can be very mean, you know."

"Oh yes, I do know," Chaos said. "This will be our little secret, Tillie."

Chapter 49

Pulsar, the guy some of the white dudes avoided at Sanctuary, was known to have a mean streak occasionally. But this morning, he felt peace as he looked at the two beautiful ladies in his life. The naked one, hair every which way, was his woman, the owner of the body he wanted to explore every inch of, the owner of the mind he wanted to look into. Next to this awesome lady was a smaller, darker, chubbier one. Her eyes seemed to reflect the world, and her smile wrapped him in sunshine. He was happy, but he wondered how long this moment could last. He'd had such bad relationships in the past that he'd given up thinking about a future. But today, he was letting himself dream of even better days ahead.

He put his brawny brown arm over his sexy woman, who had the little lady attached to her right breast. Pulsar marveled at the tones of brown—his rich chestnut, Sophia-Emma's angelic gold, and Loving's rose shade and lingering summer tan. This was America now, a country of shades and contrasts, of coordinating colors that wanted to blend, bleed, and create new ideas, new lives, and new experiences. What a stunning picture the three of them made. While caught up in the moment, he at last knew he had made the right decision about coming to this place.

A while ago, Pulsar and another man from Africatown, Alabama, had sneaked into American Paper one night and vandalized its property, painting skulls and crossbones on smokestacks, tanks, and offices. They'd taken documents that told stories of board meetings where members discussed ways to conceal information about the toxins they were releasing into the air and dumping into the Hog Bayou.

"At last, my bros and sistahs know they have been poisoned by the company that hired them to sweep their floors, the company that handed out Butterball turkeys each year," he had told the newspapers as the police escorted him to prison.

He'd been willing to go to jail for his civil disobedience. Fortunately, he was later released on bail; his neighbors and family had paid it. But then the corporate mafia, who controlled Mobile Bay and much of Alabama, started saying that Pulsar was really a long-time crook. They said they had pictures of him selling dope to teens in Africatown and nearby Plateau. They said he had been a "man of interest" in the investigation when a cop was found dead in Three Mile Creek. All of a sudden, he was the only suspect for all the crimes committed in the previous three years around Africatown. He panicked and ran off, following the directions to Sanctuary that his friend, George Haney, had given him. That was seven years ago. As far as Africatown people knew, he was either dead or was hiding out in the shadows of the crime world.

For the last seven years, most of the people at Sanctuary had believed the story that he had had to leave his home in Africatown because his father was abusing him. That wasn't completely the truth. If it had been, he could have moved away and split ties much sooner. No, he was scared of the white mafia, corporates, and police on the prowl for black blood. Pulsar had turned his back on all those who had bailed him out. Today, he felt like a coward, a pure coward with no backbone.

Even though he was grateful to Sanctuary for taking him in, and though he was enthralled by the woman he'd met here—one he hoped would stay with him for the rest of his life—he missed Africatown, a one-of-a-kind African American community that had been settled by formerly enslave people after the Civil War. These slaves were different;

they were the last illegal slaves brought to America from the Kingdom of Dahomey in West Africa in 1860. They had preserved their language and their customs as ethnic Yoruba and Fon people. Pulsar's dream was to one day return to his hometown, but he would have to wait until he could get up the nerve to face possible imprisonment and, worse, those who had once trusted him.

Pulsar wondered if Loving would go there with him. *Probably not,* he thought. She had so many bad memories associated with that state—her mother, her former lover. Was she with him today because she was trying to deal with the pain of losing her man just three months ago?

His loves were now beginning to stir. Maybe his thoughts had ruptured their peaceful sleep. He kissed Loving's shoulder.

Loving turned her head toward him, smiled, and said, "You know, you're kind of cute in a dark sort of way, and I don't mean your skin color. Someday, we need to really get to know one another so we can love soul-to-soul in addition to body-to-body."

"I agree," Pulsar said. "But first, breakfast. I thought you two would never wake up."

Chapter 50

Zhen Bang was at Loving's door when she, Pulsar, and Sophia-Emma returned from breakfast. If Zhen Bang hadn't recognized the baby, Loving would have completely passed as just another mother at Sanctuary.

Zhen Bang wasn't smiling as she said, "Just got a call in the office from your friend Chaos. She wants you to call her back. Says it's important. Didn't you tell her not to call here again? Doesn't she realize that folks out there track you by phone calls?"

Loving could tell that Zhen Bang wasn't comfortable with the situation Chaos was putting the community in.

"I did send her a letter like you suggested," Loving said. "But she probably hasn't received it yet. Do I call her back or what? Maybe she knows something. Chaos wouldn't put me in danger if it wasn't important."

"Crevice has a dental appointment in Charlottesville today. I'll give her your friend's phone number and have her call her from a pay phone."

"My gut tells me something's wrong." Loving was holding her baby closer, as if someone was already at the kitchen door about to break in. "I need to see that extra-secret place where we can go if folks come looking here."

"Now, don't jump to conclusions, Loving. Maybe she left something here, or maybe Craig has asked her to come visit. It's probably nothing."

"Oh, it's important I know Chaos. She knows when to be invisible and when to stick her neck out. You're not leaving this room until you show me where to go if authorities—or anyone worse—enter our gates out there. Pulsar, can you monitor the gates today so I can go hide? I also need to pack food and stuff for us to sleep and—"

"Stop this right now," Zhen Bang insisted. "Guess I misjudged you. You're nothing but a coward. Now let me out so I can catch Crevice before she leaves any minute."

Loving moved aside and clung to Pulsar, who held her tightly.

"I'll be checking in and out throughout the day, Loving. But I can't station myself at the gate every minute." Pulsar was also losing patience with his lover.

"What if Zhen Bang asks others to just take an hour as guards? I can't let people take my baby. No way."

"I'm getting out of here. Go ahead and pack a bag. Get some food from the kitchen," Zhen Bang said. "Stay in your room. Be quiet. We've got your back. As far as we know, no one here is in danger. Relax, girl. Relax. You don't want to scare your baby, do you? Do you?" She shook her head in disgust as she opened the door and went to find Crevice.

"None of you understand. My mama is probably up and around now. She'll stop at nothing to put me in my place. She just wants me to be single or walking down the aisle with a blond man, and she wants me to be without Sophia-Emma."

Loving suspected that Zhen Bang didn't comprehend the dangers she and her baby were facing. She never should have come here. They didn't care.

Pulsar sat down on the bed, pulling her with him. "Loving, don't worry. I know the place they'll put you. Believe me, you don't want to be put in that hole unless your life depends on it. When I get a break, we'll go over there and check it out, if you think that'll ease your mind. But after you see it, you may want to take your chances here," he said.

211

Chapter 51

As planned, Zhen Bang gave Crevice Chaos's phone number. She instructed the young mother to ask Chaos to provide the information she had for Loving. She was also to stress that Chaos was not to contact Loving in any way until Loving told her all was clear. Crevice would make her call from a pay phone and keep the conversation short and to the point. In the meantime, she was to keep her eyes open and stay out of the public eye. Zhen Bang trusted Crevice to follow through. After all, as a longtime member of Sanctuary, she had a serious head on her shoulders.

Pulsar sneaked the red-headed Loving, now wearing glasses on a regular basis, over to the secret spot, where she and Sophia-Emma would go if authorities were somehow able to get into the compound. She followed Pulsar beyond the lake and up a hill overlooking the horse pasture. They stopped at a level spot next to a huge, nondescript rock the size of an upside-down bathtub. To her surprise, the rock wasn't a rock, but a covering, like cities often use to fit over utility wires here and there. Pulsar moved the covering and revealed more dead oak tree leaves. He brushed them aside and revealed a large piece of plywood. After he lifted the plywood, Loving saw the spot where she and Sophia-Emma would hide out. She peered down the hole. She estimated that there might be enough room for four people to stand up or two people to sit down. But it was so dark, so cold, and so spooky.

"They expect me and my baby to hang out in this foxhole? Sophia-Emma would be scared to death. She'd cry and give our location away. No way can we go in that grave. What was Zhen Bang thinking?"

"Remember, this is a place of last resort, Loving. Take it from me, no one's going to find you here. Hey, I'm a wanted man. No one's found me after seven years. And I didn't color my hair, change my style, or start wearing glasses, either," Pulsar tried to assure her.

"And you didn't come here with an innocent baby," Loving insisted. "And while we're talking about running from authorities, why don't you level with me and tell me what you did? Did you kill someone? Do I need to be afraid of you now, too?"

Pulsar looked through her like she was glass. "Not quite. I'm just a bail runner. I was afraid to go to jail, so I ran. And if you don't want my help, if you don't trust me, then I'm out of here. You're being cruel and selfish, and I'm not a ball you can kick around."

"Hell, you're hiding out here just because you're afraid of jail? Here I go again. Did you kill someone or rob a bank? People go to jail every day."

"Easy for a white person to say. Black men in Alabama prisons get eaten up by the system. Yes, I'm a coward because too many of my neighbors never made it back home after their sentencing." He stepped farther away, looking as though he would explode at any minute.

"Where I come from, our community is slowly dying because of chemicals in the air, water, and even the ground we've grown our gardens in. One day, I snuck into the paper plant and vandalized it so badly that it had to be shut down, maybe for good, and for that I'm extremely proud. But I got caught. My community bailed me out, and I skipped town, simple as that."

"Sounds kind of cowardly to me. Go home and face the music. Get on with your life."

"Easy for you to say. Besides, now that I've met you, I have even more of a reason to stay. At this moment, you're speaking with white privilege. If anyone else were talking like you are now, I would floor them. Only thing is, I still love you, damnit."

Loving and Pulsar looked into each another's eyes. Loving was crying. Pulsar was still fuming. Yes, this could be one of the best hidden secrets in the Southeast. Maybe this was where they needed to be, but were there other places where they could get lost? Mexico? Canada?

"Okay, Pulsar. I am sorry. But I think it's about time we quit being cowards, don't you? What have we done wrong? You were trying to save your community. I'm trying to save a baby nobody wanted. Maybe we're both nothing but scaredy-cats," Loving said.

"Let's talk about that more tonight, Loving. For now, I have to go to work. Why don't you go to the commie store and get stuff to decorate your hideout? I'll alert you if I see any G-men or G-women get through our barbed and electrified front gate."

Both of them, plus baby, started back toward the lake. Loving felt a shiver go down her back. She looked down at her baby, who was curled into her bosom under her Moby. Envisioning such a sweet angel screaming in a dark, damp hole made her want to vomit.

Chapter 52

Crevice told herself that she was doing this traitorous deed for little Dorothy-Fire. She left the dental clinic with a numb mouth and two less wisdom teeth. Maybe she would be able to sleep at night from now on... unless guilt interfered. Meeting her outside was a strange-looking white guy with a shaved head and a body covered with tattoos. Some of them were words she wouldn't repeat to Dorothy-Fire. Sometimes she had to do the better of two evils and collaborate with people who repulsed her. Sure, she was cooperating with the devil, but Sanctuary would protect Loving and her baby. They had secret spots no one would ever find.

"You ready for the call?" the strange man asked her as she approached her van.

"Ready as I'll ever be, Stu." Crevice unlocked the van. "We're going to the first phone booth I see. You can listen in if you promise to keep that damn mouth of yours shut."

"Hell, don't get nasty with me. This wasn't my idea. Just doing what Jim said I had to do. There's a phone booth over near the deli. I'll be right next to you and won't say a word. Just be yourself, and before you know it, you can go home and see your little girl."

"I don't know why I ever told y'all that I'd help you out," Crevice said after they got in the car and started driving to the deli. "Remember, I've had nothing to do with this. I need Sanctuary for a few more years. Jim's still going to set up an account in my name, isn't he?"

"I'm not part of your agreement. Settle that with Jim."

"Well, here we go," Crevice said as she pulled up to the phone booth.

They barely fit into the booth. Crevice could feel Stu's breath on the top of her head as she dialed Chaos's number.

"Yeah, what do you want?" Chaos said as she picked up the phone.

"Hi, Chaos," Crevice answered. "I'm with Sanctuary, and I was told to take whatever message you're trying to get to Loving. She can't talk to you right now. I'll get your message to her."

"What's going on up there? Why won't you guys let her talk to me? As far as I know, you're a total stranger. This call isn't coming from Sanctuary."

Crevice tried to reassure Chaos. "Chaos, we're giving Loving some extra protection right now because she's scared that her mother may send authorities to Sanctuary to take her baby. I was sent to make this call from another location so we could keep Loving's privacy intact. So, what do you want me to tell her?"

"Just that her mother and some white nationalist guy are working to find her and take her baby away. She needs to be on guard. That's it."

"I'll be sure to tell her that. Thank you for letting us know. Now, I need to tell you not to contact her under any circumstance until you've heard from Loving herself," Crevice concluded. "Now goodbye."

"Well, I'll—" was all Crevice heard as she hung up.

"That's what we thought," Stu said as he bent down to kiss Crevice.

But Crevice would have none of that. "This is business, Stu. Stay off my lips and follow me back to Sanctuary. When we get there, you don't know me. Understand?"

She took him back to his black truck at the dental clinic, where another thug was waiting for him. They both followed Crevice as she headed back to Sanctuary. Crevice estimated that she would be back in time to gather the eggs and breastfeed Dorothy-Fire before dinner.

Chapter 53

Loving looked at her watch. For some reason, she was feeling uneasy. Something bad was about to happen, and she was scared. Since she had become a mother, she could identify with does and mother bears, who could sense danger.

She expected that Pulsar would be back in a few minutes. One thing she appreciated about her man was that he was a man of consistency. He worked hard, but when dinnertime rolled around, he would leave his job and wash up for dinner.

When her door opened, she put Sophia-Emma into her stroller. To her surprise, Zhen Bang was at her door with Pulsar.

"Loving, I want you to stay in your room tonight," Zhen Bang warned as Pulsar rushed over to put his arm around his woman. "It's probably nothing, but Pulsar has noticed a strange vehicle approach inside our gates. Crevice has told me that Chaos's message to you was that some white nationalists have talked with your mother, and they're working with her to take the baby from you."

Loving looked down at Sophia-Emma, picked her up, and held her tight. Her eyes filled with tears. "I'm not going to take this baby and crawl in a hole out there, though I have a flashlight and a bag packed. No, they're going to have to kill me before they get my baby."

"Zhen Bang, thanks for coming over. I think I can handle this now. You can go," Pulsar said with authority. "Loving and I need to talk alone now."

"Okay." Zhen Bang looked doubtfully at both of them. "Just stay in your room. Lock your door. The rest of us will play dumb. I'll be in the office, if things get tense."

After Zhen Bang had left and closed the door behind her, Pulsar sat Loving down on the bed. "I've not been at work today, Loving. Instead, I've been making a few plans."

Loving started to protest about not being included in his planning, but he ignored her.

"Now, listen here for just a few minutes. I know what we can do. I'm ready to go back home to Africatown. After listening to you today, and after thinking about how I've not been facing the consequences of my actions seven years ago, I've decided that I have to take care of some unfinished business there. I want to go tonight, and Sophia-Emma will be going with me."

Loving was stunned. She almost laughed at Pulsar's so-called plan. "No way, Pulsar. I won't let you take my baby from me. And you're going back to Alabama. That's where they're looking for her. Why would I let you take her from here, where no one knows us, to that hotbed of racism in Alabama? If you want to leave, go. But Sophia-Emma is staying here with me. I've known you less than a week, and now you tell me you're taking my baby?"

"Just hear me out, Loving." Pulsar got off the bed, turned toward her, and kneeled. "This is what I think will work. You stay here, and I take Sophia-Emma with me to Africatown. I head on out of here. I'm a black dude doing my thing. You know no white dudes are lookin' for me. They lookin' for you and your baby. Maybe they find you. Maybe they don't. If they do find you, you'll convince them that you no longer have a baby. Maybe you gave her back to her real mama. You'll think of something. Tell 'em that you decided you weren't the mommy type and that you just needed some time after your old boyfriend got bumped off. They leave. You wait a few days. Notify me when the coast is clear, and I'll come back. Or you could join me somewhere in Tennessee or

North Carolina. We'll decide what to do after that. Maybe we'll stay here, or you'll join me in Africatown, or we'll go to Canada or Mexico. But we have to do something right now unless you want to take your darling little girl over to that hole and hide right now. I think we have a chance to completely stump 'em."

"I need time, Pulsar," Loving cried, but she knew inside that she would not separate from her baby, even for a few minutes.

"Sorry, babe. Your time has run out. If you don't decide in two minutes, you risk having that baby torn from your arms. I've seen those guys. They're in a souped-up black Ram truck. They're searching each dorm. I've got a car gassed up, and I know another way out of here. You can trust me, Loving. You know that."

Loving, who had been crying uncontrollably, stopped abruptly. "I can't release my daughter to anyone. Anyone. You hear me, Pulsar? No one, not even you. Now let's go, the three of us. I'm willing to take my chances. I don't need two minutes. I'm out of here with you and Sophia-Emma."

Against his better judgment, Pulsar nodded in agreement. After all, time had run out. Loving grabbed the sleepy baby from the stroller, and the three of them snuck out of the bedroom window that faced the woods. Pulsar led the way to the old Ford Galaxy. He started the motor after they got in, and they sped to the compound's back gate. The entire time, Loving was gazing out the rear window, looking to see if the black truck was following them.

As one would suspect, the white nationalists had anticipated that Loving would try to escape as soon as they got into Sanctuary. Crevice had agreed she would act as lookout for an extra thousand bucks. All she had to do was ring the bell on the lodge's porch, and the intruders would come out and pursue Loving and her baby. The plan worked without a wrinkle.

Before long, Loving saw the black truck racing through the dust their car was leaving behind. This wasn't in the plan, but at least if they overcame them, Loving would be there to defend her baby. She forced herself to remember some of the close calls she and Peter had been through. They could still evade these creeps.

"Pulsar, you know the back roads around here better than these flatliners from the red clay of Alabama. Speed up as fast as this thing'll go. When you get far enough ahead, turn off the road and let them go on. In my opinion, it's the only way."

"Thanks for telling me something I already knew, sweetheart. But remember, they have a four-wheel drive truck to maneuver. I have only this junkyard sedan."

Loving remembered her first crooked trip in the dark of night months ago. She recalled how many hills and curves they'd went around before finding Sanctuary. Surely, now that it was getting dark, they could lose these thugs behind them, but she wasn't about to bet on it. She had begun to search for a plan B when, behind them, she saw scores of people coming out of the ditches that ran along both sides of the road. As far as she could tell, they all wore black clothes. They stood in the road and locked arms, slowing the black truck. Loving covered her eyes. She knew what would be coming next. Some of these folk were going to be run over and killed. But she peeked a couple seconds later and saw that the truck had stopped. It was now surrounded by fellow anarchists who, she assumed, were harassing the two men. She assumed the men weren't willing to murder people just to complete their gig.

"We need to go back and thank those comrades." Loving tugged at Pulsar's shirt sleeve.

"You can thank them later," Pulsar responded as he picked up speed, so much so that Sophia-Emma began to cry in fear.

"There, there, sweetie," Loving said as she held her baby closer to her breasts.

"I guess you're right," she said to Pulsar. "I'll bet Chaos had these folks camp out here, knowing that these guys would be coming for us any time. I've got to talk to that girl. In the meantime, where are we going now?"

"One thing's for sure: We're not going back to Sanctuary," Pulsar said. "There's a stool pigeon somewhere in that group. And I think I know who."

"You do?" Loving asked. Then she was silent for a few minutes. "You mean Crevice? Do you really think she was the Judas?"

"Sure wouldn't be surprised," Pulsar said as he navigated the turns and twists on the road, wondering if another team of white nationalists was waiting ahead. "You know, Loving, I think we need to not get on the interstate at the regular spot. Most likely, if they had you, they would meet up with the higher-ups at a major stop, like a rest stop. We need to go farther north," he surmised.

"You know, I agree with you," Loving said. "We also need to drive most of the night on side roads. No car seat for Sophia-Emma. Do we have registration on this car? We are just asking to get pulled over."

"To top all that off, I'm black, and I have a bad case of a hot temper," Pulsar added.

"All we can do is stay at the speed limit and sort out our plans tomorrow." Loving opened the glove compartment to search for a current registration. "By the way, do you have any money?"

Chapter 54

"We have almost a full tank of gas. Let's be happy we have that, aight? Thank God you can breastfeed Sophia-Emma, so we can handle her hunger for a while. We'll think of something. For now, our main worry is not being caught by these cracker lunatics."

Loving stared at the ring on her right hand. The diamond sparkled back at her as she raised it toward the moonlight. Her grandmother on her father's side had given it to her at graduation. It had been worn on the left hands of four grandmothers before her. So far in life, things had never gotten so bad that she had needed to pawn it. Tonight, though, she decided that even her ring wasn't so sacred that she wouldn't sell it so they could get to a place of safety.

"I've got my ring, Pul—"

She was interrupted by a mild jolt from the back of the car. She turned around and saw the passenger in the car behind them aiming a gun straight at them. Soon, he was honking his horn.

"Speed up, Pulsar! We need to get out of this guy's firing range, like, now," Loving yelled.

Pulsar nodded and pushed the gas pedal down as far as it would go. The Galaxy, a V-8, took off like a rocket. The silver SUV behind them kept up. The driver rammed into their rear bumper again.

"I'm already going as fast as this babe will take us. I don't know what more I can do," Pulsar said, longing for the simpler times, back when Loving had only been another cribbage player.

To make things worse, another vehicle, its lights on bright, was heading toward them in their lane. Pulsar had the choice of either heading into the left lane to avoid a collision or diving into the deep ditch to their right. Or they could stop and run. Pulsar chose the left-lane option. The car heading their way veered over into the same lane. Pulsar felt like the mouse between two hungry, vicious cats, saliva dripping from their open mouths. He pulled off the road and slammed on his brakes.

"What in the hell are you doing?" Loving screamed. "We can't let these crazies kill us. Get back on the road."

"I'm tired of running," was all Pulsar said. "This is my last run."

Before Loving could chastise him more, there were men with semi-automatics on both sides of the vehicle.

"So, what now, Pulsar? Roll down our windows, get out, and run so these cowards can shoot us in the back, or do we just exit and make some small talk about the moon with these idiots?" Loving asked sarcastically. "Maybe if I offer my ring, they'll call this all off. Think so?"

The gunmen answered the question for them. They broke the car's rear windows with their guns and reached in to the front doors, unlocking them and opening the doors.

"Out," one of the men ordered.

Loving and Pulsar complied, Loving covering Sophia-Emma's head with a blanket. Immediately, they felt the muzzles of the guns at their backs. Loving and Sophia-Emma were shoved into the SUV, while Pulsar was forced into the old green Mercedes that had been heading straight to them. Evidently, their abductors knew that by separating them, they would be more likely to cooperate.

As Loving sat in the back seat of the SUV, all she could think was that she had neglected to kiss Pulsar before they parted. Would she ever see him again? Would this hired team of rednecks and white nationalists kill Pulsar? Lynch him to make an example of him for dating a white woman? After a few miles on the road, Loving felt a small pang of relief when she noticed that Pulsar seemed to be going to the same place she was. But she also considered that maybe her captors wanted to have her witness their treatment of a black man. She begged God to not let that happen. Never.

"Why are y'all getting involved in our personal lives?" Loving finally worked up the courage to ask.

"We're just following orders, ma'am," the skinhead with a swastika on the back of his hand answered. "Now, let me ask you a question. What in the world makes you want to hang out with a monkey?"

"That man has more class in his little toe than you have in your entire body," was Loving's only answer.

"We'll see about that, dear lady," the driver said, playing with his sandy beard, which went down to his shoulders.

"Where are we going? You can take us back to Sanctuary, and we'll pretend none of this trouble ever happened." Loving decided to let the hungry Sophia-Emma nurse.

The skinhead stared at the scene behind him. Loving couldn't help but wonder what was going through his mind. Was he turned on by the sight of her breasts? Was he sickened to see a white woman nurse a dark baby? Either way, he made her uncomfortable.

"Can you turn around?" she asked the man.

"I'll look wherever I want in my own car, bitch. You're lucky I don't have my pistol aimed at the two of you right now."

Loving looked down at Sophia-Emma and held her closer. Maybe she could shut that man out of her life. Maybe if she closed her eyes, when she opened them again, she would realize all of this had been a bad dream, and she could just take her little girl for a stroll over to the lodge for breakfast. When she opened her eyes and realized this wasn't a dream, she begged her old partner, Peter—now that she was aware that heaven really did exist—to use his power to convince these creeps to change their minds.

Loving pulled Sophia-Emma away from her breast, lifted her up to her shoulder, and started to burp her.

"You know, a white baby would be easier to care for," the driver said as he looked at her in the rearview mirror.

"A baby's a baby, guys," Loving said. "It's only a small minority of crazies like you two who think color makes a difference."

"We'll see about that," the skinhead said. "Enjoy it while you can. Our folks have other ideas about what to do with your sweet little baby."

Loving was now more than scared—she was enraged. She wanted to remove Sophia-Emma from her lap, stand up, reach for the smart-aleck's firearm, and blow both their heads off. Anything less than that wouldn't do the trick.

She turned around to see if she could get a glimpse of Pulsar in the vehicle behind her. She could barely make out his profile in the backseat. But she did notice that the SUV had its right turn signal on. They were turning into a driveway full of ruts, much like the one at Sanctuary. Half a dozen barking hounds ran up to the two vehicles. A light turned on in a trailer farther down the road, and the gruff voice of a woman cussed at the dogs. They obeyed.

Chapter 55

The captors wasted no time forcing their captives out of their cars. The skinhead opened the backdoor and nearly pulled Loving's right arm out of its socket as he pulled her and Sophia-Emma out of the car. Once they were out, he slapped Loving across the face.

"That's to teach you a little respect, bitch," he said as he spit tobacco at Sophia-Emma. He could tell Loving was seething.

Loving glanced over at Pulsar. The driver of the other car kicked him in the groin as he attempted to get out of the car. He swore at his assailant as he bent over in pain.

"Leave us alone. We haven't done anything to you," Loving demanded.

The pudgy supremacist angrily yelled back, "That's not what I heard. You and your previous boyfriend made concerted efforts to destroy traditions that glorified our southern forefathers. How dare you say you didn't do anything to deserve what you're getting now. How dare you!"

"And I wish I'd done more. And we would have if one of your criminals hadn't killed Peter. If that person's in prison now, I hope he rots there."

Loving looked over at Pulsar, who was still being used as a punching bag by the kidnappers. She broke away from her attacker to join Pulsar as he fought. But before she knew it, she was flat on her back, her baby lying on top of her. Sophia-Emma began to cry from fear and shock.

Loving's attention now shifted to her baby, though her lover was being overwhelmed by attacks from two aggressors. She didn't know if she would be able to get up, but the muddy driveway had softened her fall, and in a few minutes she was back on her feet, punching her attacker with one arm and clutching Sophia-Emma with the other.

"You son of a bitch."

With a bloodied hand, she went after the three captors between her and Pulsar. Before she knew it, though, the bearded one once again grabbed her arm. He nearly threw Sophia-Emma into a patch of muddy grass by a tree, then tied Loving's hands behind her back. Her baby, who was frantically crying, was taken into the trailer by an old woman Loving thought was a witch.

While havoc continued taking place outside, blood mixing with mud, spit mixing with slugs, the old woman looked over Sophia-Emma inside the dimly lit trailer. She had told those men out there to do what had to be done in order to honor General Robert Lee, Jefferson Davis, and uncles who had fought for the lost cause. She, too, believed American negroes were threatening white society by marrying white girls. She saw them paired up in the malls. She couldn't even shop there anymore. Poor white men were emasculated and couldn't get jobs because they were now the lowest of the low, under the negroes and greasers.

Despite her opinions, she couldn't force herself not to hold the baby to her chest. She couldn't stop herself from wiping the mud from Sophia-Emma's little chubby hands and feet. As she raised Sophia-Emma to her shoulder, her baby eventually stopped crying. The wiry-haired old woman sat down on a lime-green, plastic-covered kitchen chair and laid the baby face-up on her knees. The two's eyes met. They stared. They understood. One spoke with her mouth, while the other communicated with her intense eyes.

Chapter 56

"You boys have had your fun," came a yell from the trailer's doorway. "Come on in now, and bring the mama and her black ape in here."

Loving noticed that the roughing up immediately stopped. Their captors marched them both, guns against their backs, into the trailer. Pulsar tried to break away a couple of times, but when Loving ran over to him and begged him to play along until they could get Sophia-Emma back, he reluctantly walked by her side, fingers intertwined with hers behind her back.

Once inside, Loving lunged toward Sophia-Emma and snatched her from the old woman. Again, the baby was startled and began to cry.

"Miss nigger lover, you gotta be gentle with babies," the old woman scolded. She spit something into an old Chock full o' Nuts coffee can.

Loving noticed that all of a sudden, the three white men—she had a hard time thinking of them as men instead of animals—sat obediently, shoulder-to-shoulder, on the old peach-colored couch that sunk in the middle.

The old woman gave a warm, wet rag to Loving and said, "Wash you self up. That baby don't need a dirty, stupid mama. I can't do anything about your stupidity, but no sense in you being dirty while you hold your little babe."

Loving was stunned by the slight gesture of kindness from the old woman. She studied the lady's appearance and guessed that she was probably in her early sixties. Her bushy white hair may have been red at one time. Some was tucked behind her ear, but most of it was around her face. She kept brushing a few wild wisps away from her face as she talked. She was wrapped in a faded, cloudy-day-gray, terrycloth house coat. Her bare feet spread out like those of ducks.

"Thank you, ma'am," Loving said in a grateful tone that even surprised herself.

"Now I want to talk to all of yous. No interruptin' me, y'all hear? Miss whatever your name is, I want to introduce my boys to you. The one with the shaved head is Merle, my youngest. There in the middle, the stout one with the beard, is Kyle, and over here at the end of the couch is my oldest and shyest, Bobby Joe. They can be somewhat rough at times, but living out here, my boys need to be tough and protective of our rights as the real Americans. Although we're getting the shaft these days. Oh, and my name is Ina May. We're all Goinses.

"Now I understand, miss, that you have this baby here that isn't really yours. She belongs back with her colored mama. My take on all this is that you can always make your own pretty, white, blue-eyed baby. But tonight, that there baby's eyes, they did talk to me.

"Give me a smoke, Bobby Joe." The old lady rested a bit and took a book of matches from her housecoat. She lit Bobby Joe's unfiltered cigarette and spit a strand of tobacco into the coffee can.

"Now, here's how I see it. The boys here will tell you that some of us mamas out here in the holler have carried down special anointin's from our ancestors. That means we can converse with all other females, two-legged or four, without words. I'm an old woman, and I have never been wrong while interpretin' what another female says, especially youngins."

"Aw, Ma, there you go again, bringing up your special anointin's. You know no way is that happening," argued Kyle as he kicked off his muddy boots and put them on the yellowed newspaper that served as a rug by the door.

"You hush your mouth, young Kyle. Your daddy knew my powers. I told him that that old mule out there wanted to kill him, and she did, didn't she? God rest his soul.

"Anyways, while my boys were out there messin' with you two—not sayin' I didn't tell 'em to—me and that little chocolate baby there, we met eyes, and we d'cussed some 'portant matters. You have a very smart youngin there, miss whatever your name is. Our eyes did talk two times. I wanted to make sure, and here's what she said. She said that she's got no mama. She was put here to bring harmony among us people, kin or not, darkies or whites.

"Now, you believe me when I say that if we don't let that baby stay with this misguided woman, we've got trouble in store for us. That youngin there, she tells me that she was sent here to bring harmony by Almighty God Himself. She tells me that our Savior, Jesus Christ, came down long time ago, but now is a woman's time. You know, I kinda can see that."

"Ma, that black buck over there ain't no friend of God. He's fucking that white woman, who stole that baby from a white plantation down in Alabamy," Merle whined.

"What'd I tell you boys? I'm not judging this young, misguided pair. I asked the baby who she wanted to stay with. She insisted that for now, those folks are to care fer her. I know, that don't make no sense, but who am I to question the Almighty God?"

"Ma, you're getting old. You know we can make a thousand dollars by taking this baby back to Alabamy. We can't go back on our word. That Mr. Christian ain't gonna believe your hogwash here tonight. We'll be blackballed. Cain't show our faces in town. They're all gonna laugh at us, if not kill us," Kyle complained.

"Better thems than the Almighty Lord. My mind's made up. That little girl also told me with her eyes that God will bless those who bless this child and care for her. So that's what I'm doing. Little one over there, you're not forgettin' me, air ya?"

Loving felt her baby turn away from her breast and nod to the old woman. They both smiled.

"Now that that's settled, I'll get back with that Mr. Christian. I'll invent something to tell him. I gotta sleep on it. I think you all need to bunk down with us tonight, and I'll send you on your way come mornin'. Merle, go get that old mattress out in the barn, bring it in har, and I'll have 'em sleep on the floor. But mind you, what's your name, no hanky-panky in this here house with that darkie fella. He sleeps on the couch, and you sleep on the mattress with this godly baby."

Loving didn't know what to say. This was certainly not something she had ever even dared to imagine happening. Maybe there was something to this God thing, after all. Maybe her baby was gifted, just like Ina May had claimed. But even if she was just an old woman being crazy, Loving would take it. Maybe she could even stretch her luck a little more.

"Mrs. Goins, my child will bless you and your family, I do believe, one day. But today, she needs to be cared for just as a baby. I have nothing for her. Nothing. Would it be safe for us to go back to Sanctuary tonight? We need to settle up with the people there and get the stuff we need."

Mrs. Goins once again focused her gaze on Sophia-Emma. Loving watched them communicating. Here was this old woman talking to a three-month-old baby. She had heard that many mountain women displayed supernatural psychic powers, but she didn't know babies could, as well.

"Young lady, I wouldn't recommend you go back to that commune. There are squealers there who will endanger both of your lives. Maybe someday, when things calm down. But now, uh-uh." Ina May brushed her frizzy hair back behind her ears again.

"We have no money and no identification on us. We took the car from where we were staying. No car seat for Sophia-Emma. We're truly on the run," Loving explained.

"But remember, you have your baby, and your baby has Jesus. Can't get any better security than that."

Chapter 57

After Ina May and her boys were all bedded down for the night, and after Loving had nursed Sophia-Emma to sleep, she and Pulsar nursed each other's wounds.

"I'm so sorry I've gotten you into such a mess," Loving whispered into Pulsar's ear as she kissed each bruise, scratch, and bump on his body. Pulsar reciprocated. "One day, we'll be safe. No Kyle or Merle or Bobby Joe to punch, spit, and poke at us," Loving softly said to her lover. "I'm really sorry that you, a proud, strong Black man, have had to endure such cruelty and verbal abuse from people who look like me. I wish I could stop it."

"That day will come," Pulsar tried to reassure her. "Just believe it. I do. For now, I could stand to have some pain relievers. Want some of that moonshine over there in that Ball jar? It might help us sleep a little better."

After each had a glass of the homemade booze, the pain did subside. But Loving was also gabbier than usual.

"Did I ever tell you about Promised Land?" Loving asked.

"Just bits and pieces here and there," Pulsar answered as he fondled her breast. "Tell me more."

"It's about a thousand acres of green beauty that nestles up against the gentle Alabama River, not far from Selma in Dallas County. But I guess you know that, with you being from around Mobile. But what you don't know is that someday that land will be yours and mine and Sophia-Emma's. My goal—listen to this—is to divide most of that land between the natives we stole from and the descendants of slaves who worked our land. All I want is a small plot that's big enough for horses and a garden. That's all I need. What do you think?"

"You going to buy a few dozen mules, too, since my ancestors were promised a mule, as well?" Pulsar kissed Loving and laid his head on the throw pillow masquerading as a bed pillow. "I can't wait till we drive into Africatown, hopefully in a couple days. I'll take you to our little museum that tells our story. Some of us were the last slaves to be brought into the country from Africa. We were sent up your river to other plantations, but we all came together after the war to make our own town with our own schools, language, and foods. "Many even took back their original African names..." His voice trailed off as he went to sleep.

Loving moved back down to the old mattress, which smelled like a wet barn. Tonight, unlike nights since her adolescent years, she would say a prayer of thanks. Never would she have guessed that things would turn out the way they had. She would also pray that Ina May's boys would behave themselves tonight. For some reason, she didn't think they were too happy about what their mother was determined to do.

Chapter 58

Loving missed her normal bed. Although she and Pulsar hadn't been together for a long time, she missed having her body next to his. As the howling coyotes were answered by the hounds, she distracted herself by looking at her sleeping baby, so small but so big, waiting to change the world. Would a sword also pierce her heart one day, as a holy man once prophesized upon seeing God's son? Such idle thoughts. Ina May was crazy. But as long as she really believed in her powers, Loving could pretend to believe, too.

Then she thought of the future. Would she, Sophia-Emma, and Pulsar end up in Africatown? Would she, as a white woman, be welcome there? Would state officials come and take her baby away? Maybe it would be safer to leave the country, perhaps go to Canada. Another option might be to face Alabama Human Services and legally adopt Sophia-Emma. Didn't Ina May say that she had no mother?

The next thing she knew, there was a hairy arm wrapped around her from behind. She squirmed. At first, she thought that Pulsar had joined her and Sophia-Emma on the floor mattress, but the arm didn't feel like Pulsar's. And the smell. The body reeked of beer and sticky flesh. She immediately sat up.

"Get the hell out of here," she screamed at the man behind her.

Kyle immediately stood up. He was naked.

Within seconds, Ina May was in the living room with her ball bat. "You filthy son of a bitch, get back in your room with your brothers," she scolded her son as the bat whacked his butt. "Ought to be ashamed of yourself. Leave that white woman alone. She is a beautiful flower, not to be sullied by the likes of you. I'm sleeping in the hallway the rest of the night, and if you try this one more time, you're out in the barn with that mule."

Loving was in shock. She felt dirty and wanted a shower. "Mrs. Goins, I need to take a shower. I can't sleep after this. I don't know if I'll be able to sleep for a month or ever after facing this abuse."

"Aw, get in thar. I'll watch the boys. Mighty sorry Kyle couldn't keep his hands off of you. Did he, you know, *know* you? He's always givin' me nothin' but trouble," she said.

"No, but he was naked—as you know—and he was just about to. He's an awful man. Awful! I can't wait to get away from here. You may think my baby is a saint, but I'm not. I won't forget this."

Loving left the room, turned on the shower in the bathroom, and endured the yellow water as it dissolved the dirt all over her body. As she wiped down and put back on her dirty clothes, she heard Sophia-Emma cry. She went out, scooted past the old woman, and took Sophia-Emma into her arms. She knew there would be no sleep tonight.

Pulsar's fingers rested on her shoulder. He whispered, "I'll kill that bastard, I swear."

"No, you won't," Loving insisted. "We leave here tomorrow, one way or another. But I'm not forgetting this anytime soon."

Chapter 59

Morning couldn't come soon enough for Pulsar and Loving. Thankfully, Sophia-Emma seemed to be oblivious to all the dysfunction that had been going on around her. Loving was the first to get in the bathroom while Ina May puttered around in the kitchen. As much as she hated this place, the smells coming out of the kitchen and permeating the air were making her salivate.

"Come and get it, or it's going to the pigs," Ina May yelled from the kitchen.

Her three boys skedaddled into the kitchen and started spooning scrambled eggs, sausage patties, biscuits, and gravy onto their flowery paper plates.

"That's enough, you hogs. Leave some for our guests," Ina May ordered. "I want that lil girl over there to have a taste of my goat-milk gravy."

Loving washed her hands and shook the water off, not wanting to contaminate her hands all over again by drying them off with the yellow-stained towel hanging from the doorknob.

"Just hold off on any food for my baby. She gets only me now," Loving instructed.

"That's ridiculous," Ina May retorted. "See those boys there? They were getting pablum as soon as they could swallow. Slept all night. Did 'em no harm. Doctors these days know nothin' 'bout baby raising up."

"No doctor is telling me what to do," Loving defended herself. "No solid food hits this baby's mouth till after she's six months old."

"Well, I'll be, girl. You're goin' to starve that lil one. Remember, she's got special powers. Don't want to get that girl mad at you."

"We just want to get on the road, ma'am," Loving said. "What car, by the way, you gonna let us drive out of this hellhole?"

"Now, you watch your language. I don't have to do nothin' in this here hellhole you seems to think this is, lil miss high n' mighty."

"Your son crawled in bed with me—naked, mind you—last night. Is that what you brought your boys up to do? I think y'all need to kneel down and ask God, who my daughter seems to know better than me, for forgiveness," Loving demanded.

Ina May didn't say a word.

Pulsar looked at Ina May's boys, giving each "the eye," warning them to lay off of his woman.

Knowing food would be hard to come by without money, Loving and Pulsar took what was left on the cookstove for themselves. They nodded to Ina May, telling her that her cooking was definitely top notch.

"Now, mind you, Mr. darkie and Ms. nigger lover, I would rather drown you in the pond out back than see you live on, but I know that that baby of yourn, Miss Sophia-Emma, wants you to care for her for a few years. And we-uns can't get in the way. So we won't, and my God Almighty has told me we will be blessed. My faith is strong enough to move that mountain across the road into Mary-Land, so we will git y'all back to your car and send you on your way with two hundred dollars from my Hershey's can here. That's all I got. Plus, we'll make up a good story to get the others off your tail. After that, you're on your own.

"Now, Kyle, after that lil trick you played last night, when you couldn't keep that pecker in your pants, you're stayin' with me while Merle and Bobby Joe help our young couple and sweet lil Sophia-Emma get on their way."

"I think you're a wise woman, Mrs. Goins," Loving said as she raised Sophia-Emma to her shoulder. "However, your sons left our car in the middle of the road and broke out our windows last night before they brutalized us. We need one of your vehicles, along with a title. You need to sell it to us for one dollar. And it'll be your job to turn our car over to Sanctuary. I'll leave their number. They'll probably prefer to come get it themselves."

Ina May was silent once more. She sat down on her long, sagging couch, tightly closed her eyes, and seemed to be conversing with her God. She got up and walked over to Sophia-Emma, who was getting agitated while her mother just stood there. Their eyes met again. Big brown saucers fixed on emerald-green, bloodshot little marbles. After a minute, both shook their heads and smiled.

"Your little girl tells me that you should get our SUV, damnit. We need that four-wheel, I tell her, but she assured me that all would be well. That's enough for me. Bobby Joe, go get my cigar box, which has our 'portant papers in it. I'll sign it over to y'all."

"Ma," Bobby Joe protested. "We need that Toyota to git into town, to haul feed and chickens into town, and to go huntin'. You know that other Mercedes jalopy ain't worth crap."

"Hush your mouth, young man," his mother ordered. "I know what I'm doing. If you dummies hadn't acted like maniacs last night, I wouldn't have to be doin' this. Kind of 'an eye for an eye' thing. Blame your brother Kyle over there."

Bobby Joe obediently fetched the cigar box and brought it back to the kitchen. Ina May made her marks on the title, gave them $200 from the coffee can, and took back one dollar as payment for the truck. Loving wrote out Sanctuary's phone number and Zhen Bang's name on a napkin. The men in the room just looked on as the women in power threw their weight around.

Outside, Pulsar positioned himself behind the driver's seat, with Loving leaning as close to him as the seat belt would allow. She swore she saw Sophia-Emma and Mrs. Goins wave at each other as they sped out of the boondocks.

Chapter 60

Willie Nelson was singing "On the Road Again" as Loving and Pulsar drove the souped-up SUV onto a road that eventually had two yellow lines down the middle of it.

"So much to do, Pulsar." Loving was making a list—get a car seat, buy diapers, get rid of the old rags Ina May had put on Sophia-Emma, and buy food, gas, and clothing. Two hundred would cut it close.

"Where are we going first, my love?" she asked Pulsar, who seemed to be making his own plans.

"We're going to Africatown," he answered. "I'm going to get right with my people and the courts. I'm tired of hiding. And once I get my baggage dealt with, I suggest you do the same. Get Sophia-Emma legit as your daughter. Our daughter. Settle things with your mama. You know what you want. You're an adult. Don't let her treat you like a child."

"But you forget, Pulsar, that she and the white supremacists were working together to take Sophia-Emma. Do you think she'll meekly accept defeat? You don't know my mama."

Loving continued to work on her list, adding *adopt Sophia-Emma* and *put Mama in her place.*

Chapter 61

Loving felt like a rock had fallen into the pit of her stomach when she and Pulsar crossed into Alabama on Interstate 85. By now, she had crossed through most of the items on her list. She glanced back at her daughter, who was now asleep in her Goodwill car seat. Alongside Sophia-Emma were some paper bags of food for the road, including cans of pork and beans, whole wheat bread, and peanut butter. They'd also bought diapers and a couple changes of clothes.

"I'm scared, Pulsar," she said when she saw the big billboard saying *Welcome to Sweet Home Alabama.* "Do you think we'll really be welcome in this hole of despair? I left in fear, and now I have to come back even more scared. I haven't changed at all except that I'm a red-headed, middle-class-looking bitch. I have the same colored baby with me, and I love her even more now than I did back then."

"When you escaped from here a few months ago, you were what your old lady probably called riff-raff, and you had a newborn no one but you wanted. This time, you both have me," Pulsar teased. "Don't underestimate what I add to the picture now."

Loving squeezed Pulsar's hand and thought of the approaching holiday season. She imagined meeting Pulsar's family, making resolutions, and going to Christmas celebrations. There would be time to work things out with her mama later, when the old lady was ready.

"By the way, now that we seem to be a real couple, will you tell me your real name? Tell me about your people," she coaxed the handsome bearded man beside her.

"About all I can tell you about my people is that we're descended from the last cargo of slaves brought to America. My people came through the Mobile Bay in eighteen sixty. There were about up to one hundred and sixty of us on the Clotilda. After the Civil War, many of the Clotilda's passengers chipped in to buy our land near the Hog Bayou, about three miles north of Mobile. My people are the Joneses. And my name is Alan Jones. We believe someday the ship will once more rise from the dead."

Loving pondered over Pulsar's story for a few minutes. She had never heard this in any school she'd attended. One more example of the victors writing the history.

"That's a courageous story from a noble name. Will you one day go back to Alan Jones, or will you stay Pulsar?" Loving asked.

"Guess I'll decide that when the time is right. You?"

"I'm beginning to like Loving. But like you, time will tell."

Loving habitually ducked whenever they passed an Alabama trooper vehicle, along with other cars that had the blue lights on top. One nice thing was that Sophia-Emma was sleeping through all these worries and bitter memories. Noticing this, Loving decided to escape from her bad memories of life and death in Alabama by getting some shut-eye, as well. She leaned over toward Pulsar's shoulder, and his warmth and strength seduced her into a deep sleep.

In her dream, she saw the tombstones, not her family members' atop the red oak hill, but the multitude of unmarked graves down by the river. Ellie, Sally, and Cecilia were calling her. They sang the old spiritual "Dese Bones G'Wine Rise Again" in a three-part harmony, comforting Loving's worried spirit while also seeming to call her home.

She awoke with a start when the SUV hit a skunk in the road. Within seconds, she smelled the skunk's odor, and it reminded her of her years back home.

"Where are we, Pulsar?" she asked.

"Just passed Auburn. Think I'll stop in Montgomery for some gas."

"Not Montgomery, please," Loving requested. "That's where Peter was killed. I can't bear to see any familiar sights there."

Pulsar grimaced, and Loving knew that he was uncomfortable when she brought up Peter.

"We'll stay out of Montgomery, then. Probably lots of people there we don't want to see, either."

"You'd better believe it," Loving said. "They grow like mold around here."

Pulsar assured her they could pass by Montgomery with the fuel they had. They would get off at an exit that advertised gas somewhere west of the city.

"Can we stop over at my old home, Promised Land?" Loving asked. "I don't want to see my mama or anyone else there, not right now. I just need to visit a place down by the river where I used to hang out a lot. In my dream, I was remembering some old graves over there that probably need some tending before winter sets in. Shouldn't take more than an hour."

Loving, who'd put her former name, Amanda, on the shelf, couldn't do the same with her deep love for Promised Land. That sacred piece of land—its birds, its flowing lazy river, the crawling critters, the sweet scents, and even those sleeping and crying ghosts in their graves—continued to beckon to her. Her heartbeat was in unison with the living and unliving there. Her spirit spoke to the souls still yearning for freedom, reparation, and justice. Even the ghosts of her ancestors ached for forgiveness. They wanted to be set free from all the pain they had once caused the natives who had wandered those hunting grounds. Those natives had been there before barbed-wire fences separated them from the land that had once fed their families for generations. They had been there when no Europeans had even conceived of this continent.

Along with that, the broken bodies of slaves continued to wrestle with grief, wondering why their lives had been wasted, why their women were raped and their babies were taken from breasts, and why lovers were whipped or hung before their tear-filled eyes and broken hearts.

There was a time when they called her every night. Now she could hear them calling Sophia-Emma, too. Today, both she and Sophia-Emma would return to Promised Land and listen to their cries. Perhaps Pulsar would also hear the voices of his people.

Just then, they both heard Sophia-Emma's familiar coo. Loving turned to touch her chubby hand. They exchanged smiles. She looked over at Pulsar, and he was smiling, too. Three smiles at once. She hadn't seen this in days.

Chapter 62

Today, it was different when Ina May's old Toyota pulled up to the spot where Loving had heard the graveyard voices so many times. This time, Pulsar walked with her, and they took turns carrying Sophia-Emma in their arms.

All of a sudden, Loving heard the spirits again. This time, she lay flat on the cold ground. Pulsar and Sophia-Emma stared at her as she seemed to lose any awareness of them. Loving started to whisper and sing the old spiritual song she had heard the old women singing in her dream.

"Well the Lord He thought he'd make a man
Dese bones are gonna rise again
Made them out of mud and a little bit of sand
Dese bones are gonna rise again"

"Do you hear them singing, Pulsar?" Loving asked the bewildered man standing above her. "They're happy today. They love us. They say one day our dream will come true. My mama don't know it yet, but this whole plantation is going to come to life one day. You and me, we're going to be family for Sophia-Emma."

Loving raised her right arm so Pulsar could help her stand upright. He kissed her—a long, soft, tender kiss that convinced her all the more that he was the man meant for her forever.

"Want to see the women who talk to me every time I come to this spot? C'mon over here and meet 'em." Loving led Pulsar, still with Sophia-Emma in his arms, over to the graves she'd tended so often through the years. "This one here is Sally, next to her is Ellie, and over here with little Sofie is Cecilia." She pointed out the primitive, time-worn rocks covering frost-stunted grass.

Pulsar abruptly handed Sophia-Emma to her mother and peered down at the big rock over Cecilia's grave. His fingers followed the letters of her name from beginning to end, and then he looked over at the smaller stone, which belonged to Sofie.

"There they are!" he cried.

"There who are?" Loving asked as she and Sophia-Emma joined him on the cold ground.

"My great-great-great grandmother," Pulsar responded. "We have a story about her in our family. She had always said that she would one day be buried with the free, but during the war she was raped and killed by Union forces somewhere up the river in Alabama. We never knew where, so it was just a mystery where she ended up. If this is our Cecilia and her baby girl, she was among the last slaves brought over here from Africa. She belongs to my people."

"You got to be kidding me. We must move her to Africatown soon." Loving wrapped her arms around Pulsar, leaving Sophia-Emma on the ground, where she began to prowl around. She scooted over to little Sofie's grave. They could hear her cooing to Sofie there.

"What's going on with Sophia-Emma?" Pulsar asked as the two of them turned their eyes to the baby.

"I know my baby," Loving said. "She and Sofie are communicating. From her tone, it seems like she's taking orders, asking questions. That baby never fails to amaze me. You know, I've mostly scoffed at the supernatural, but there is something about my little Sophia-Emma I can't explain. This is one more mystery. Now that you and I and our baby are beginning a new life, I think it's time to start keeping a journal about her. I can no longer hold all her little miracles in my heart."

Pulsar and Loving saw a shadow fly over them. They looked up and saw an eagle that was very much like the one that had circled Sophia-Emma last September. It flew low, moving in a circular shape over the family. They heard its chirping-cawing song, like he had important news to share. Loving knew not what the message was, but she did absorb the emotions she felt. There would be great joy in years ahead, but also great sorrows. Only few in this world could endure what was to come, but there would always be a sacred peace in this old graveyard. The eagle seemed to tell Loving that someday her promises to the guests buried along the Alabama River would be fulfilled through her daughter Sophia-Emma, the baby who was protected by this mighty spirit-bird one day not too long ago.

Hadn't the prophet Isaiah promised, "And a little child shall lead them"?

Epilogue

Loving leans back in her chair in the small bungalow where Pulsar grew up. His mother insisted he and his family take it over so she could move into senior living nearby. Her journaling finished for the day, Loving pats her womb, where new life kicks back. Out her window, she can see Hog Bayou in the distance. Since Pulsar had temporarily shut down some paper plants years ago, more birds had been flying in and nesting there. She hears that the fish are jumping, just like they were when Pulsar's ancestors settled in the area after the Civil War.

Her life in Africatown has gone well. Eventually, the town folk got used to Pulsar having a white woman and a blended baby, whom he had brought back with him after he disappeared for more than seven years, and most have come to accept this return of their own Prodigal Son. Neighbors weren't too happy that he'd lost the bond money they'd lent him by skipping bail. But thankfully, the company dropped the case, so Pulsar no longer has to hide from the law. Today, he's a proud grassroots organizer for a water justice network in the state. And slowly, he's paying back those in the community who trusted him so long ago.

Loving is now an artist and a homeschooling mama, and she often thinks about all the small miracles and wise remarks her smart daughter has shared with the community. The matriarch of the town, Mildred Washington, is another older woman who communicated with Sophia-Emma through her eyes when she was a baby. They now often walk down by the creek, sharing only God knows what. That's okay, Loving tells herself, since Mildred's like the grandmother Sophia-Emma has never had in her life.

Loving has kept up with news about her mama through Tillie, another older woman with a special bond with Sophia-Emma. A few times a year, the three of them meet over by the Alabama River, always at Sophia-Emma's favorite spot: where Promised Land slave graves are. Tillie and little Sofie now want privacy when they talk. The eagle always soaring above seems to watch.

Because of Sophia-Emma's constant demands, late one night when the moon was full, Pulsar and other men from Africatown snuck into Promised Land, dug up Cecilia, and took her home so she, finally free, could at last rest in peace among her people. According to Sophia-Emma, little Sofie loves the river too much to move. But maybe someday she will want to reunite with her mother.

Tillie says Mrs. Foster, who "is too mean to die," still carries a grudge against Loving, but she's softening little by little. She even occasionally mentions Loving—Amanda—with a tiny smile on her face instead of a scowl. She has named her church as the recipient of Promised Land, and it will be converted into some big Episcopal conference center when she passes on. This puts a damper on Loving's hopes of using that land to pay reparations to the descendants of the slaves who once built the grandeur that became Promised Land. Also, her plans to convert some of the land over by the river into hunting areas for descendants of native people has gone by the wayside. She hasn't completely given up yet, though. Bigger miracles have happened. Most of all, she just wants to hug her mama again and reconcile when both are ready.

Chaos has traded places with Loving, in a sense. She moved in with Craig, and they visit over at Sanctuary now and then. Chaos and she talk frequently.

Sanctuary soon discovered that Crevice was the Judas figure who spilled the beans about where Loving was. For a year, the community met as they tried to decide what to do about her betrayal. In the end, true to the nature of Sanctuary, Crevice apologized and was allowed to continue living there with Dorothy-Fire. The money she was paid to squeal on Loving was forfeited to the community, which in turn was used to buy a vehicle to replace the one Loving and Pulsar had abandoned on the road when they were kidnapped. Someone thought they saw some country boys driving the previously abandoned car on backroads over by Lynchburg one day.

And speak of the devil, then there's Ina May and her boys. Ina May cooked up a good story for that Christian fellow. She told him that Pulsar and Loving had escaped to Canada and had given their baby to a First Nations community, knowing she would fit in there better than she had with them. Ina May has also forced her boys to find themselves wives from a nearby "holler," except for Kyle, who's currently in the seminary studying to become a Catholic priest. She says he's determined to serve God, but the studies that go with that are nearly intolerable.

The white nationalists and anarchists are still at it on the streets and country roads. Loving would be lying if she said she didn't miss that life. At least today she has her dreads back, and when she can, she dresses in black. But now she's fighting with, not for, the people who have been hurt most by white people. She's following their lead, and being a follower is, well...nice.

Loving's thoughts wander back to those days when she lived in her Very Wicked van, fighting the white supremacists by harassing them and destroying their property, fighting greedy capitalism by confronting societies that supported it. Some of this was needed. Some was not. She hopes that those who can will continue to fight the unjust system that is devouring much of society, tearing families apart and making greed look good.

When Loving found her daughter, Sophia-Emma, then lost Peter, so much had changed. She somehow thought that if she ran away, she would find peace. She did for a short time, and she was able to bond with her new baby. But a person can't hide away forever, always aware that someone will come hunting for them someday.

Today, her enemies know where she is. Her mother knows she's living with the three-fifths people now. The white supremacists know where she is, but they've gone on to fight for their mere survival as the Southern Poverty Law Center in Montgomery uses their antics to take them to court and fundraise. Also, Linksters—children born in Sophia-Emma's generation—are now, while still concerned about race, are also confronting other threats, like global climate catastrophe and the military industrial complex." Africatown itself, located in the Mobile Bay, is threatened, mostly because too many well-meaning people have fiddled while Rome was burning.

She knows that one day her first child will leave on a mission that is burned into her mystical genes. Probably sooner than she likes. But for now, she has an authentic-looking birth certificate, thanks to Amigo's excellent skills. He's slow but professional.

Yes, life can be joyous when you're not running away from it. And this new person who's doing somersaults inside her right now brings her even more bliss, no matter what its gender. He or she will be loved, just as Sophia-Emma has been loved. He or she will bring new experiences, not better or worse, just different. This baby will grow up in a loving community that Loving hopes no one will have to run away from again, ever.

Loving's eyes move to the most recent sentence she has written in her journal:

Sophia-Emma constantly amazes me. Today, she said out of nowhere, "Blessed are the ancestors long abused. Justice is theirs through their children."

Discussion Questions

1. Why are the dead who are buried by the Alabama River wailing?

2. Why do you think so many Americans are hesitant to let go of Jim Crow practices and beliefs? Are these belief systems similar of different than white supremacy?

3. How do you envision living on an old plantation or in a time when they flourished?

4. What part does the eagle flying over the abandoned baby play in this novel?

5. Do you think mothers and daughters often don't see eye-to-eye on matters? Do you think Amanda (Loving) and her mother will one day reconcile?

6. Compare the female characters of this book, such as Amanda (Loving) Foster, her mother Louise Foster, Sophia-Emma, Medie, Crevice, Chaos, and Ina May. Who would you describe as an angel? A betrayer?

7. Share your thoughts about Sanctuary. Have you lived in or visited an intentional community?

8. Was Loving on the rebound when she made love to Pulsar? Do you think the relationship can last?

9. How would you have proceeded if you wanted to adopt an abandoned baby?

10. Have you ever been in a conversation using only your eyes? Do you think there are times and circumstances when such communications are necessary?

11. Is Sophia-Emma simply an abandoned baby, a prophet, an angel, or a goddess? Do you think she has a human mother?

12. Would you prefer this story to be fictional or factual?

Acknowledgments

This book would still be running through my head if it weren't for the following persons' helpful advice and editing skills. My gratitude goes out to experienced writer and mentor Joanne O'Sullivan; Rhoda Weaver, who read my manuscript for sensitivity; housemate Jane Crumby, who read and critiqued it all in one day; and to Brianna Nichol, my editor. Lastly, my never-ending thanks go to my daughters Miranda Watson, Renee and Matilda Bliss, my patient partner William Nocho, and my deceased sister Betty Murphy, who made all of this product financially possible. I love you all! Even my eight-year-old granddaughter, Madeline Stringer, did her part by taking the picture of me for this book.

About the Author

Rachael Roberts Bliss grew up on a traditional farm and went to church every Sunday and Holy Day at St. Patrick's Catholic Church in Dunlap, Iowa. She knew she wanted to be a writer when she saw tears in her father's eyes as he read her last school newspaper editorial in the *Dunlap Reporter.*

During those middle years between book learning at Estherville Junior College (now a part of Iowa Lakes Community College) and The University of Iowa and retirement nearly fifty years later, Bliss helped create and raise five children, and worked in television and print media, but found more fulfillment working for social justice nonprofits that focused on hunger, the environment, poverty, and peace and justice. Her last job was as an Americorps VISTA volunteer in her sixties.

Now living in Asheville, NC, Bliss has in recent years taken courses in photography and writing at Asheville-Buncombe Tech Community College and the University of North Carolina-Asheville's Great Smokies Writing Program. When she's not pecking away on her laptop, she's playing grandma with her eight grandchildren or demonstrating for peace and justice at home and throughout the world.

You can keep up with her ups and downs on:

Twitter: @PeoplePowerGran

Facebook: www.facebook.com/rachaelrobertsbliss

TURN THE PAGE FOR AN EXCERPT FROM THE NEXT BOOK

The Goddess of Promised Land: Lamentations

You have merely begun to read about the ever-changing life of Sophia-Emma Foster, or the Spirit-Goddess. Next up, meet her in *The Goddess of Promised Land: Lamentations*, as a teen trying to figure out her mission here on earth. And since the Divine Feminine has relentless energy to change the world, save time for *The Goddess of Promised Land: Revelation*. Sophia-Emma has surprises in store.

THE GODDESS
OF PROMISED LAND

❧

LAMENTATIONS

How doth the city set solitary that was full of people? (Lamentations 1:1)

Was she afraid?

Damn right, but there was no one around to tell.

Sophia-Emma, teen and nerd, a few minutes ago had sneaked out of her family's backdoor ahead of Hurricane Abram. She wanted to once more savor—maybe for the last time—this small world of Africatown, Alabama, USA, where she'd lived, played, and wandered for most of her life.

Abram was picking up speed, making the lone explorer hurry to her favorite places before the monster storm came in to rearrange the struggling town's furniture. It was only late June, and already the Gulf was getting out-of-its-mind rowdy. Some folks 'round there kept blasting recent ancestors for ignoring the early signs of climate change back in the nineties. Yet all those huge tanks at Magazine Point said that everyone was guilty, even present-day folk. A tangle of pipelines was still flowing into this tank farm through some pipes for as long as sixty years. Sophia-Emma was now fearful whenever she heard a hurricane was forecasted to hit her town. Could the pipes endure one more onslaught? Would this be their version of Katrina?

She shifted her gaze to the now empty two-mile-long Cochran-Africatown Bridge above her head. The trucks that carried industrial cargo across it were now parked somewhere in safe places that would protect them from approaching Abram. How Sophia-Emma wished her community hadn't approved its construction long ago before she was brought here as a baby. The marshes, fishing wharves, small homes, and grocery stores were now all gone. In their place, only sprawling tank farms, barges, and coal terminals. The once pristine Mobile Bay River Basin had been ruined with chemical spills and outright dumping.

Not too long ago, one of the Africatown residents had painted a mural of the Clotilda at the base of the bridge. Sophia-Emma had passed by it many times before today. The painting told the story of a buried ship that in eighteen-sixty illegally brought over the Atlantic the last captured Africans, more than up to a hundred-sixty captured enslaved Africans. Many of their descendants still lived here in this tiny town they had built after they regained their freedom following the Civil War. She wondered how the incoming storm would mess with all of their descendants and the things they cherished.

Sophia-Emma knew she needed to get back home, but there were so many last looks to file in her melancholy mind. She looked over at the old cemetery where all the dead residents were buried facing east toward their African ancestral home of Benin. Old-timers talked about being part of the Yoruba tribe that had existed from times immemorial.

Giant raindrops were now plopping on Sophia-Emma's head. The wind was picking up, but for the most part, other storms off the Gulf started like this, too. She walked on, wanting to visit Hog Bayou and Shell Bayou. Then there was Third Creek where it met the Mobile River, flowing near Kimberly Clark and the Asphalt plant.

"Stop it," she shouted to the wind as she zipped up her waterproof jacket. She felt her bushy, dark hair blowing across her face, along with needle-like sand caught up in the wind. But she couldn't stop yet.

Before long she was walking against the wind. In other storms during her short life, the wind would come and go. But now the wind's velocity was building and building with each second. The petite girl fell flat on her face, but even that didn't stop her. She was up and moving so she could get to some last looks at the factories and refineries.

Finally Sophia-Emma could barely stand up against the wind and the sand-ladened rain. The skin on her face felt as though it was being sliced to shreds. She turned around, thinking she had been defeated, and let the wind blow her home the long way, flowing with the blasts rather than against them.

Other noises now bombarded her. She was too afraid to look behind herself, but the storm seemed to be throwing tree branches at her back. Meanwhile, the rain was drenching her, so much that she couldn't even see where she was headed. For the first time, the wandering teen wondered if she'd be the first victim of this hurricane. Would she die out there in the streets?

"Damn it, Wind," she screamed at the top of her voice while being drowned out by Abram's slams and punches carrying her along his cruel gales. Boards put up over windows were being violently pounded. A couple palm trees were being plucked out of the ground like weeds. Street lights were dimming as electrical wires, now broken by falling branches and debris, sparkled like dying embers of a campfire.

"I gotta find some type of shelter or I'm done for," Sophia-Emma told herself as the power of darkness was overcoming her. All she could hear in response was the wind howling, rain drops pounding, chaos, the end of the world.

Once again, she screamed until her voice took on the sound of fingernails on a chalkboard simultaneous with wheels squealing around a sharp corner.

"I say to you, Wind. I say to you, Rain, no more. Stop this ruckus right now!"

Silence. Her world was now quiet. She heard a pine needle drop. Then she cried out in relief, gratitude, and fear.

Sophia-Emma noticed neighbors in the hood slowly and cautiously starting to emerge from their homes. They didn't pay her much attention, for which she was relieved. She knew they were probably as confused as she about what the hell Abram was up to. This lull couldn't mean the eye of the storm was over them, signaling that half the storm was over. No, he seemed to have gone to sleep or simply called it quits. Yes, people were avoiding the live electrical wires scattered everywhere, but why did the wind become tame so suddenly, as though a gentle giant had walked through their little town and swept away hurricane winds and rain with his broom?